WHAT MY SISTER Didn't KNOW

JANIE De COSTER

STREET Essence

Published by:
G Street Chronicles
P.O. Box 1822
Jonesboro, GA 30237-1822
www.gstreetchronicles.com
fans@gstreetchronicles.com

Cover design:
Hot Book Covers, www.hotbookcovers.com

ISBN 13: 978-1-9384427-2-8
ISBN 10: 1938442725
LCCN: 2013940808

Join us on our social networks
Facebook
G Street Chronicles Fan Page
The G Street Chronicles CEO Exclusive Readers Group

Follow us on Twitter
@GStreetChronicl

Dedication

I dedicate this novel to my grandchildren:
Shania, Jered, Toure', Ethan, Jullian, Jaylen, Madison and Bryana.
The world is at your feet if you put God first.
Remember…All Things Are Possible With God

Isaiah 47 : 10

You felt secure in your wickedness, you said, "No one sees me"; your wisdom and your knowledge you astray, and you said in your heart, "I am, and there is no one besides me."

Life Lessons

Why are life lessons so hard to learn? Could it be through our
difficulty in understanding, that life doesn't go as we sometimes plan?
There are bumps in the road we cannot see,
until we feel them underneath.
Twists and turns shatter our faith,
leaving us feeling as if we have been abandoned by grace.
Then there are times when our eyes shine so bright,
bringing out smiles of happy delight.
The laughter within us runs deep as a well,
cascading down with happy stories to tell.
But as we grow older, life lessons become clearer.
We must take the bitter along with the sweet,
until our time on this earth is complete.
Life lessons are not a book that can be easily read,
they are a journey through life to be lived instead.

Out in the Cold

Sometimes I feel as if I'm out in the cold,
clad only with emotion covering my body and soul.
When I look around me, I see smiles of good cheer;
however, they exclude me as I wipe away my tears.
Better days are coming, sings the song of old.
But will it come to me, I ask, shining like silver and gold?
My heart is heavy as I wait upon that day.
Like a child at Christmas, on bended knees I pray,
to have the most precious gift there is, happiness, I crave.

Acknowledgements

I want to give honor and praise to my Lord and Savior Jesus Christ for giving me this gift of writing. Never in my wildest dream did I think that I would be an author. But God saw something in me that I didn't, and now here I am.

I would like to thank my loving and supportive family. Steven, you've been there since day one and I want you to know that I appreciate you so much. My children, Lataisha, Krystal, Raphael and Stephon, thank you guys for believing in me. I can't tell you how many lonely nights I've spent in this journey but it's worth it all to see my work in print. To my brother Samuel and my sister-in-law Sylvia. I thank you two for your prayers and your loving support. Samuel, God has given both of us special gifts and I'm happy knowing that we both are using our gifts to glorify our Heavenly Father.

I'd also like to thank the authors I've met along the way. Leigh McKnight, thanks for being a true friend. Altonya Washington, thanks for being so nice. I love your humbleness…you are inspiring. Thanks Tamika Newhouse for supporting new authors. Thanks Rhonda Mcknight, Rose Rock and Vanessa Miller for your advice. Thanks Ella Curry for giving me a moment to shine on blog talk radio. I especially like to thank my publishers George Sherman Hudson and Shawna A. of G Street Chronicles for giving my novel a new home. I look forward to more novels to come. And last but certainly not least, I'd like thank every reader who picks up a copy or downloads this novel. Remember my novel is not only to entertain but educate.

God Bless You All
Janie De Coster

*If we say that we have no sin, we deceive ourselves
and the truth is not in us.*
1st John 1:8

PROLOGUE

"**M**ommy, may I have another pancake, please?" Brice asked, looking up at his mother.

"Okay, honey, one more and that's it," she said, placing another buttermilk pancake on his plate. "Now hurry and eat it, son," she urged as she slipped on her mocha-colored knit sweater.

Mornings were always hectic for Gade. She had to drop her son off at school and then make her way over to The Good Samaritan Hospital where she worked. As Brice gobbled down the last piece of pancake, Gade stared at him in awe.

His almond-colored complexion, honey-brown eyes, and curly brown hair gave him a handsome appearance of a model. She knew by the time he entered high school, girls would be flocking around him like mad-crazy.

Lamonte startled her out of her thoughts by kissing her gently on the cheek as he grabbed a cup of fresh brewed coffee. "It might be another late night for me, babe. I've got three men out sick with the flu," he said, swallowing the last of his java.

"No problem, honey. I'm sure Brice and I will find something to do with ourselves until you get home." She watched Brice struggle with his Spiderman book bag, which was almost as big as he was.

Gade picked up her leather briefcase and grabbed her keys from the black and white marble countertop. "Come on, Brice, let's get going before we both are late," she ordered, stopping a minute to give Lamonte a quick peck on the lips.

"Mmm, that tasted better than the syrup on the buttermilk pancakes I just had," he chuckled, gazing at her.

Lamonte was so complimentary. Had been since the very first day they met. He was a good husband and father, and she loved him.

Brice opened the sunburst-designed door and was about to walk out.

"Hold it, son," he ordered as he bent his tall, six-foot frame down to his son's eye level. He gave him a high-five as Brice let out a soft giggle. "Who loves you, kid?" Lamonte's voice boomed.

"My daddy!" Brice yelled, jumping up and down.

"That's right, my boy, and you have a good day at school, you hear?"

"Okay, Daddy." Brice had a spring in his step going out the door.

Lamonte smiled at his wife, giving her a sexy grin. She smiled back. "You too, baby."

Gade pressed the automatic door button to unlock the car. She had made it to the pearl-white Navigator when Lamonte hollered out, "Oh honey, I almost forgot. When you were asleep last night, my brother called. And guess what, Babe? He's coming home. After all these years, my brother is finally coming to his senses. He's even going to help me run the business, just like we had planned in the beginning. And to top it all off, Brice is finally going to get to know his uncle!" He beamed with joy.

Gade stopped dead in her tracks. It was a cool mid-April morning, but she felt her temperature rising, making her sweat. The phone call she was dreading had finally come. Unbeknownst to her husband, she was more aware of his brother's plans than Lamonte would ever be.

In fact, the man wasn't coming home as Lamonte had thought. He was already here. He had blessed her with his appearance a couple of days ago, and thanks to him, their lives would never be the same.

"Babe, did you hear anything I've said?"

"Yes, honey…I heard every single word, and it's great that your brother is coming, home," she stammered. "We'll talk about it tonight, hon. I'm going to be late," she uttered, avoiding his eyes as she got into the SUV.

She started the engine and pulled away from the curb as Brice yelled from the window, "Bye Daddy!"

As she drove down the freeway, Gade's mind went back in time to the very day Joe Nathan Burrels had walked into her life almost six years ago. Although it had been that long, her feelings for him lingered, and the evidence of their sin remained as she glanced at the beautiful face of her son in the rearview mirror. This is how it all began.

SIX YEARS EARLIER

It was the 4th of July, a day of celebration, but Gade was as bored as she could be. Lamonte, her first true boyfriend, had enlisted in the military a couple of years earlier and he was on his last tour. He had been away for almost a year, but he was due to come home soon and she couldn't wait. She was thinking about how much she missed him, when her older sister Saphire bounced into her bedroom unannounced, as she always did.

Saphire was everything Gade wanted to be. Bold, Bodacious and Beautiful, just like the license plate on her gold Lexus stated. Saphire was a big woman, but curvaceous. Big-breasted and very outgoing, she reminded Gade of the comedy queen, Monique.

"Lil' Sis, what are your plans today? Don't tell me you're going to stay in this stuffy old room and shrivel up until your man gets home?" Saphire smirked with a toss of her head.

"I'm fine, okay? And no, I'm not going to stay in this room. I do have plans," Gade stated a little too quickly.

Saphire threw her head back and let out a throaty laugh. "Yeah, right, and I'm having dinner with the Queen of England." Dropping her plus-size frame on the foot of Gade's canopy bed, she crossed her thick legs. Gade gave her a twisted look.

Saphire was always ragging on her about her unpopularity. In fact, they argued about almost everything under the sun. But it wasn't always that way. Things began to change when she reached her teenage years. They drove their mother nuts with their tiffs, as she called them. Mom could never understand why her two lovely daughters just didn't get along. Gade had very few friends, due to her shyness. Well, actually, she wasn't that shy. She was just quiet and reserved.

As she stared at her baby sister, Saphire said, "Get up girl, we're going to a picnic!"

"Who says I want to go to a picnic?"

"I did, and you're going. It's Clay's family reunion picnic at the park, and for some strange reason, he invited you as well. So get to stepping," Saphire said firmly as she stood up and strutted out the door.

She sure has some nerve, Gade thought. *Ordering me to attend a picnic where I won't know a blazing soul.* Then her thoughts went to Clay, Saphire's boyfriend. He is such a nice guy; too nice for her sister, that's for sure. The man treats her like a princess. God only knows why he puts up with her behind, because all she ever does is boss him around. They had been dating for the past three years, and Saphire wasn't the faithful girl Clay thought she was. But like they say, love is blind and Saphire had Clay's eyes wired shut.

"Why not go to the picnic?" she mused. "After all, I'm not doing anything else."

FAMILY REUNION IN THE PARK

Clay met them at Leimert Park, a popular place where celebrities were known to hang out. There were also several flourishing jazz clubs in the area. The park occasionally held crafts and art shows, which always drew large crowds. Clay's tall lean frame flipped over a tree trunk and he landed back on his feet on the soft velvet green grass. He got a kick out of showing off his athletic abilities and Gade admired that.

The women watched as he made his way over to them. "Hey, Sugar Plum," Clay greeted Saphire as he wrapped his arms around her plump, but shapely figure and gave her a kiss on her full lips. Then his eyes landed on Gade. "I'm glad you could make it," he said and smiled.

"Anytime, Clay, and thanks for inviting me," Gade murmured, walking over to the picnic table decorated in red, white and blue. A large bouquet of fresh-cut red roses sat in the middle of the checkerboard tablecloth as it swayed in the summer breeze.

"Oh, no you don't, Little Bit," Clay chimed in. "Go on over there and grab yourself a plate," he instructed as he pointed to the huge green tent that was swamped with family members standing in a buffet line.

Gade did as she was told, and after standing in the long line for what seemed like hours, she came back with a large plate of buffalo wings, baked beans, cole slaw, rolls and a slice of sweet potato pie, which was her favorite. She balanced it all with a cup of sweet tea in hand.

Saphire and Clay were standing nearby, talking to a couple who looked to be in their sixties. Gade noticed the way her sister was pouring on the charm as the older woman with silver streaks through her hair reached out and gave Saphire a motherly hug.

She then heard Clay yell out, "Look, Saphire, there's my Aunt Florine and Uncle Simon!" He pointed to a couple who looked to be in their late

forties standing near the barbecue grill a few feet away. "I haven't seen them since I was knee-high to a grasshopper," he said, and chuckled loudly as he pulled Saphire in their direction. "Come on, Sugar Plum, let me introduce you," he commanded. He turned to Gade. "Hey, Little Bit, come on over. I want to introduce you as well." Clay was obviously having a good old time, but from the look on her sister's face, she could tell this was really the last place she wanted to be.

With a nod of her head, Gade smiled and said, "That's all right, Clay, you and Saphire go right ahead. I'll meet them a little later. Right now, this girl is about to get her grub on." She snickered, pouring the packet of Cool Ranch dressing on her steaming wings.

She watched Clay and her sister as they disappeared into the thick crowd. Gade was on her third wing when she felt a light tap on her shoulder. She quickly turned around, and her heart nearly stopped. A drop-dead gorgeous man was staring down at her. She attempted to speak, but a piece of meat got stuck in her throat.

She tried to cough it up, to no avail; it wasn't budging. The handsome hunk, noticing her distress, stood her up and performed the Heimlich Maneuver. Within seconds, the meat popped right out of her mouth. Gade was relieved, yet slightly embarrassed, as a small crowd had gathered around them with panicked stares and murmuring.

"Are you okay?" the hunk asked, his eyes filled with concern.

Gade reached down, picked up her cup of iced tea, and swallowed hard. Her throat felt tight as the cold tea went down. "Uh-huh…I'm fine. Thank you. Thank you so much," she managed to whisper as she took in the full view of the man that had just saved her life.

He was over six feet tall with a muscular body. His golden complexion was flawless, and his hazel eyes seemed to glow in the sun. His short brown hair had waves, and he possessed a dazzling smile.

"I'm so sorry. It's all my fault, I shouldn't have startled you," he said apologetically as his hazel eyes gazed down into hers. "I saw you sitting here alone, and I just wanted to ask if I could join you. Now look what I've done," he stammered.

"No, no…it's okay, really," she assured him as the crowd began to disperse. "You know something, you just saved my life."

With a shrug of his shoulders, he returned, "Well, I, uh…guess I did." For a moment, they both stood in silence, reveling in what had transpired.

"How did you know to do that?" Gade asked, bewildered. Being in the medical field, she always saw courses offered to the public on CPR, but to actually have a stranger perform it on her was sensational.

"I've taken some classes at the Y, and I guess the training just stuck with me," he responded with a chuckle.

"How can I ever thank you?" she asked, lowering her eyes from the intense stare of his hazel ones.

"You all right?" he asked, without acknowledging her question and taking in a full view of her short curvy body.

"Yeah, I'm fine, really," she answered evenly.

"That's great, just great," he said, obviously relieved. "Well now, getting back to your question, how about having dinner with me tonight?" he asked with a crooked grin.

Gade paused for a moment, as thoughts of going out with this fine man sent tingles down her spine. The vibes he was sending made her very nervous. "Um…I don't know about that." She was thinking of her boyfriend, Lamonte. She hadn't gone out with another man since they started dating almost a year and a half ago. She believed in being faithful. That's the kind of person she was. But there was something different about this man. The attraction she was feeling for him was magical, dangerous. "You just saved my life, and I don't even know your name," she exclaimed, trying to stall as she debated her situation. They hadn't been introduced properly.

She extended her hand, and he took it gently. "My name is Gade Michaels," she stated with a warm smile.

"And mine is Joe Burrels, and I'm only asking you out for dinner, not to marry me. Although I wouldn't mind that either," he replied, giving her hand a squeeze.

Gade felt her pulse quicken at the thought of being in bed with this

fascinating man. Imagining his strong arms holding her, his fingers touching every inch of her body, was making her weak in the knees. She felt ashamed for thinking such sensuous thoughts about a man she didn't even know.

Clearing her throat and her mind from such lustful thoughts, she answered. "Well, since you put it that way, why not? But let's hold off on the wedding until at least the second date."

She chuckled as they let go of each other's hand. Reaching down into her big canvas bag sitting on the picnic bench, she pulled out a pen.

She scribbled her address on a paper napkin she'd retrieved from the picnic table. Just as she handed the paper to Joe, Saphire and Clay walked up. "What do we have here?" Saphire asked, looking at the man as if he was a delicious bowl of butter pecan ice cream.

Saphire played with the lace of her tight baby blue top that had the word "sexy" written on it in rhinestones, bringing extra attention to her full-figured breasts. Unlike Gade, Saphire was well endowed. Her D cups captured the eyes of men, as if they were diamonds, while Gade's B cups faded into the background like a shadow on a cloudy day.

Growing up, Gade envied her sister so much; she would go as far as stuffing her bra with tissues just so she could look as voluptuous as Saphire did. All through high school, she had only two boyfriends. Every time a boy showed interest in Gade, once they met her sister their interest in Gade suddenly died. Saphire had twenty or so at her beck and call, but still found time for her meager crumbs. Next to her sister, with a name like Saphire and a body to match, she always felt like she didn't stand a chance.

She silently watched her sister cast her spell on Joe, and wondered if he would now renege on his dinner date with her, and take her sister instead. In fact, that was the reason she'd stopped bringing guys over to their home.

It was like choosing between steak - Saphire, or her as the hamburger. Gade spoke quickly. "Um, Saphire, Clay, this is Joe Burrels. Joe Burrels, this is my sister Saphire and her fiancé Clay." Gade emphasized the last word.

Saphire's eyes narrowed as she gave her sister an evil stare. She knew

darn well that she wasn't engaged to Clay, and had no such plans. She steamed silently, but she managed to give the man a sexy stare.

"Nice to meet you, man," Clay said, breaking the silence and reaching out to shake Joe's hand.

"Yes, I certainly agree. It's very nice to meet you," Saphire crooned as her eyes traveled over his tan muscular frame. She took in the shape of his full lips and licked hers.

"By any chance are we related?" Clay asked, searching Joe's face for some family resemblance.

"Nah, man, I don't think so. You see, I was just invited here by a friend, Sam. We're here shooting hoops. There's a basketball tournament going on today and he invited me to participate. I'm also here visiting my family," Joe quickly added as he saw the expression on Gade's face.

Just as he was aware of Gade's demeanor, he also couldn't help but notice Saphire's hourglass figure as his eyes roamed over her shapely body. Her D cups demanded attention like a drill sergeant in front of a group of fresh rookies. Both women were captivating in their own way, but like a kid in a candy store, he had to sample only one bar at a time. So, he turned his attention back to Gade.

"You guys missed the whole thing," she began excitedly. Clay and Saphire's brows went up as they stared blankly at Gade. "This man just saved my life!"

"Saved your life, what are you talking about?" Saphire asked. Her eyes were glued to the fine hunk of man before her.

"Just exactly what I said, he saved my life. I was sitting here eating my wings and I choked on a piece of meat. The next thing I knew, he was performing the Heimlich on me. Didn't you, Joe?" Gade asked.

"It wasn't such a big deal." He shrugged. "I'm just glad I knew how to do it." He smiled as Saphire continued to gaze at him. Gade saw her sister staring at her new friend.

Gade was relieved to find there weren't any sparks, on Joe's part, that is. But the way her sister was drooling at the mouth, made Gade wonder if she needed to call the dog catchers to pick her up.

"Ahh, man, that's really amazing!" Clay exclaimed, oblivious to the fact that his woman was practically propositioning the stranger. "Thanks for being there, bro. I don't know what we'd do without Little Bit here."

"Yeah thanks," Saphire uttered slowly, giving Joe a flirty grin.

"Don't sweat it. Anybody would have done the same thing. Especially for such a beautiful woman," Joe answered as he looked at Gade. She couldn't help but smile widely while Saphire drew in her lips. Envy played in her eyes. "Well, you guys, I must be going. I know Sam is wondering where I've gotten off to." He turned to Gade, and giving her a small smile, he said, "I'll see you tonight." Then he did something she didn't expect. He reached over and gave her a small hug. The hug may have been brief, but it left a lasting impression.

"Nice meeting the both of you," Joe said as he released Gade. Noticing the deep stare coming from Saphire, he met her gaze. His stare lingered for just a moment. Without another word, he trotted off, leaving both women staring after him, lost in thought.

"Sounds like somebody's got a hot date tonight," Clay exclaimed as he smiled at her.

"I sure do," she bubbled.

Saphire cleared her throat. "Clay, why don't you go join your cousins over there. I think a game is about to begin," she said, her face scrunching up as she looked in the direction of the basketball court. The sun was at its highest peak, and so was her temper.

"Yeah, I think you're right, Sugar Plum," he replied as he hurried over to the guys.

Gade braced herself for Saphire's lecture. "Go on, say what's on your mind." She sighed as she took a seat on the picnic bench.

Saphire parted her full lips and folded her arms. "Well, Lil' Sis. For one, how in the hell did something as fine as that find its way over to you? And two, what is with you, agreeing to go out with him so fast? You don't know the man from Adam," she questioned with a wave of her hand.

Gade raised her eyebrows. "Mmm, that's never stopped you before, now has it? All a man has to do is breathe your way and you're ready to

jump his bones."

Saphire gave her sister a hot look. Pursing her lips, she said, "I think the choking incident must have cut off your brain circulation."

Gade let out a burst of air. "I'm not a little kid anymore. I can make my own decisions, and I've chosen to go out with him. He saved my life, for crying out loud! What lunatic would do something like that and then turn right around and do me harm?" she reasoned.

Saphire paused as she took in her sister's observation. After a brief moment, she said, "Yeah, you might be right about that. A nice little dinner for the girl he saved. What a great conversation piece to brag about with his friends."

"Oh, so you don't think he could possibly find me attractive?" she stated, her feelings crushed.

Saphire shook her head. "Now there you go again with your little insecurities. I didn't say anything about your attractiveness. I'm just concerned because he looked so much older than you. More my age, don't you think?" Saphire was pouring it on. "Plus, you've got a boyfriend," she continued. "Have you forgotten all about Lamonte?" she asked, throwing her black-and-burgundy braided hair over her shoulder.

"You have some gall, you know that, Saphire?" Gade spat out, standing up. "You're trying to lay a guilt trip on me and I'm not buying into it. I'm going out with Joe, and there's nothing you can do about it." Saphire was about to respond, but Gade interjected as she held up her hand. "You're such a hypocrite. Look how many times you've gone out with other men, when you, my dear sister, have a boyfriend as well," she said smugly, looking over at the basketball court as Clay and his cousins pounded it out over the ball. Clay took control of the ball, dribbled down the court, and with the swiftness of a bird, he slam-dunked it.

Victory shouts rang across the park as Clay pranced around the court, giving the guys high-fives. Saphire's eyes narrowed. She gave him a quick smile before turning her attention back to Gade. Closing her thick fingers around Gade's arm, she hissed, "What goes on between my man and me is our business.

Pulling her arm out of Saphire's tight grip, Gade returned, "And what I do and who I see is my business."

Oblivious to the tension between the sisters, Clay and an elderly man approached the women. "Hey girls, I got somebody I want both of you to meet," Clay announced, out of breath. He wiped the sweat from his face with the thick white towel he picked up from the table. Standing beside Clay was a short stocky man who looked to be in his late sixties. Clay pulled Saphire into his arms. "Uncle Hesekiah, this is Saphire, my future wife," he said, remembering how Gade had introduced her before. He liked the thought of Saphire being his wife, and he was planning to make it official one day. "And this is her sister, Gade."

Gade let a short giggle escape from her throat. If only Clay knew that marriage was the last thing on her sister's mind.

"Well, I'll be doggoned-boy, you sho' got you a fine one here!" Hesekiah stared at Saphire as his eyes stretched as big as saucers.

Gade wondered if the old man was getting a cheap thrill just by looking at her sister's big breasts and shapely body. Clay glanced down at Gade, who was just finishing up her last piece of sweet potato pie.

"Little Bit, are you still chowing down? No wonder you're so small, you eat like a bird." Clay laughed as he let go of Saphire and sat down beside her.

Hesekiah lowered his beady eyes and focused on Gade. "My lawd, you're a pretty little thing, you just need more meat on your bones, like yo sister here," he said as his eyes fell back on Saphire's chest.

Gade folded the paper plate and its leftover contents. She proceeded to wipe her hands with the paper napkins she pulled from the picnic basket. People joking about her weight didn't bother her anymore. She was used to all the jokes and the names she had been called, from lightweight to bantam feathers.

She might be small, but she had curves. Her petite frame earned her plenty of stares from the opposite sex. She was sporting a short hairstyle that was popular at the salon. Her honey-colored complexion was flawless. With her light brown eyes and dimpled cheeks, not to mention her just

waxed eyebrows, and with a recent facial, she was feeling pretty good about herself.

And why shouldn't she? A fine as wine man had just asked her out and she was elated. But doubt began to creep into the back of her mind. Was it the way her sister said? Was Joe Burrels just being a good sport?

Or was he actually interested in her? Then it hit her. Hadn't he said that he saw her sitting alone and he wanted to come over and talk to her? A small smile played at the corners of her mouth. Joe liked her, she was sure of it, and the feeling was definitely mutual.

Feeling more secure, she got up, gathered her paper plate, cup and used napkins, and threw everything into the nearby trash can. Gade extended her hand out to Hesekiah and said, "Nice meeting you, Mr. Hesekiah."

Hesekiah took her small hand into his rough one and shook it, holding on a little too long for Gade's comfort. She retrieved her hand and glanced at her sister and Clay. "I'll see you guys later, I'm going home now," she announced as she sashayed away.

"Hold up, I'll take you home!" Clay bellowed.

Shaking her head, Gade said, "Nah, that's okay. You and Saphire go on back to the picnic. I'll take the bus. I want to go downtown anyway and browse the shops a little. I might pick up something from Melrose. Something exotic for my date tonight." She giggled as she gave Saphire an impish look.

She strutted off in the direction of the bus stop when she heard her sister's sassy voice say, "Gade, don't you go and do nothing stupid, you hear me!"

Gade turned around. "Don't worry, sis, I won't do anything you wouldn't do." She made quick strides out of the park, and never looked back.

GET ON THE BUS

Gade found a seat next to an elderly lady who reminded her of her nana. With salt-and-pepper hair and skin the color of coffee beans, the lady gave her a warm smile, which Gade returned with a smile of her own. She sat down, leaned her head back, and settled in for the ride.

Thinking of her sister, she wondered who the hell she thought she was. Sure, she was her one and only older sister, but Saphire certainly wasn't her momma. Saphire always got on her nerves, telling her how to run her affairs when she needed to be concerned with her own. Their mother, Josey, was forever breaking up arguments between the two of them.

Gade admired her mother. She was a strong woman who had raised them by herself since the day their trifling ass daddy walked out of their lives. Josey held down two jobs to support them when they lived in the projects. Their mother was determined that her girls would have a better life.

The proudest moment of their lives was when their mother became a homeowner. She purchased a three-bedroom, two-and-a-half bath home in a middle-class subdivision in LA. She showed them first-hand what a little sweat and determination could do.

Gade wasn't sure if the work and determination to have a better life was the real reason her momma worked so hard. Her belief had been that it was an attempt at masking the pain she felt from their father, Russell, leaving her for another woman. Gade remembered the cheap birthday cards and Christmas presents that came in the mail as the years went by.

She was too young to really understand what was going on, but one thing she knew for sure, the memories of her mother's tear-stained face as she sat before the Christmas tree that first year, remained etched in her young mind. From her child's point of view, Christmas was supposed to

have been the happiest time of the year for everyone. Moms and dads doing everything possible for their homes to be filled with great cheer, in anticipation of the man in the red suit making his grand entrance. But not in their house. It was as if someone had died, leaving their ghost behind.

As the years passed, so did the sadness. Christmas began to be a time of joy and happiness for them again. Their mother tried to make up for the lack of affection from their father, who Gade had long ago labeled as a sperm donor.

Years later, Saphire graduated with a degree in business, while Gade had chosen the medical field. And now, even though they were in their early twenties, they both still lived at home. The house was more than big enough for all of them, plus they just couldn't see leaving their mother alone, like their father had done.

Gade's light brown eyes scanned the crowd. Two middle-aged women clutched their shopping bags tightly while a teenager sat behind them with his Walkman in his ear rocking to the rhythm of the beat. Looking past them to a couple of rows down, she saw two white businessmen with black leather briefcases. They each wore black Armani suits.

Surely, they could have afforded a luxury car, she thought, not realizing how intently she was staring at them. The one who could have been a carbon copy of Tom Cruise met her gaze and winked at her, snapping her out of her trance. She gave him a slight smile and quickly averted her eyes. This must be her lucky day, she mused. Catching the attention of two fine guys within hours of each other was something of a record to remember, that's for sure. Noticing she was nearing her stop, she reached up and rang the bell. As the bus slowed to a stop and she stepped off, from the corner of her eye she saw the white guy still smiling at her as the bus pulled away.

WHERE DID HE GO?

Saphire couldn't get her mind off the fine hunk of a man her sister had met at the picnic. Who was he and where did he come from? He wasn't a relative of Clay's, which was good, but she had to find the answers to these questions. She pondered this, as Clay stood close by, running off at the mouth with his uncle Hesekiah.

She peered at the old man as he took a long drag of his cigar and then blew out the smoke. Earlier on, she'd liked the sweet aroma, but now it was making her ill. "Excuse me, you two," she interrupted, standing up from the picnic table.

She was bored listening to the men talk about nothing that held any interest for her. "I'll let you men catch up on old times while I go and mingle for a while." She leaned over and gave Clay a quick kiss on the lips.

"But Sugar Plum, our second game is going to start in a few, and I wanted you to see me and my smooth moves as I clobber my cousins again," Clay bragged, looking over at his uncle.

"Yeah, the boy was always good at throwing that ball." Hesekiah chuckled. Saphire noticed how his pot belly jiggled when he laughed.

She wondered if Clay would look like that in his old age. Surely not, she mused, taking in his muscular physique. Letting out a defeated sigh, she made herself grin. Seeing Clay play basketball was the last thing she wanted to do, but on second thought, maybe that fine man Joe Burrels was still hanging around.

Mmmm, she smiled to herself. She could feel the glare of Hesekiah's old eyes on her. "Well…okay," Saphire relented, sitting back down next to Clay. She stared out towards the basketball goal as a group of men gathered there. She was hoping to see Joe Burrels and his fine self somewhere in the mix.

A GIRL'S NIGHT OUT

Gade studied herself in the full-length mirror. She sported a black and white Gucci dress that accentuated her small curves. Her three-inch black stilettos added inches to her short stature. She wore a small amount of makeup, just to accent her high cheekbones. Satisfied with her appearance, she peeked out from her second-story bedroom window that faced the tree-lined street.

As she awaited the arrival of her new date, her nerves were frayed. She sat down on the edge of her full-size canopy bed to calm herself down. From Gade's understanding, her mother also had a date tonight. Many years passed before her momma would even give a man the time of day, much less date one. Her dad really did a number on her.

Her mother's motto was, fool me once, shame on you, fool me twice, shame on me. Josey always told Gade and her sister that they would never have to worry about a stepdad, because no man was ever putting his legs under her table, let alone lying in her bed, permanently, that is. But as young as they were, she couldn't fool them. She was certain her mother was getting her freak on whenever she stayed out at night on the pretense of working late.

It was a fact that a man was occasionally in their house at one time or another, because she and her sister had found men's socks every once in a while mixed in with the laundry. But neither of them had the nerve to confront her about it. Josey's business was her own, as she reminded them often. Gade's thoughts faded as she saw a gold Expedition slow down and then stop in front of her house.

Her heart began to pound loudly as the honey-colored stallion got out of his SUV and strutted up the driveway to her front door. Within minutes, Josey's voice boomed upstairs, beckoning her to come down for her date.

With each step Gade took, her nerves rattled her, until she stood with the man who had saved her life earlier that day.

After returning home that evening, she'd recited the whole story to her mother. Now, Josey was treating the man like royalty, Gade saw as she peeked at them seated on the sandalwood-gold couch.

Joe was holding a small gold-rimmed saucer, part of her mother's best china. A thick slice of her famous homemade chocolate cake sat on top of it. Joe placed the saucer down on the oak coffee table and stood up when he noticed Gade's presence.

Joe was even taller than she remembered, and finer, too, Gade mused as her eyes took him in. The navy blue shirt framed his broad shoulders and the designer jeans showed a slim, yet muscular build. Josey smiled at her daughter as she entered the room. "I guess I will leave you two alone now," she murmured as she also stood.

"Thank you for the cake, Mrs. Michaels, it was delicious," Joe commented as he gazed at her mom. "Why thank you. You're quite welcome," Josey said, smiling broadly.

Joe knew Josey liked him from the instant he walked in the door. Women were smitten by his charisma and he knew it. "And by the way, Mrs. Michaels, I see where your daughter gets her looks." Joe gave Josey a dazzling smile that he knew would cement their friendship.

She saw her mother blush for the first time in her entire life. Joe was definitely a charmer, and he had her mother hooked. Josey beamed as she gave her daughter a Kool-Aid smile and left the room.

"Are we ready?" he asked as his eyes traveled from her face all the way down to her black stilettos. From the alluring stare he had given her, Gade knew he liked every inch of her petite frame, and that made her smile.

WHERE IS MY SISTER?

Saphire breezed into the kitchen and headed straight for her momma's cooking pot. From the smell of things, dinner was almost ready. Saphire removed the stainless steel lid, and the aroma of beef stew teased her nostrils as she inhaled. "Mmmm," she said.

"Girl, if you don't get your nose out of my pot," Josey huffed as she made her way into her medium-sized country kitchen.

"Oh Momma, can I please have a bowl?" she begged as she looked at the big chucks of potatoes and carrots as if they were diamonds.

"That's tomorrow's dinner after church," Josey announced as she took the lid from Saphire's hand and placed it back on the pot.

She studied Saphire quizzically. "Didn't you eat enough at the family picnic?"

"Yes, Momma, I ate a little something, but I had more important things on my mind." She smiled vaguely as she took a seat at the breakfast table.

Josey loved her oldest daughter dearly, but she had sinful ways just like her father. Saphire was always scheming for some reason or another, and Josey felt like she could trust her no further than she could throw her.

"Oh, I see, Clay was too busy showing you off to his family, huh?" Josey smiled as she searched her daughter's face for clarity.

"Well yeah, he tried," she responded dryly, looking down at her French-manicured nails. It was time for a touch-up.

"How come you don't sound too happy about it? Didn't you have a good time?"

"Momma, it was okay, I guess. I mean, I didn't know anyone there other than Clay's parents, so what did you expect?" Saphire answered curtly.

"Well, you don't have to bite my head off. I just asked if you had a good time, for God's sake. I mean, you were with Clay…and God knows he's

the life of the party all by himself." Josey chuckled.

Saphire smacked her lips. In her mother's opinion, Clay was the next best thing since the light bulb. Sure, he had his props. He was a hardworking man; in fact, he was working towards establishing his own business. And he was a wiz at repairing things, which he hoped would lead him into getting his own shop real soon.

Now, Clay was also your ordinary, everyday type of guy. He was into family, church and spending quiet evenings at home. When she was with him, she felt as if they had been married a dozen years. All they needed was a house with a picket fence, a couple of snotty-nosed kids, and a dog running around to complete the picture.

She wanted more out of her man. Hell, she needed more. Being the kind of woman she was, a man like Clay Matthews, as nice and dependable as he was, just couldn't satisfy her. Her mind fell back to the sexy bowlegged specimen at the picnic who called himself Joe. She'd bet he could satisfy her in more ways than one, she mused as she imagined them buck-naked in bed at some high-rise hotel.

She was getting turned on just thinking about it. *Mmmm, why did Gade have to meet him first?* She fumed silently. Speaking of Gade, where was her baby sister anyway? "Momma, where's Gade, shouldn't she be home by now?" she asked, interrupting her mother's rambling.

Josey was telling her about one of her church members who needed to have hip surgery, but she had long ago quit listening. Josey stopped and raised her eyebrow. "You didn't know about that nice man saving your sister's life at the picnic?" she quizzed.

"Yeah, yeah, I know all about that." She smirked as she crossed her thick brown legs.

"The man came by here tonight, and they went out to dinner. Joe Burrels sure is a good-looking man, isn't he? And very gentlemanly, too," Josey added with a smile.

Saphire's spirits dropped. She was hoping Joe was simply being nice to Gade, and not actually serious about taking her out, but evidently, she was wrong. Licking her cranberry-colored lips, she said, "Well, in my opinion,

I think he is too old for her, Momma."

Josey's eyes widened as she observed her oldest daughter carefully.

"I mean, he looks to be more my age, maybe even a little older, don't you think?" She stared at her mother with a slight hint of lust simmering in her eyes.

Josey's heart skipped a beat. Staring into her daughter's face, she knew that look in her eye all too well.

It was the same look Saphire's daddy had whenever he saw fresh meat in the neighborhood. She and Russell couldn't even go grocery shopping together without arguing about some woman to whom he was giving extra attention. Russell was just a big flirt, which led into him being a big womanizer.

Dismissing the memory, Josey spouted, "Age doesn't matter much these days, Saphire, plus, your sister has a level head on her shoulders. She knows how to handle herself." Josey got up from the table and poured herself a cup of coffee from the pot she had percolating.

"What about her boyfriend, Momma? How do you think Lamonte would feel about all of this? He's out there in some horrific scene with his squad doing Uncle Sam's job, while his girlfriend is out on the town with some man she just met hours ago," Saphire complained, throwing up her hands.

Josey burned with anger now, knowing all the times Saphire had stepped out on poor Clay. She had to use all of her fingers and toes to come near to the count of men Saphire had gone out with since she'd started dating him three years ago. He was such a good man, and totally head over heels in love with her daughter. Clay would kiss the ground Saphire walked on if she asked him to. Now, here she sat with the innocence of Mother Teresa.

Josey frowned. "I don't believe you have the nerve to rag on your sister like that." Deep lines creased her forehead. "Don't let me start naming guys you cheated on Clay with. For if I do, we will probably be in this kitchen all night," she sneered.

Saphire let out a deep breath as she felt the anger rising in her chest. "That is so different, Momma," she mumbled with a roll of her eyes. "I can't help it if I have a lot of men for friends."

She got up, retrieved a glass from the cupboard, trekked over to the sink and filled it with water. She walked back to the breakfast table and sat down.

Josey gazed into her eyes. "Friends? Please, don't insult my intelligence, Saphire!" she snapped. "You might fool Clay with your little lies, but you sure as heck can't fool your own momma."

Saphire returned her mother's glare and she reasoned, "Momma, I'm not trying to fool anyone. Clay knows all about my friends and we...we have...an understanding."

Josey looked her squarely in the eye. "What kind of understanding? He stays faithful while you go out and screw around with whomever you please?" she said with disdain.

Throwing up her hands, Saphire stood. "That's it, Momma. I can't even have a civil conversation with you these days without always having to defend myself!" she replied hotly. Taking in a deep breath to calm herself, she said, "Look, for the last time, there is nothing going on between me and my friends." Josey gave her a look and shook her head. Saphire let out a sigh of exasperation. "You know what? I've had it with you and your suspicions. Think what you want, I'm going to bed."

She took a big gulp of water and placed the glass down in the stainless steel sink, not bothering to wash it. She brushed past her mother without saying another word.

Josey stared after her with her hands on her hips. "Like they say, if you can't stand the heat get out of the kitchen!" Josey shouted after her.

She hated it when she and her oldest daughter got into such heated arguments, but she just couldn't let her get away with dissing her sister like that. Sure, Gade had a boyfriend, and Lamonte was nice. However, she had always felt that her baby girl could do so much better for herself.

Lamonte was so young and unpredictable. Those soldier boys always were, in Josey's opinion. No, what her Gade needed was an older, more settled guy, and from talking to Joe earlier tonight, he seemed to be just the ticket. She was going to do everything she could to make Gade see that as well.

DELICIOUS MEAL, AMONG OTHER THINGS

Gade sat quietly in the elegant restaurant with its dim lighting as Joe mesmerized her with stories of his travels. She learned he had been to Paris, the Virgin Islands, and Puerto Rico, which was a place she'd always dreamed of seeing one day. He told her he was a business consultant for a large company, which kept him on the road, and he had enjoyed every minute of it. She studied his light hazel eyes that bored deeply into hers as if he was looking for buried treasure.

"I hope I'm not boring you with my stories," Joe commented.

"Not at all, the way you describe everything to me, I almost feel as if I was there with you," Gade mused.

Joe took in the glow of her face from the candlelight. He wanted her.

"Maybe one day you will be," he responded.

The tone of his voice sent a chill racing down her spine. This man was doing things to her body as well as her mind. Joe took a small sip of his champagne as he waited for Gade's response.

"Maybe," was all she said as the waitress appeared with their food.

The filet mignon and steamed vegetables teased their senses. As she took a sip of the white wine, she devoured the features of the handsome man who sat before her. He was the perfect gentleman, and so knowledgeable. *How in the hell did I snag such a fantastic man?* She asked herself.

"Are you having a good time?" he asked as he reached over and took her small hand in his. He rubbed the top of her slender fingers with his thumb. Sparks flew through her.

Clearing her throat, she smiled. "Yes, I'm enjoying myself immensely. It's the best time I've had in a while," she admitted. The restaurant dance floor was scattered with couples taking advantage of the soft jazz that filled the air.

"Care to dance?" Joe asked, his eyes never leaving her face.

"Sure," she responded as they both stood up.

On the dance floor, Joe pulled her close as they swayed to the soft rhythm of the love ballad "Killing Me Softly," by Roberta Flack. Killing me softly was how she was feeling as she took in the masculine scent of his sexy cologne. He held her small frame firmly against him as she fell into a romantic trance. Was it the champagne, the soft music and the closeness of this fine man that put her there? She questioned as her eyes fluttered. For a brief moment Lamonte's face flashed through her mind, but he was like a faraway dream she just happened to remember. Here and now, Joe Burrels was all she wanted to think about, and being in his arms was all she wanted to feel.

PILLOW TALK

The house was dark, except for the night light her mother always left on at the bottom of the stairs. Gade carefully placed one foot lightly on each step, hoping she wouldn't hear the familiar squeaking it usually made.

Finally, she reached the top of the stairs, and she sprinted into her room, quickly closing the door behind her. She exhaled as she whispered a thank you to God as she reached for the light switch. She flipped it on and almost screamed.

There, on her canopy bed, sat her sister, Saphire. "What in the hell are you doing in my room?" she bellowed.

"What does it look like, Lil' Sis? I was waiting for you to bring your little ass home."

Gade let her black stilettos drop to the floor with a thud as she walked farther into the room. With a tilt of her head, she remarked, "I don't see why you had to wait up for me. Last time I checked, I was twenty-one years old, and I don't need your adult supervision."

Saphire's eyes flickered up and down her baby sister's body, in search of any signs of disarray or perhaps hickeys, even. Anything that would suggest that something sexual had transpired.

"So tell me, did you do the nasty with him?" Saphire asked, scooting to the edge of the bed.

Gade let out a sigh. "That's really what this is all about, isn't it? You just want to know if I bedded him." Gade crossed her thin arms. She gave her sister a perturbed look. "You're one long ass trip. For your information, no, I didn't bed him, unlike you, of course. I like to get to know my man's mind before I know his body," she snapped as she began pulling off her clothes. "Now get out of my room so I can go to bed," she ordered.

Saphire stood up from the bed and approached her sister. Standing face-to-face, she had Gade's short stature beat by almost two inches. She had gotten under her skin for the third time today.

First, at the picnic for meeting such a handsome man, second, for having dinner with the man, and third, for being a smart ass about it. She stared down at Gade and hissed through tight lips, "I'm trying to watch out for your little naive ass, a'ight?"

Gade rolled her eyes.

"You don't know a damned thing about playing the field. You've only had two real boyfriends in your entire, secluded little life."

Gade winced at the words spewing from Saphire's mouth and she began to steam. Giving her a salty look, she spat, "You think you know everything about me, don't you? I may have slept with a football team of men, for all you know. Just stay out of my business and I will stay out of yours, you know what I mean. I'm sure Clay would love to know about your latest."

Saphire knew she had the goods on her, so she decided to step down a bit. With her voice softening, she said, "Listen to me, Lil' Sis. It's a jungle out there and I don't want to see you getting all caught up into something you can't handle. You're my blood, and it's my job to keep you safe."

Gade peered into her sister's eyes. Was she really seeing a glint of sincerity in them? Maybe she did come off a little too strong with her, and maybe she was looking out for her baby sister. Gade's shoulders slumped as she let her guard down. Saphire had a way of making her feel like the guilty one. She sighed. "I'm sorry, Saphire, maybe I was being too hard on you. I apologize."

Saphire reached out and gave her sister a hug. "Apology accepted, and I'm sorry, too, for what I've said. You know I can get carried away."

"Hey, let's do something we haven't done in a while," Saphire announced in a bubbly voice.

Gade frowned as she tried to figure out what on earth she was talking about. "What's that?" she asked with a raised brow.

"Girl talk, silly. You know, what we used to do whenever one of us

went out on a hot date." Saphire chuckled.

Gade gave her a blank stare as she took a seat on her bed. She must have been referring to the times Saphire went out on a hot date and came home telling her all about it.

Without waiting on a response from Gade, Saphire stated, "I'm going downstairs to get us some milk and cookies." Looking back over her shoulder, she added, "You can tell me all about your date with this new man of yours, and I can tell you what happened at the picnic after you left today." Saphire was grinning like the true devil she was.

"Well, all right," she relented as her sister bounced down the stairs.

G STREET CHRONICLES
~A NEW URBAN DYNASTY~
WWW.GSTREETCHRONICLES.COM

HE'S BACK IN TOWN

Lamonte dialed Gade's digits from his cell. She answered on the third ring.

"Hello," her sweet voice rang through the phone.

"Hey boo, just calling to let you know I'm home!" he said excitedly.

"Oh…you are?" Gade stammered.

"Yep, and I can't wait to kiss those juicy lips of yours, amongst other things," he laughed.

Gade managed a slight chuckle of her own. "But I thought you weren't going to be here until the weekend," she said, trying not to sound disappointed. Today was Wednesday, and she had no idea he would arrive this soon.

"Our tour ended earlier than we expected. I had the opportunity to take an early flight home, and here I am. What's wrong, baby? You don't sound as if you're happy that I'm home."

Gade cleared her throat. "Now Lamonte, you know that's not true. I'm glad you're home, baby," she murmured, finding her voice. "You just surprised me, that's all."

"Well, that's good, because I'm coming by tonight to take my woman out to a fancy meal and a night out on the town. Then, I want to ravish that sexy body of yours. It's been months since I've kissed those tender lips. I miss you, Gade."

Feeling the love for her seeping through his voice made her cringe with guilt. A slight moment of silence fell between them as she struggled for a response. None came.

"Well, I'm not going to hold you, I know you're at work, so I'll see you tonight," he concluded.

Gade's mind had wandered to a faraway land, the land she shared with

another man. A land she would now leave, for her ship had come to take her back home.

Coming out of her short trance, she muttered, "Um, sure baby. See you tonight."

"Love and kisses, boo," Lamonte quipped as the line disconnected.

Gade closed her cell as she sat at her desk. She'd known Lamonte would be coming home soon from his tour of duty, but she had pushed the thought out of her mind. The truth of the matter was, she didn't have much time to think about Lamonte at all, since Joe kept her very occupied.

She had known him now for a little over three months, and they were spending almost every day together. Glancing at the clock on the wall, she saw it read 4:30 pm. She would soon be off at five. Then it dawned on her, she and Joe had plans for tonight. She let out a deep breath. With regret, she knew she had to call and cancel.

Joe knew all about Lamonte. She was very upfront with him about their relationship. He knew Lamonte was in the military and that he was due to come home soon. He didn't seem to have a problem with it. In fact, he bragged to her how he would make her forget all about her camouflage man, and true to his word, he had done just that. Until now.

Her mind floated back in time to the heated night they shared at Joe's apartment. She envisioned the scene between them as they sat on his black leather couch. They had just finished a delicious meal of country-fried chicken, garlic potatoes and green beans he had prepared himself.

After dinner, Joe was all up in her Kool-Aid, tasting every bit of her soft brown flesh. He started at her upper body, kissing her earlobe, neck, and then making his way down to the center of her cleavage. She shivered as she felt the warmth of his breath upon her breasts.

He kissed her ever so gently, then proceeded to release her breasts from the low-cut blue poplin blouse she was wearing, exploring one with his hot tongue. A moan escaped from the center of her soul, making her body tremble with desire. Would she let this man make love to her? For the very first time in weeks, she thought of Lamonte, and with all of the strength she could muster, she put on the brakes.

She had to before they reached the point of no return. She didn't sleep with Joe that night, but they did everything else. The man had her singing like a parrot. Joe did such fantastic things to her body, that it made her ask the question, how could a man make love to a woman without actually making love? The man had skills she didn't know existed.

Eventually, she could no longer resist. He was like an aphrodisiac. Lying in his bed as he stood above her, she tingled from fear and excitement.

He peered into her apprehensive eyes and whispered, "I'm going to make love to you in sixty-nine ways."

And sixty-nine ways it was. She drifted in and out of consciousness as he stroked her. Her eyes rolled, her lips uttered small moans as she rode the waves of passion and pleasure. Joe Burrels was a Golden Adonis, and he'd earned that name.

"Are you going home or are you going to just sit here and daydream?" Martha, her co-worker, asked, looking up at the clock. Gade jumped up, startled. The clock read five pm.

She couldn't believe she'd been daydreaming about Joe for the past thirty minutes. Gade managed a weak smile as she gathered her things and headed for the door. "See you tomorrow, Martha!" she called out over her shoulder.

Once in her car, she sat for a minute, contemplating what she should do. Her man was home, and he wanted to spend time with her, which was understandable. But what about the new man she had met? He wanted her as well. Now she realized the truth of what Saphire was saying the other night when they had what she called their girl talk.

Playing the field was definitely a hard thing for her to do. Could she pull it off? After all, her sister had been doing it for years, and everything seemed to be working out fine for her. Clay never suspected a thing, no matter how many lies Saphire threw at him. She closed her eyes and opened them again. Her mind was filled with questions.

She started her car and headed home. Once in her room, she stripped off her clothes and jumped into the shower. Being in the warm, steaming water helped calm her and somehow cleared her head. She worked out a

lot of problems while basking in the soothing effects of the water, and she hoped it would work again with the problems she was facing now.

The water felt good as it cascaded over her body. Flashes of both men appeared before her as she wrestled with her decisions. Should she leave a relationship of a year and a half, which was solid and safe, for someone she'd met who made her feel so good, but she had only known a few months?

Gade turned the water off, and she reached for the thick white towel from the rack that hung over her bathroom door. She began to dry her petite body. For the very first time, the water didn't work. She was no closer to making a decision than when she first climbed into the shower. She was an honest person, and she couldn't play the field like her sister did. She just didn't have it in her. She sat down on her bed and picked up the phone on her nightstand. As she dialed Joe's digits, her heart began to pound.

Joe's cell vibrated on his side. Answering it, he heard Gade's sweet voice on the other end. "Hey sweets, what's up? I can't wait to see you tonight."

"Well, that's what I'm calling about," she began. She tried to control the unsteadiness in her voice. "I'm...going to have to cancel our date tonight, Joe. Lamonte is back and he's picking me up later."

"Oh, so I guess that means we are over and out," he said pointedly.

"Don't be upset, Joe," she pleaded.

There was a moment of silence and then he uttered, "Well, I guess a girl's gotta do what a girl's gotta do. It was nice knowing you, Gade Michaels," he stated and disconnected the call.

Gade sat planted on her bed, listening to the dial tone of the phone. Her mouth almost dropped to the floor.

How could he just hang up on her like that? Wasn't it he who said her boyfriend didn't matter? Her fingers began to hurt because she was clutching the receiver so hard.

Gade placed the phone back into its cradle, put her hands over her face and exhaled. She felt as if someone had come along and knocked the wind right out of her. She had only known the man for a few months, so why was it hurting her so deeply? She lay down on her bed and grabbed the

blanket her nana had had lovingly crafted for her when she was a child. She used her favorite colors, which were yellow and white. Nana had long been gone, but her memory remained vibrant in Gade's mind. Gade was her favorite and everyone knew it. She felt so safe and secure when she wrapped up in her nana's blanket. And now Lamonte was here.

"Saphire, go downstairs and keep him company until I get dressed," she said frantically. Gade went through her closet hurriedly.

Saphire stood in the doorway with a disturbed look. "Lil' Sis, I don't know what's going on here, but you need to get your act together." She shook her head as she walked out of the room.

As Lamonte told her stories of his last days in Germany, Gade's attention span began to waver. How could Joe do this to her? Surely he knew she was having real feelings for him. She remembered clearly what he said about Lamonte.

He wasn't a problem to him, he swore, but now all of a sudden he was. It just didn't make any sense. Maybe Joe thought she wasn't a real woman. An experienced woman would have handled things differently, she thought, feeling her insecurities seeping in again.

"Earth to Gade," Lamonte said, waving his hand in front of her light brown eyes.

"Baby, what's going on? I don't think you've been listening to me since we arrived. Maybe I've should've taken you someplace else," he said, disappointment in his voice. They were seated in Christina's, an elegant restaurant by the oceanfront. Christina's specialized in fine cuisine.

"Lamonte, are you kidding me? This place is the bomb!" Gade stated as she took in the expensive decor. The greenery, coupled with the dim glow of the champagne-colored chandeliers, gave it a romantic atmosphere.

"So why are you acting as if we are sitting in Burger King?" he asked. Gade knew she was getting busted. She had to come up with something quick to ease Lamonte's mind. She smiled as Lamonte gave her a boyish pout. "Baby, I'm sorry. I'm just a little down tonight, but believe me it has nothing to do with you or this restaurant. It's family problems that are getting to me," she admitted.

"Family problems?" he questioned.

"Well, to be perfectly honest, it's that sister of mine. She found out that I made a low grade on one of my exams, and she has been riding me about it. Even going as far as threatening to tell Momma, and she knows I don't want that."

"Yeah, I know how your mom can get." Lamonte chuckled.

Gade tilted her head. "Having Momma know about a low grade is like having the police in your face," she laughed, hoping Lamonte was buying the white lie that she was selling.

"Well, don't worry about it, boo, you're a smart girl. You will bring up that grade in no time." Lamonte reached over and took her hand. "And as far as that sister of yours is concerned, well, she's just jealous because you got all the brains in the family." He smiled.

Oh, how she hated the lie she'd spoon-fed him. But she just couldn't tell him the truth, now, could she?

She could only imagine how he would feel, knowing that she had the hots for some older guy she'd met while he was away. How could she tell him she was in his bed just days before? The frightening part about it was, she just couldn't get the man out of her system, and wasn't sure if she wanted to.

Gade gave Lamonte a small smile as the waitress brought their drinks. She had chosen the Strawberry Bellini, and she quickly took a bigger sip than she usually would. She had to dull the pain that Joe left lingering in her heart.

THE BODY SHOP

Saphire popped her head under the hood of the lime green Caprice that Clay was working on. She watched as he fiddled with several wires. His co-worker, Jimmy, was behind the wheel of the car. "Give her some gas!" Clay hollered out as Jimmy did as he was told.

The car sputtered a bit, and then she purred like a kitten. "That's it, man, I knew you could get my baby going," Jimmy responded with a satisfied smile. "Yo, Saphire, you got yourself a genius here," Jimmy rattled, getting out of his car.

Saphire gave him a small grin as she looked up at Jimmy. He definitely fit the description of the term grease monkey. His skin was dark and ashen, which gave it a rubberish appearance and the short fro he sported had long ago lost its luster. The natural black color of his hair was now a dusty gray.

The brother looked as if he could use a good bath. *Maybe if he ran himself through the carwash next door, without his vehicle, of course, he might look like something recognizable when he came out,* Saphire thought to herself. She turned away from Jimmy's stare as she tried to stifle a giggle that was making its way up. The vision of him going through the carwash brushes was hilarious.

Clearing her throat, she took in a light breath. "Clay, are you ready yet?"

Her voice was laced with attitude as she checked the time on her Gucci watch. "You know you have to go home and do some scrubbing before we go out tonight," she continued as she watched him close the hood of Jimmy's car.

She couldn't stand the scent of oil and dirt that Clay's chosen profession exposed him to. Why couldn't he have been a businessman who wore Armani suits every day? A man who carried a leather briefcase to work at some corporate office, she mused as an image of Clay walking into

an upscale office building filtered through her mind. Instead, she had to endure his greased-up uniforms and dirty fingernails.

"Ughh!" she groaned solemnly. It wasn't like the man wasn't smart. He had a business degree under his belt, but he didn't have the desire to do anything else except work on dang-blasted cars.

Saphire shifted her weight from one side to the other as she waited impatiently. A thought crossed her mind while she watched Clay's process of closing up the shop. What would the world be like if there weren't people to repair things that were broken, including cars? Car repairmen were a much-needed commodity. But why did her man have to be one of the ones who repaired these cars?

Clay noticed the frustration on her face. "I'm coming, Sugar Plum, and don't you worry, I will get myself spic and span clean for my woman," he chuckled, breaking into Saphire's little daydream.

He reached out to give her a quick peck on the lips, but Saphire stepped away with a twisted look on her face. The man must have lost his everloving mind. She couldn't risk the chance of him getting grease on her brand new Gucci short set that cost her nearly eighty bucks, and that was the discounted price.

"Don't you even go there, Clay Matthews," she smirked, holding out her hand.

Clay chuckled harder. He had no intentions of really kissing her. He knew how fastidious she was. Ms. Video Queen, he called her silently, but never to her face. "Sugar Plum, I'm riding with you, I can pick my ride up later," he said, walking in the direction of her Lexus.

She narrowed her eyes and cocked her head. Did she just miss something? The plans were, she was supposed to be riding with him, not the other way around. Saphire hesitated for a moment. She remembered she kept a bottle of air freshener under her front seat, and the blanket she and Clay had used at his family picnic was still in the back seat of her car. She had totally forgotten to take it out. He could sit his greasy behind on that, she concluded as she followed him to her car.

LET'S GO CLUBBING

Saphire's girlfriends LaShon and Mia were right on the money. The new club, Spotlight, was rockin' like the 4th of July. Disco lights cast multi-colored patterns as the patrons jammed to the beat of the music on the dance floor.

The club was practically full, but there was still enough room for one to move around without rubbing elbows, unlike some of the other clubs she had visited. The dress code was casual, yet classy. The women wore the latest styles. Gucci and Roca were all in the house.

Even her own man looked mighty tasty in his Roca outfit, one that she'd bought for him, of course. If it was left up to Clay, a pair of Levi's and a pullover shirt would have sufficed. She was even amazed that he was at the club at all. Usually, their Saturday nights consisted of a movie and then a quick meal at the local Waffle House or IHOP. If he was in one of his off key moments, he would have talked her into a video rental with pizza delivery at his place or hers. But lately, Clay was beginning to follow her lead.

She concluded that he may have had his fill with her complaints of him never wanting to do anything really fun. On the other hand, that mother of hers might have whispered some little lies into his ear, making him suspicious of her. Her mother really got on her nerves with that sort of crap.

In retrospect, she had to admit, her mother had every reason to think the way she did. Truth be known, she did have some things, or should she say someone, to hide. Bobby Stanley was her best-kept secret. She met him at the gas station, of all places, as she stopped for gas on her way to work.

She worked at Goodman & Goodman, a relatively new, but very successful law firm, as a paralegal. She was dressed to the nines, as they say. Her navy blue Donna Karan suit fitted her hand-in-glove and her

three-inch matching pumps showed off her shapely thick legs.

"Don't you dare touch that gas pump," a voice uttered out of nowhere.

Saphire turned and looked into the handsome face of a tall, lean man. He was sporting a smooth baldhead with a trim mustache. Sexy wasn't enough to describe him. Saphire held onto the gas pump handle, frozen in her tracks.

He made his way over to her, took the gas nozzle out of her hand and proceeded to pump gas into her Lexus. "I wouldn't want a pretty woman like yourself messing up that fine suit you're wearing the hell out of," he said, showing her a dazzling smile.

The man was outrageously flirting with her, and she felt herself blushing as she watched the pump reach ten dollars, then fifteen, and it kept right on going. She sized him up as she took in his tall and trim frame. He was dressed casually in a brown button-down Polo shirt and matching trousers.

Not bad, she mused, eyeing his backside. The handsome man didn't stop until her tank was full. "Why did you do that?" she asked, giving him an intense look.

"Because I wanted to," the man stated, closing the cap on her gas tank. "Where are you off to this early in the morning?" he asked, giving her an up and down stare. Returning his gaze, she smiled but didn't respond. She was wondering where all of this was leading. "Mmmm, dressed as fine as you are makes a man want to wrap you up like a Christmas present," he chuckled.

She couldn't help but also chuckle at his remark. "I'm on my way to work," she answered evenly, "and you didn't have to fill up my tank. I don't even know you."

"Well, what can I do to change that?" he asked, leaning his long, slim backside against her car passenger door.

Her lips curled into a wicked smile. "Well…my name is Saphire. Saphire Michaels."

"And mine is Bobby Stanley." He extended his large hand and took hers. "And I would love for you to have dinner with me tonight."

As they say, the rest is history. Bobby became her secret lover. For

months now, they had been sexing it up like crazy. They were meeting at faraway places, and even in nearby hotels in the middle of the day. Bobby was a happily married man, which didn't bother her, not one little bit. No expectations and no commitments; right up her alley.

She called the shots and Bobby placed no demands on her. He was the very opposite of Clay. He was full of excitement, and he knew how to please, tease, and appease. They had the greatest time when they were together. When their sexcapades were finished, they each went on their merry way until next time. And that was exactly the way she wanted it.

Coming out of her trance as she and Clay danced to the beat of Usher, she looked at him and smiled. They were having such a good time at the club. She danced so hard, she couldn't cut another step if she wanted to. Catching her breath, she scrimmaged her way over to their table. "That's it for me," she huffed as Clay took his seat on the opposite side of her.

"Is this the same Saphire Michaels who I thought was such a party animal, if my memory serves me correctly?" he taunted as their eyes met. "You said that I would be the one begging for mercy," he reminded her with a hearty laugh.

Pursing her lips, she quivered. "Okay, Clay, you win. I guess I'm not up to par tonight." She began fanning herself with her hands.

It was getting pretty heated in the club, or was it her guilt catching up with her. If Clay only knew the real reason her energy level was down, he would probably be cussing her out right about now. Earlier that day, she was with Bobby. They met at the Sleep Inn Motel across town, and sleeping in was the last thing on either of their minds. The man had more moves than the Energizer bunny, and now her body ached in places she wouldn't even mention.

Clay ordered their drinks, and within minutes, two Pomegranate Ginger Cosmopolitans were sitting in front of them. She sipped slowly on hers, while Clay gave her a quizzical look. "Are you okay, Sugar Plum? You seem kinda distant tonight."

"I'm fine," she murmured as she repositioned herself in her seat.

Clay continued to stare at her, which was making her feel a little uneasy.

"Oh, another thing, Sugar Plum. I was trying to call you around lunchtime today, but you never picked up your cell." He watched her reaction carefully, the same way her mother did when she thought something was up.

She felt another sudden rush of heat flooding her face. Did he suspect something? No, he couldn't, she decided quickly. After all, she was the expert at hiding her dirty laundry. She almost choked on her drink, but she managed to swallow hard and cleared her throat.

"Oh, um, I left my phone in the car when Lashon and I went into the restaurant. We were at the mall for lunch, and we did a little window shopping," Saphire clarified as she lowered her eyes from Clay's questioning stare.

"Oh," he responded, taking another sip of his drink.

"Clay," Saphire said, letting out a sigh. "I'm really tired tonight. Let's just go home, okay?"

He glared at her as if she was a stranger sitting before him. "You're ready to go home?" Clay looked into the face of his silver Rolex and then returned his gaze back to Saphire. "It's still early, Sugar Plum. We've only been here an hour or so."

"For heaven's sake! Can't a woman be tired? And plus, I'm beginning to get a headache," she snapped, placing her hand on her forehead. "I think my monthly visitor may be on her way," she said, hoping he was swallowing the lies she was putting out.

"Ahh man, and I was hoping we could get our freak on tonight. It's been a while," Clay grumbled.

Not responding to Clay's statement, she reached for her Gucci clutch purse. "I'm going to the ladies room," she announced, standing up and walking briskly away from the table.

She needed to get away from Clay for a moment to clear her head. She didn't have a headache and her monthly wasn't due for a week, but having sex with him tonight was just something she did not want to do. Not after her fling with Bobby earlier that day. She needed time to recuperate, and so did her body.

She made her way through the crowd with ease. As she passed the crowded bar with patrons dressed to impress, she had to do a double-take. The figure of the man sitting with his back towards her looked very familiar.

The club was dark, but the disco lights flickered enough for her to see the silhouetted frame turn a little, giving her a better view. It was him. The man from the picnic, Joe Burrels, Gade's friend. She summed it all up in one good stare.

He was dressed to kill in his designer clothing. She noticed the almost finished drink in his hand. She figured he must have been there for a while, maybe that was even his second drink. She couldn't help but stare at him, and in that moment, his head turned and their eyes met. His face broke out into a gorgeous smile and so did hers. Joe got up from his seat and strutted over to where she was standing. He took in the sight of her full-figured body as her eyes held his.

"My, my, my, what do we have here?" he mused as his eyes floated over her curvy shape and thick legs. She smiled widely as she took in a whiff of his intoxicating cologne. In her sexiest voice, she purred, "Oh, so you remember me?"

Peering into her hazel eyes, he answered, "How could I ever forget such a beautiful face as yours?" He grinned and stepped a little closer to her. Goose bumps began to form on her arms as she gazed into his handsome face. "May I buy you a drink?" he asked, touching her arm slightly.

The touch of his slender finger ignited a spark. Clutching her purse, she nervously darted her eyes around the club. The place was so packed with people; she couldn't see the table she and Clay shared. It was tucked away in the far corner of the club. She wondered if Clay was still sitting there waiting for her return. She sure hoped so. *What the hell,* she thought. If Clay found them sitting together, she would just tell him that they ran into each other, which was the absolute truth.

"Well, okay, but it has to be a quick one. I'm not alone," she admitted as she followed Joe back over to the bar. Once seated, he ordered their drinks then turned to face her.

"My guess would be that you're with your future husband," Joe stated as he stared into her eyes.

Saphire lowered her eyes from his intense stare. "Um…yes, I mean no. He's not my fiancé. I don't know why my sister would give you such an impression. We're just dating, that's all," she explained as the bartender placed their drinks in front of them.

They each took a sip of their Martini. Joe smiled, showing off the deep dimples in both of his cheeks. Taking in his features, she wanted to strip him down to his bare skin, and expose what she knew would be a ripple of taut muscle, tight hips, and fine goods. That's just how sexy he looked.

"Are you here with anyone?" She gazed in the direction of the bathroom, which she had never entered. She feared her sister Gade may have been in the ladies' room and would come out any minute, like a bat out of hell at the sight of her sitting at the bar with her date.

"No, I'm here all by my lonesome," he revealed.

Saphire had a hard time believing what he'd just said. "Come on, now. Surely, you are playing me. A handsome man like yourself, here all alone? Well, that's just terrible," she teased, giving him another one of her enticing smiles. "Why didn't my sister come along with you?" she questioned.

Her main objective was to find out if the fire had died down between them yet. Gade wasn't exactly the type to keep a real man interested for very long, and since she didn't see Joe hanging around their home, she hoped with everything in her that this was the case.

"Let's just say we've both been busy." Joe replied not wanting to reveal what was really going on between him and Gade.

Saphire shifted her position on the barstool. The lower half of the ruby-red wrapped dress she was wearing fell away, exposing her shapely legs, which Joe couldn't help but notice.

Joe cleared his throat as he tore his eyes away. Lifting his eyes, he focused on Saphire's lovely face. He wanted to get to know the sexy woman who sat just inches away from him, but he didn't want to seem forward. "I'm not going to keep you here too long. I don't want to be the cause of any friction between you and your…friend," he stammered.

Amused by his concern, Saphire still wasn't ready to leave this man. There was definitely friction going on all right, and it was coming from the desire he was stirring within her. She felt as if a small fire was burning in the pit of her stomach and traveling to…well, parts below.

She wanted this man, even though Gade saw him first. At that very moment, Saphire made a decision. To her way of thinking, all is fair in love and war.

"Maybe we can get together, you know, another time, another place," Saphire hinted in her sexiest tone of voice.

Joe hesitated for a moment as he registered what she was implying. An all-knowing smile crept across his lips as he retrieved his business card from his black leather wallet and placed it in the palm of her hand. "Call me," he said, as he slid off the bar stool and disappeared into the thick crowd.

She turned the gold-embossed card over and then she slipped it into her Gucci purse. Just as she snapped it closed, Clay appeared.

"There you are, Sugar Plum. I was looking all over for you. What are you doing at the bar? I thought you were on your way to the ladies room," he quizzed.

"I went already and I just stopped at the bar to get myself a glass of water to take an aspirin, if that's all right with you. And another thing, why do you keep calling me Sugar Plum? You make me sound like a chick on some country-ass cable show," she fumed as she stormed out of the club.

Clay followed her out with a grim look on his face, wondering what in the hell had gotten into her and why was she directing it at him?

MY SISTER IS HOME

Gade heard Saphire plodding around in her room as she lay in bed. Looking over at the clock on the nightstand, she noted that it beamed 2:00 a.m. out in red. That was entirely too early for her sister to be home when she was out partying. Saphire was known to come home with the rising of the sun. The only reason she was still up herself, was because she had been studying for the medical exam she had to pass if she wanted to make it through this semester. Gade fluffed her soft pillow and closed her eyes again. Saphire and Clay must have had another fight, she concluded. When was that boy ever going to learn that Saphire was a leopard and leopards don't change their spots?

She took in a long breath and turned over. She couldn't let herself get caught up in her sister's problems. God knows, she had her own to deal with. Thoughts of Joe and the short time they had been together just wouldn't leave her alone.

That man had stirred something in her she'd never felt before, and as much as she loved Lamonte, those feelings for Joe consumed her like a roaring fire. It had been two weeks now since Joe hung up on her. She'd hoped that maybe he would call once he cooled down, but she now concluded he'd meant it when he said he was over and out.

She hadn't even confided in her mom that she was no longer seeing him, and she wasn't going to share that secret with Saphire. She noticed the way she had focused on Joe at the picnic that day. It was as if he was baby back ribs and she could suck him down to the bones.

Turning over again, she sighed. As far as they both were concerned, she and Joe were still a hot item. Her mother even told her she made the best choice by sticking with Joe. Lamonte was a nice guy, but she thought Joe had a little more going for himself, being older and wiser. Mmmm, if only

Mom knew. The man had everything a woman would need and want in this life.

Gade glanced at the clock again, 2:45 a.m. "Why can't I just go to sleep," she murmured to herself. She swung her legs off the bed and picked up her cell from the nightstand. She stared at Joe's number flickering in the dark face of her cell. She wanted, no, needed to talk to him. Like a dieter craving that second slice of chocolate cake, she felt the need to see him stir within her.

Her thumb pressed her call button. As she waited to hear his voice, her throat felt dry, but the palm of her hand was damp with sweat. Her heart beat like a drummer boy's rhythm. The phone rang and rang and then suddenly she broke out of the trance she was in.

What in God's name was she doing? She was about to hang up when she heard Joe's sleepy, but sexy deep voice. "Hello, Gade, are you there?" he asked.

"Um…yeah…I'm here," she answered softly. How did he know it was her? Then she remembered the Caller ID.

Silence fell between them as she groped for words. "I…don't know why I called you, sorry." she muttered. She was about to hang up when she heard his voice calling her name.

"Gade, get dressed, I'll be there in about fifteen minutes."

The phone went dead. Did she hear him right? He was coming over in fifteen minutes. Gade threw the covers back and jumped up. She grabbed a tee shirt and a pair of shorts, pulled them on, and stuck her feet into a pair of pink flip-flops. She was ready, or so she thought. What about her hair? It was all frizzed and she wasn't going to let him see her like this.

She snatched the black comb from her vanity and ran it through her hair in record time. She sailed down the hall to the bathroom and brushed her teeth in one hot minute. As soon as she made it back into her bedroom, she pulled back the white Priscilla curtains, peeked out her bedroom window, and there he was.

Joe's gold Expedition was parked out front in the soft glow of the street light. She questioned her actions once more as she made her way quietly down the stairs. What was she doing? Her head was saying one thing, but her heart was saying another. Her heart had won.

A LOVER'S NIGHT

Gade could feel Joe's breath at the nape of her neck as he softly snored. Joe's perfectly shaped lips were parted slightly as she lay entwined in his arms. Their lovemaking had been sensual, hot and liberating. Gade stared down at his sleeping face. She wanted this man, but uncertainty stirred within her once again. Saphire's words seeped into her mind. She was playing a dangerous game, running two men at the same time. Sure, Saphire could handle it; that's the way she always rolled. *But I might just be in a little over my head*, she pondered.

Loving two men in different ways is a huge demand on one's heart. She should know, she thought, as Joe's arms pulled her closer against his smooth chest. Staring out into the semi-darkened room, she revisited every argument she and Saphire ever had concerning the games she played with men. Gade even remembered calling her sister a garden hoe, which was a terrible thing to say about one's own sister, and now she was beginning to fit the description. Joe stirred as his eyelids flickered. Gazing down at her, he kissed her softly, then more firmly as his nature grew. Gade fell into step as they proceeded to make love yet again.

* * * * *

Saphire sat in her beautician's chair reading the latest issue of Vibe magazine. Tanisha was giving her one of the styles she saw Monique, the comedy queen, sporting at one of her shows a couple of months ago. Tanisha could really lay on the styles at Hollywood Hair Salon. She kept a long list of clients, and getting an appointment with her could be grueling at times. Monique was one of Saphire's favorite entertainers, especially after being told that she favored the actor. She had the same round face and dark eyes. And when her hair was done in one of Monique's signature

styles, she knew she could be considered at least a cousin of hers.

Saphire continued to read about different celebrities, and she couldn't help but drool at the sight of their magnificent homes as displayed in the magazine. *I am going to have my own dream home just like them,* she mused. Living with her momma was cool, but at some point in her life, a woman needed her own place. Even if Momma's house was big enough.

Tanisha nudged Saphire's head over to the side. "Girlfriend, what's wrong with you? That hurt." Saphire frowned, pulling her eyes away from the magazine.

Tanisha snapped her Juicy Fruit gum. "If you want this hairstyle to go right, you need to keep this big head of yours still," she ordered as she continued chewing. "You need to stop drooling over those mega stars anyway," she muttered, turning Saphire's chair around so she could face her.

"Tanisha, girl, I'm telling you here and now, one of these days I'm going to be styling and profiling just like my favorite actor Monique." Continuing to look through the magazine pages, Saphire shook her head. "You know, somebody told me the other day that I resembled her," she said proudly.

"Well, it must have been some man trying to get into those oversize hot pants of yours, I'm sure," Chaniece squealed. Chaniece was another hair stylist with a booth in the famous salon. She and Saphire had known each other since their elementary school days.

Saphire couldn't stand her ass then, and she sure as hell couldn't stand her conceited ass now. They always competed against each other, in the way they dressed, the men they chased, and for the attention of the popular social circle they hung around.

Both women drove Lexus automobiles; the only difference was, Chaniece's Lexus was three years newer than Saphire's, and she reminded her of that almost every time she visited the salon. She would gloat and repeat, "Isn't it time for an upgrade, Saphire?"

A couple of women who sat across the room began to snicker at Chaniece's remark, and it angered Saphire. Her blood boiled.

Chaniece thought she was so damned fine because she was a mixed

child. Her mother was white, and her father, a brother. Chaniece's hair was long, silky, and the color of dark caramel. She had an hourglass figure with a backside like J Lo's. Yes, guys were after Chaniece, just like they ran after her. The difference between the two, Saphire felt, was that she had class, style and flair, whereas Chaniece was a ghetto hoochie wannabe. And she was about to put her half-breed ass in her place.

"Oh, so you got jokes," Saphire smirked while rolling her eyes. "Just because you're a half-breed, don't make your ass fine. Truth be known, you look like a little brown mutt snooping the sidewalks for crumbs of food."

"Oh no she didn't!" Chaniece screamed out as her eyes rolled. Moving away from her client, she stepped around the chair and put her hands on her trim hips. "Are you calling me a dog?" she glared.

Saphire nodded her head as she stared directly into Chaniece's green eyes. "I call them as I see them," Saphire sneered with a wave of her hand.

"Why you big-ass hoe!" Chaniece steamed, making her way over to Saphire.

Big Sandy, the owner of Hollywood Hair Salon, stood behind the checkout counter at the front of the salon. Peering over her thick glasses, she saw what she thought was going to be a ruckus, and she wasn't having it. Sandy was a round woman who stood six feet tall.

Within two quick strides, she blocked Chaniece, interrupting her path. "Listen here, ladies, or should I say chicks, I'm not having this street crap up in my place of business. I'll throw the both of you out on your asses without a second thought," she warned. "Now what's it going to be?"

Her eyes darted between the two battling women. Saphire picked up the Vibe magazine and buried her head in it. She couldn't afford to be thrown out in the middle of getting her hair done. She had a hot date tonight with Bobby, and this time it wasn't at a hotel. He was taking her to the House of Blues. His wife had gone to visit her mother for a week, so they had time for real dates instead of the usual quickies.

Neither woman said another word as Chaniece made her way back over to her client.

"That's what I thought, and this crap better not happen again!" Sandy exclaimed, making her way back to the front counter.

STOP BUGGING ME!

Clay was getting on Saphire's last nerves. He was back on the 'let's get married' wagon. He stood in the middle of her mother's living room pleading his case. This was one of their in-dates, as Saphire called them. Clay ordered a pizza, which was on its way over, and he had a couple of new movie releases on the Maplewood coffee table. "Sugar Plum, we have been seeing each other now for about three years. I know I'm not rolling in dough, but I'm making a decent living," Clay argued as he plopped down on the brown leather couch. He leaned over and folded his hands.

Saphire gave him a look, but said nothing as she chewed on her bottom lip and let out a soft breath.

Clay asked, "Aren't you tired of living here at your mother's house? God knows I'm tired of staying with mine. We should have been out of our parents' houses months ago. We're both in our twenties, it's time to cut the apron strings, don't you think?"

Saphire sat on the couch with one leg folded up under her. Taking in Clay's observations, she realized he had made some good points. Sure, she wanted her own home. Always dreamed of it, but she wanted a fantastic home. Not just some two-bedroom rental and definitely not a cramped apartment. No, she wanted luxury and that's why she had never left home.

She had goals in life, and she couldn't be deterred from realizing them. She was saving her money, and when the time was right, she was going to buy herself that luxurious home, just like the stars owned in the magazines she loved. Clay interrupted her thoughts as he grabbed both of her hands, forcing her to look directly at him.

"Saphire, and yes, I called you Saphire, not Sugar Plum." Clay chuckled lightly. Now he had her undivided attention and she knew the next few

words out of his mouth were going to be important and deep. "All I'm saying is we need to be thinking about our future, baby. I love you. You are the best thing that ever came into my life and I will spend the rest of my days making you happy, I swear I will," Clay said as tears glossed his brown eyes.

Saphire felt like the Grinch who stole Christmas. Here in front of her, was a man who was expressing his true undying love and admiration for her. This loving, wonderful man wanted her for his wife. Not just a lover, a one night fling, or for the sex escapades she was guilty of participating in, but his wife. And to think, all she thought about was her own damned selfishness. Shame on her for just focusing on her own freedom and the men she had hidden in the bushes. None of them was offering her what Clay had.

Hell, half of them couldn't even if they wanted to because they were already married. Saphire sucked in a deep breath. The time had come for her to make a decision. An important decision, she realized as she looked into her man's eyes. *Well, why not?* She thought. *Maybe I could do this marriage thing.* After all, she did love him.

Saphire cleared her throat. "Okay…Clay Anthony Matthews, I will marry you," she murmured.

Clay stared at her with his mouth wide open. "What…did…you… say?" he stuttered.

"I said I will marry you," Saphire said more audibly as she grinned from ear-to-ear.

Clay jumped up, pulling Saphire right along with him. As heavy as she was, she wasn't too heavy for Clay's strong arms. He picked her up and turned her around and around while hollering out in the process.

Saphire's mother, Josey, was in the kitchen when she heard all the commotion. She came briskly into the living room and her eyes widened at the sight of them. Clay was spinning her daughter around. "What's all this whooping and hollering about?" Josey asked with a bewildered look.

Clay put Saphire down and ran over to Josey, who was about thirty pounds lighter, and easily picked her up. He spun her around as well.

"Man, I believe you done lost your mind," Josey said, giggling like a child.

"Nooo, Ma'am, my mind is perfectly fine, Miss Josey," Clay sputtered, out of breath as he put her feet back on the ground. "Miss Josey, Saphire and I are getting married!" Clay beamed excitedly.

Josey looked over at Saphire who had a sly grin on her face.

"That's right, Momma, I agreed to marry him," Saphire mumbled as she walked over to Clay, and placed her arm around him.

Josey gave her daughter a 'how could you do this' look, but quickly plastered a smile on her face. Josey felt so sorry for her future son-in-law. Deep in her heart, she knew Saphire was going to make his life a living hell.

WE'RE GETTING MARRIED

A few days had gone by since the big announcement. Gade had trouble believing it was true. Saphire was actually going to settle down. The girl must have fallen down somewhere and bumped that big head of hers. Gade walked into Saphire's room and saw her sitting at her vanity table, applying her cucumber facemask, nightly routine she adhered to. She watched her for a few moments before she spoke. Gade couldn't understand why Saphire didn't say a word to her beforehand. Usually, she would have been the first one to spill a secret.

"Saphire, are you really going to marry Clay?" Gade asked her point blank. That's the kind of person she was. *Straight as a line in the middle of the road,* she remembered her nana's famous words.

Saphire placed the lid on the cream bottle, then swiveled around to face her. She gave her sister a twisted look. "Why would you ask me such a dumb-ass question like that? The man has been asking me to marry him for months now, so I finally gave in. What is the problem?" Saphire turned back to the vanity mirror.

"Yeah, and for months you kept turning him down because you knew you didn't want to marry him, so why the change?" Gade asked flatly. "And Saphire, please, for once be honest about it."

Saphire's expression softened a bit as she turned back to face her sister again. "Clay loves me. He really loves me just the way that I am." Her face brightened. "He puts up with all my antics and my bad temper," she added with a laugh. "Don't you see, Lil' Sis? He knows me better than anyone. He wants to make me happy, so why not marry him?" Saphire faced the mirror once again and slowly peeled off her green facemask.

Saphire went through this ritual every night. Gade had to admit, her skin was smooth and blemish-free. She also had taken good care of her

skin, but she wasn't a fanatic about it, like her sister. Gade uncrossed her arms and leaned against the doorframe as she peered into her sister's eyes. "He loves you, I know that, but do you love him as much as he loves you, Saphire?"

Letting out a low breath, Saphire sighed. Gade had stepped on a nerve, and she felt her bad temper rising. Why couldn't she just accept what she said and leave it alone. Looking at her once again, she answered, "I love him, all right? And that's all you should know. Now please get off my back!"

"Yeah, if you say so," Gade said as she took a step back. "I hope you know what you're doing."

Saphire grimaced. "Don't you have a life of your own to attend to, Lil' Sis? In fact, what's up with you and Lamonte? I don't see him knocking down your door. By the way, are you still seeing him?" Saphire braced herself for Gade's response.

"Yeah…but…I've been kind of busy with studying and my part time job," she stammered.

The truth was, she was seeing less and less of Lamonte, and spending most of her free time with Joe. Lamonte kept calling of course, and asking her out, but she always gave him the same lame excuse she'd just rolled off to Saphire. Since that night Joe picked her up, they'd made an amicable agreement about their relationship. He'd vowed to give her time to sort out her true feelings, because he didn't want her to feel as if he was pressuring her to make a choice.

He wanted her to be happy and sure about what she wanted. After all, he was the new kid on the block in Lamonte's neighborhood. *He is such a mature and wise man,* she thought, as a small smile crept up at the corners of her mouth. Just thinking about the man made her smile, but sadly, she hadn't been able to do much sorting. She needed time to struggle with her dilemma, Gade reasoned. Lamonte was a wonderful guy, and they clicked on every level, so why was she so into Joe? Was it because he had the bad boy persona that attracted young girls like herself? He was older, daring, and mysterious. Joe never talked much about his family. He just said he

wasn't close to anyone because of his rocky childhood. However, he did say his parents were still alive, and he had one half-brother. That was about it, so she just left it alone.

"Gade...Gade!" Saphire called out, breaking her trance. "Lil Sis, I don't know what's been up with you lately, but I don't think it has a damned thing to do with school and those stupid exams!"

"My exams are not stupid, for your information, Saphire Michaels. And one of these days, I am going to be a doctor, making triple the money you do," she said mockingly.

"Let me tell you something, sweetheart. Sometimes you don't need brains to get what you want in this life, and working to get what I want never demanded a lot of brains on my part," Saphire smirked back.

"Oh yeah, I forgot your motto. Why use your brains when you can use your back?" Gade snapped.

Saphire simmered as she looked at her sister. She had better be glad she was her blood, because Lord knows, if she wasn't, she would have smacked the living daylights out of her. "Let's change the subject while we both are still in our right minds," Saphire hissed as she slammed the lid onto the cucumber cream.

Gade knew the slip of her tongue was about to get her a free ass whipping courtesy of her big sister. She always wondered why she and her sister didn't get along better than they did. They loved each other, she was certain of that but....

"Since you brought the subject up of one's back, have you been sneaking around lying on yours with what's his name...Joe Blow?" Saphire asked mischievously.

The remark Gade made about her had stung, and she wanted to get even with her sister. Why did they have to fight with each other this way? It was as if they hated each other, but that couldn't have been further from the truth. She loved her baby sister.

Saphire held her breath as she waited for Gade's response. She silently prayed that her answer would be no. No, they were no longer seeing each other, would have been music to her ears because she and Joe had been

seeing each other since that night she met him at the club. The very next day, she'd phoned him, and that evening they met at his place. It was a sin and a shame how they went after each other. Like dogs in heat, they say, but the saying wasn't enough to describe the lustful night they shared. And just as she thought, the man was a damned good lover. He taught her some things even she hadn't learned through her vast experience with the opposite sex. Now looking at her sister's lopsided grin, she knew what her answer would be, and in spite of herself, she felt like a heel. Slightly, that is. After all, Gade wasn't married to the man. As far as she was concerned, he was a free agent.

Gade couldn't help but grin when Saphire asked the question. Who was she fooling? Joe brought out the best in her, and yes, she was still seeing him and sexing him up every chance she got. The man was like the rising of the sun. Something beautiful to look forward to everyday.

"So I guess that grin of yours has answered my question." Saphire sighed, turning back around to face the mirror on her vanity table. "What are you going to do about Lamonte?" she inquired, staring at Gade's reflection in the glass.

Gade shrugged her shoulders as she moved over to her sister's full-size bed and plopped down on it.

Saphire took in a deep breath. "There's no need for me to ask this, but I'm going to take a chance anyway," she said, standing up and looking her sister squarely in the eye. "Have you been intimate with him? I mean, you only met him what, a few months ago…" her voice trailed off.

A brief silence fell as Gade lowered her head and folded her hands. "Yes, we have been intimate, Saphire, more than once," she admitted as she crossed her ankles. Saphire let out a deep breath, and it pissed Gade off. Lifting her head and staring back at Saphire she huffed, "You act as if I'm the Virgin Mary. I've had sex before and you know it."

Saphire broke away from Gade's intense stare and went over to her walnut dresser. She pulled open the top drawer and pretended to look for the silky fuchsia-colored pajama set she planned to sleep in that night. The set was right in front of her eyes, but at the moment, she just couldn't bear

to look into Gade's face anymore. She pulled the set out and closed the drawer with a thud.

She spun around, mustering up her courage, and looked into her sister's face once more. "Gade, what are you doing?" she asked in the firm voice she always used on her when she wanted to get her point across. "You and Lamonte have been together for almost a year and a half now. You guys are good together. Are you going to give it all up for someone you don't even know? Be sensible, Lil' Sis. Use that smart brain of yours. The man may end up breaking your heart and then what would you do? Especially knowing you lost a good man like Lamonte in the process."

Springing up from the bed, Gade heaved a sigh. "Don't you think I thought about that?" Walking around in a circle Gade said, "That's all I've been thinking about since Joe came into my life. Sometimes I ask myself, why did I even have to meet him? If only I hadn't, I wouldn't be going through this right now." She rubbed her forehead before continuing. "Then…then I think that if I never met Joe Burrels, I would have missed out on experiencing such a loving, exciting, and interesting man. Not only in bed, but being with him as a total package. The man keeps me laughing," she grinned as she looked at her sister with lit-up eyes. "Saphire, we have had some good times together and I don't know if I can give that up, or if I even want to," Gade concluded.

Saphire approached her sister, and with her fingertips she smoothed the auburn curly hair that framed Gade's face. She loved playing with her sister's silky hair. She always wished God had blessed her with what was referred to as good hair. Instead, relaxers and weaves had to suffice for the look she wanted. Reflecting back, she remembered running her fingers through her sister's curly brown hair when she was going through what their mother had called growing pains. Gade would run into her bedroom with tears spilling from her eyes over something that had upset her in school that day. And being the big sister she was, she'd promised to make it all better, no matter what it was. So when did things between them go awry? They used to be so close. Looking back, she wondered when the competition for guys had begun. And more importantly, when would it

end?

"Gade, listen to me," Saphire ordered as she held her sister's gaze. "Joe seems to be a loner. He is so much older than you are, and I'm sure much more experienced. And he may be…just having fun with you," she murmured. "When all is said and done, he may leave you hanging out to dry, and I don't want to see you hurt like that,"

Gade pushed Saphire's hand away from her face and glared at her. "And how do you know that, Saphire? Did he tell you this?" Gade blasted.

Saphire stepped back and attempted to answer Gade's question, but thought better of it.

Gade placed her hands on her trim hips. With a satisfied look, she said, "Of course he didn't, because this is just another one of your mind games you like to run on me." With a sneer, Gade spewed, "You are just so bent out of shape that he didn't fall for your sex-crazed ass. Instead, he saw me and liked me. He chose me instead of The Queen of Men," she emphasized with angry eyes, "and you can't stand the thought of that, now, can you?" Tears began to form that she wiped hastily. She had had enough of her sister's sabotage. "All of my life I felt like I had to compete with my big beautiful sister for men's attention. Seeing how they would look at you and then at me made my flesh crawl," she cried. "What did I have to hold their attention? Long slim arms with legs to match. A curve nowhere to be found on that bean pole body of mine. Well, big sis, times are changing. My body has changed. I've got curves now, and men look at me with interest. And for once, this fine, older and captivating man has chosen me," Gade said, jabbing her finger into her chest. "Are you hearing me, Saphire?" she asked as she glared at her.

Saphire stood silently, watching big tears roll down her sister's face. She had no idea Gade felt so inadequate. She wanted to tell her that she was just as beautiful as she was. In fact, she wanted to tell her that no man should have to justify her self-worth. Gade was a beautiful girl inside and out. She was her sister and she loved her but…Saphire remained silent.

Gade noticed the slight pause and took advantage of it. Giving her sister a stern stare, she placed her hands on both hips. Focusing on her, she stated,

"Joe Burrels has chosen me, and I'm not going to let you talk me out of seeing him. You may want him for yourself, but this time you're not going to win. The man is mine and I suggest you get used to it," she spouted as she made her way out of Saphire's room.

Just before she reached the door, Saphire grabbed her by the arm and held it tight. "Let me tell you one damned thing, Lil' Sis. Write this down in your medical notes while you are studying. I've warned you about Joe Burrels, but you refuse to listen. Believe me when I say that you are playing with fire. You can't play a player's game when you don't know the rules. Don't let it burn you up," Saphire warned through clenched teeth.

Both women stared deep into each other's eyes. A game had begun between them that day; a game that would forever change their lives, for better or for worse.

SURPRISE!

Gade swung the leather bag over her shoulder as she walked towards her car in the hospital's parking garage. Her black Camry with silver chrome sparkled in the sunlight. Her car wasn't brand new; in fact, it was five years old, but it purred like a kitten, thanks to Lamonte. He kept it in tip-top shape, making sure the oil was changed on time, and the engine was running like it should. Lamonte is so dependable about things like that, she thought, as the times they'd shared floated before her.

She thought about how he helped her with her studies and gave her massages when her neck and shoulders ached from bending over her books for long periods of time. It had been almost a month since she had last spoken to Lamonte. He kept calling her, trying to make dates that she kept breaking, and finally the calls just stopped. Now, she found herself missing him. She pressed the remote and unlocked the door. She threw the leather bag filled with her books in the passenger seat and then she slid into the driver's seat.

She started her car and pulled out into the rush hour traffic. Turning the radio to her favorite soul station, she prepared herself for the long and tedious drive home. She was tired and she couldn't wait to soak in a warm bubble bath. Her day had been long, with school and her part time job, but she had to hang in there. Her dreams of being a pediatrician were slowly coming to fruition. She loved children, and one day, she hoped to have a house full of them. Gade allowed her mind to drift as the station played soft and sensual soul music. Weaving in and out of traffic, her thoughts centered on Joe. She hadn't heard a peep from him in over a week. She'd tried calling him several times, leaving umpteen messages, but he had yet to return even one of them.

She was so afraid that what her sister had predicted weeks ago was

slowly coming to pass. Maybe Joe was finished with her and had moved on to greener pastures. A song began to play that clouded her heart and mind with emotion. It was one of Lamonte's favorites, and he'd sung it to her often. On his last tour in the military, he called her late one night and sang it to her over the phone. Lamonte had a smooth baritone voice and it flowed smoothly like a river in the summertime.

The song was an oldie by Freddie Jackson. The lyrics to "You are My Lady" played over the radio and brought tears to her eyes. Her heart grew heavy. She wondered if she had messed up big time by losing a man she knew cared about her so deeply. She had let go of something so precious, for what? A little excitement, mind-blowing sex, and…that's it? Where were the feelings of contentment, commitment and love? Those things she had come to know with Lamonte? Wiping away the tears that blurred her sight, she realized what she'd been trying to figure out for weeks. She was still in love with Lamonte Singletary. She'd never stopped loving him. Sadly, lust had blinded her, fogging her senses, clouding her heart.

She didn't know how she had driven to Lamonte's job, because she wasn't aware of taking the road that led her there. Staring at the red brick building that held Lenmark Industries, she took in a deep breath. People were making their way out to their cars. Gade searched the parking lot for Lamonte's SUV, but didn't see it. Maybe he left already, she concluded as she put her car in reverse. She was ready to back out of the parking lot when she saw the side door of the plant open and Lamonte and a white chick walk out. They were in deep conversation and laughing like a couple in love. Lamonte had his arm wrapped lightly around her waist as they headed towards a black Lexus.

He opened the passenger door for her and she slid in. He got into the driver's seat and they pulled out, driving right past her. Gade took a closer look at the chick and realized she wasn't white after all. It was Chaniece Washington, her sister's rival, better known as Half-Breed.

A GETAWAY

Closing her eyes, Saphire thought about the day she and Joe shared. They had gone to Venice Beach, just before dawn. Walking in the beach's white sand, hand-in-hand, they listened to the soft sounds of the waves crashing on the shore. Like young lovers, running free, enjoying each other, loving each other. Upon the arrival of the sun, adorned in its brightness, they had breakfast at the beach's oceanfront restaurant. Later that day, they strolled down the strip, playing, laughing, as if nothing else mattered.

Back at the hotel, Joe stretched out as naked as a newborn baby on his king-sized bed with Saphire's thick body right next to him. She was sliding ice cubes down his chest. Joe winced at the cold feel of the ice cubes, but burned with desire as her warm and sultry tongue licked up the melting liquid. They had just finished another round of hot sex and were supposed to be chilling out, according to her. He didn't know the chilling out part included a glass filled with ice cubes. Saphire dropped the last ice cube near his manhood. He flinched as the ice began to melt from his body heat. Saphire's tongue darted out like a snake's, scooping it up with one lick, then she tasted him, driving him stark raving mad in the process. Tension began to build as he climbed the throes of passion. He succumbed to the volcano as it erupted, letting his lava run free. They each struggled for air as their wet bodies luxuriated in the aftermath. Later that day, they enjoyed a day of shopping hitting the gift stores as if it was Christmas.

As afternoon turned slowly into evening, the time of departure had come. With goodbyes to be said, and memories to carry, each lover went back to the reality of their lives. A twinge of guilt stabbed at her heart. Here she stood with one man she loved, wearing the engagement ring of another she was going to marry. Sometimes she scared herself with her boldness. Surely, one day it was going to catch up with her. But not today. Today

was something she was going to cherish, she decided as she kissed the tip of Joe's chin. Saphire jumped into the shower and doused herself with her Victoria Secret's peach body wash. She had to scrub away all evidence of her and Joe's passionate lovemaking. She couldn't risk the chance of Clay smelling anything other than the fragrance of peaches.

He was picking her up at her house in about an hour. They had dinner plans with his parents tonight. As far as her family and Clay knew, she was on a business trip for her boss. Just as Saphire finished showering, she wrapped the thick white hotel bath towel around her and slipped her feet into the soft matching slides. Joe showed up at the door looking as sexy as she knew that he was.

Smiling, with a glint in his eye, he reached out for her towel but Saphire pulled away. "Now Joe, you know I've got to be going. I'm running late as it is," she said, brushing past him.

She gathered up her clothes and got dressed. Joe stood watching her, not saying a word until she was ready to leave. He let his mind wander as questions plundered the depths of his heart. He found himself being drawn more and more to this lovely woman. It had come to the point that he wanted her for more than just sex. But knowing her other obligations made his heart wince with pain.

Joe walked over to her, and put his hands on the sides of her face. He stared intensely into her hazel eyes. "How long is this going to last, Saphire?" he asked, with mixed emotion in his voice.

Saphire returned his gaze and answered lightly, "As long as we both want it to."

"It's getting complicated," Joe admitted.

"Only if we let it, Joe," Saphire murmured, moving away from him as she reached for her purse and keys. Saphire sashayed to the hotel room door. She turned and said, "Until next time, my love."

The door closed softly behind her as Joe stood silently in the stillness of the room. His eyes flickered over the king-sized bed they'd just made wonderful love on. Saphire had forgotten the silk scarf she purchased from the gift shop earlier that day. He picked it up, filling his nostrils with the

fragrance of her sweet scent as he inhaled. He wanted her and he had no plans of ever letting her go.

AN AWAKENING EXPERIENCE

Gade came to her senses after being lost in a trance. The plant parking lot was empty now. How long had she been sitting there? Gade wondered, as she looked at the time in her car. It was now almost six- thirty. She couldn't believe she'd been there almost an hour, staring blankly into space. Her face was wet with tears. Never in a million years would she have thought the sight of seeing Lamonte with someone else would affect her the way it had. Lamonte was her man, the love of her life, but now she realized that he too had moved on. The sad thing about it was, she had no right to be upset. No right at all, but–she was.

After walking into her home, Gade heard her mother in the kitchen, but she had no desire to talk to her, or anyone else, for that matter. She didn't even say hello, instead she made her way up the stairs.

Josey appeared at the bottom of the stairs, and as she gazed up at her daughter, she exclaimed, "Well, I guess I must be the invisible woman, huh?"

Gade stopped at the last step. "Damn," she swore to herself. She'd almost made it to the top but now she had to face her mother's questions. Gade turned around, hoping Josey wouldn't notice her swollen eyes. "Momma, it's been an exhausting day, and all I want to do right now is take a long hot bath and turn in early, okay?"

Josey stared long and hard at her baby girl, who was the spitting image of herself. Gade certainly had her features, honey- colored skin with soft curly auburn hair, light brown eyes with a smooth round face, and a dimpled chin. Gade had also inherited her loving heart. She knew something was wrong with her daughter, and she was going to get to the bottom of it right here, right now.

"Gade, do I look like I'm buying what you just shelled out to me?"

Josey asked with her hands on her rounded hips. Gade paused, opened her mouth, and closed it again. Josey sighed and said, "You might as well come on back down here and tell your momma what's really going on with you."

Gade relented. She dropped the heavy leather bag on the top of the stairs and made her way down. "Where's Saphire?" Gade asked cautiously.

She wanted to make sure she was nowhere around. She didn't see her car outside when she came in, but that didn't mean a thing. Saphire was known to leave her car anywhere and hop in the car with someone else, only to be dropped off at home and go back for it later. Since the altercation they had in Saphire's room a few nights ago, they had barely spoken a word to each other. Gade followed her mother into the living room. They sat down next to each other on the russet sofa. Josey was watching her favorite crime show. To Gade's surprise, Josey picked up the remote and turned it off. This was unusual because nothing and no one interrupted Josey when that show was on.

"Momma, why did you turn off your program?" Gade asked with a raised eyebrow.

Josey exhaled as she looked at her daughter. "Because there is nothing in this crazy old world that is more important than my daughters," she replied with a smile. "Now tell me, chile, what is going on between you and that sister of yours? I want to know what it is and I want to know right now!" Josey commanded.

"Well, why didn't you ask Saphire?" Gade returned, snatching her eyes away from her mother's unrelenting stare.

"Don't you dare go getting smart with me, Gade Michaels. You're never too old for me to smack you on those lips of yours," Josey snapped.

Gade knew her mother wasn't playing either. Josey had raised them with a firm hand and a thick brown leather belt, which by the way, still hung in her mother's closet. Before Gade could respond to her mother's question, Josey began to speak again. This time her voice was soft and caring.

"Anyway, you know your sister won't tell me the whole truth. But I

know I can always count on my baby girl to be honest with me," Josey urged, looking at Gade with trust and confidence. Gade lowered her eyes from her mother's. How could she tell her that her daughters were feuding over what she had always warned them about...men?

"I'm listening," Josey said, breaking her out of her thoughts.

"Momma, Saphire and I will mend our fences, all right? We've had plenty of fights before, it's not like this is our first one," she said in a soothing voice.

"Yeah, but there is something different about this one, I can tell." Josey sighed as she watched Gade closely. "I think this one runs a little deeper than the others, Gade. Now, am I wrong?" she questioned, crossing her short brown legs.

Gade could no longer hold up under her mother's intense scrutiny. Instead, her eyes focused on the dark face of the 42-inch flat screen television that was centered on the living room wall.

"I'm right, aren't I?" Josey questioned, leaning forward in her seat. "Tell me, Gade, and it'd better not be about some man either," she warned.

Gade let out a breath. "Now, Momma, how can it be about a man?" she said with a roll of her eyes. "Have you forgotten Saphire is marrying her man? And as cute as Clay is, he is not my type," Gade spouted with a faint laugh.

Josey sat, shaking her head. She wasn't a bit amused by Gade's comment. "That marriage will be a farce if there ever was one," Josey relented.

"But Momma, I thought you liked Clay. In fact, you said many times that he was the best boyfriend Saphire ever had."

"And that's the truth, but your sister is too stupid to see it. And Clay is not the one I'm worried about," Josey said, repositioning herself on the sofa. "It's that sister of yours we need to be concerned about."

"Momma, you know Saphire has never been faithful to Clay since day one, and her saying I do to him is not going to change her ways," Gade sputtered.

"Gade, you should have seen the light in that man's eyes when he asked your sister to be his wife. Lord, he was twirling Saphire around so...you

would have thought the man done won the lottery." Josey's voice trembled with pride. "His eyes were shining so bright. I've never seen a man so happy, not since…" Josey's voice trailed off as she thought about her ex-husband, Russell, and the night he had proposed to her so many years ago.

Josey cleared her throat as she tried to clear the memory from her mind. It seemed as if the past always popped up when she least expected. Coming back to reality, she continued. "The man was a whooping and hollering. He even picked me up and turned me around a couple of times." Josey laughed.

Gade folded her arms, seeing the glow on her mother's face. She hated to be the one to dim her light, but the truth was the truth. "Well, if he marries Saphire, somewhere down the line he's going to be whooping and hollering again, but it won't be under happy circumstances. You can bet your life on that," Gade hissed.

Gade rubbed her forehead. She felt a headache coming on. "Momma, I'm tired and I'm going upstairs," Gade announced as she got up from the couch.

Gade headed up the stairs, but before she reached the top again, Josey yelled out, "You didn't come clean with me, chile, but I'll leave it alone for now."

"Thank God for small blessings," Gade whispered as she made another step.

"Oh Gade!" Josey yelled again from the bottom of the stairs.

Gade cringed in anticipation of what her mother would say next. "What is it now, Momma?" Gade answered slowly while holding her breath.

"What happened to that handsome knight who saved your life at the picnic? Don't tell me you two are fighting already?" Josey chuckled.

"Momma, you can't fight what you don't see, now can you?" Gade asked quickly as she ran up the stairs and into her room.

She wasn't waiting for an answer from her mother. That would be another long road she was too tired to walk. After about an hour in her room, she heard her mother's voice calling her down for dinner. Not feeling very hungry, she decided not to go. Was it really her appetite that had failed her

or was it the expectation of facing her mother and the probing questions she knew she would ask concerning Joe. Her head felt as if it was going to explode from the memories of Joe and Lamonte as they both filled her mind.

What did she do wrong? She wrestled with that thought as she dropped down on her bed. How could she lose two men so easily? What was wrong with her? Maybe she didn't have what it took to hold on to a man. Maybe Saphire was right about her, after all. Here she was, a little, inexperienced fool wearing her heart on her sleeve. Look what she got for it—absolutely nothing. Tears stung her eyes as she closed them tightly. Her heart felt so heavy. The man she had known for almost two years, who she thought was so much in love with her, was now fooling around with that damned-near white Chaniece. And if that didn't do her in, the man she just recently met, whom she felt an instant attraction to, was now MIA–Missing In Action.

A deep frown creased her forehead. Why couldn't she work it like Saphire? The woman could juggle five men at one time without missing a beat, and they kept coming back for more. "Ugggh!" Gade cried out, sitting upright on her bed. Who was she kidding? She had no intentions of being like her sister, Saphire. She wanted stability, commitment and true love.

Didn't you have all of that with Lamonte? A voice whispered in her head. Gade picked up her red heart-shaped pillow and threw it against the wall. "How could you turn to Chaniece?" Gade cried out. Maybe she was jumping to conclusions. Maybe they were just friends. Yes, that was it! Gade glanced at the digital clock that sat on her nightstand. It read 9:00 p.m.

She'd bet Lamonte was at home right now watching his favorite show *Dog, The Bounty Hunter*. She couldn't understand why he got such a kick out of seeing people being chased down and taken to jail. A soft giggle escaped her lips at the memory of them spread out on his mother's living room floor with a bowl of hot buttered popcorn and a couple of colas.

"Lamonte, I can't believe you invited me over here to watch your stupid show. Where are the movies you supposedly rented?" she quizzed.

Lamonte gave her that dazzling smile of his and pulled her into his

arms. "Chill, baby, chill, I got your movies but first I need my candy treat," he laughed and kissed her fully on the lips. Their kiss lingered before he pulled away. Then he reached down into the cherry wood movie cabinet and retrieved her movies. Gade's face broke out into a satisfied smile. Lamonte was always a jokester, and he kept her smiling.

Thinking about him now made her mad-crazy. She had to talk to him, she just had to. She picked up the phone and began to dial his home number. After three rings, his father picked up. "Hello, Mr. Singletary, is Lamonte there?" she asked, holding the receiver firmly.

"Hello, Baby Doll, I haven't heard your voice in a while," Mr. Singletary answered. Gade had so many nicknames referring to her small size, and Mr. Singletary had just added another one to the pot. Mr. Singletary was such a nice man, and he treated her as if she were already his daughter-in-law.

"Where have you been keeping yourself, young lady?" Mr. Singletary's voice interrupted her thoughts.

"I've. . .just been busy, Mr. Singletary, you know, with school and work."

"I understand, and to answer your question, Baby Doll, my son is not here. I haven't seen him since he left for work early this morning. That boy seems to stay in the street these days. You want me to give him a message for you?"

"Nah, that's okay, Mr. Singletary," Gade mumbled brokenheartedly as she placed the phone back into its cradle.

She slumped down on the bed, wet tears rolling down her face. Here she sat with no man to call her own. Who could she blame? Searching her heart, she realized there was no one, for her plight was one of her own making. Saphire had told her more than once that she was playing with fire. Gade closed her eyes. A vision of Lamonte's face settled before her. There were flickers of flames circling all around it. Her world was on fire.

SATURDAY MORNING

The sisters were still at war with each other. They moved around their home as if they were total strangers. They spoke only when it was necessary, and it was driving their mother out of her mind. Gade had just finished vacuuming the hunter green carpet in the den when Saphire came into the room with a bowl of Special K cereal. Saphire was on another diet craze, which Gade thought would last a couple of days and then she would return to her old eating habits. Saphire's breakfast usually consisted of buttermilk pancakes laden with molasses, two eggs, hash browns and three strips of bacon.

As Saphire whizzed by her, a couple of flakes fell from the bowl. Gade gave her an agitated look. "Can't you see what you've done!" Gade snapped, shaking her head.

"Don't sweat, it, Lil' Sis, it's only cereal," Saphire muttered, bending down and picking up the flakes with her manicured nails.

"What are you doing eating in here anyway? Breakfast should be eaten in the kitchen," Gade spat out.

"And who are you, Miss Thang, to tell me where I can and cannot eat? I'm a grown ass woman and I will eat where I damned well please," Saphire huffed.

Gade put her hand on her forehead and gasped. "Oh my, how dumb can I be? Queen Bee rules the world. There is nothing that she can't do. Bed every man that breathes and walks, then still be treated like the Virgin Mary," Gade smirked as she waved her arm around.

Saphire's eyes narrowed. "Oh, am I hearing a tinge of jealousy in that sweet little voice of yours?" Saphire asked, putting her hands on her sumptuous hips.

"At least when I bed them they do come back to me," Saphire taunted.

Gade was fuming now. Saphire had pushed the wrong button. Gade parted her lips to speak, but Saphire cut her off.

Pointing her finger, Saphire said, "Nah, don't you say a single word," knowing she had Gade by the throat, so to speak. "Where are the—?" she held up one hand and counted on her fingers. "What is it now, Gade, one, no two, and if I would throw in the most recent one for good measure, I think that would make three." Saphire spewed. "Where are they now, Gade? Don't tell me they done hit it and quit it so early in the game?" Saphire chuckled as she rocked back and forth on her heels.

Pent up anger rose in Gade's chest. Her eyes focused on the big cereal bowl her sister held in her thick hands. Without another thought, Gade reached out and shoved the bowl into Saphire's voluptuous breast, staining the bright yellow blouse with its contents. Saphire let go of the bowl and it landed on the floor with a thud.

The heat was on as the two women hooked up like wrestlers. The Michaels sisters were going at it like two enemies on the playground. Hearing the commotion in the den, Josey dropped the dish she was washing into the soapy water in the kitchen sink. She came sailing into the room with the fighting women as they continued to duel.

Josey's voice boomed with fire. "What the hell is happening in here?" she raged, getting between the two. Josey separated them like a referee. Saphire's golden hair weave was rearranged in a style that resembled a wicked witch hat. Gade's Gucci pink blouse was torn from her shoulder. "What on earth has gotten into the both of you?" Josey asked with a scowl on her face. "Blood fighting blood will not be tolerated in Josey Michaels' house!" she stormed. "Do you both understand me?" she asked in a commanding voice.

The sisters muttered, "Yes," in unison as they looked into her blazing eyes.

Josey's chest heaved as she began to speak. "Now, I don't know what's going on between the two of you. For some reason you both want to keep it a secret from me. But let me tell you something," Josey continued as her eyes traveled from one daughter's face to the other. "Remember this." She

pointed her slim finger at both of them. "Secrets don't stay secrets forever, what's done in the dark will always find its way to the light, no matter how hard you try to hide it. Whatever is festering between you, I am advising both of you to squash it and squash it right now, or you will find yourselves out of this house." And with that, Josey left the room.

Gade glanced over at Saphire. As far as she was concerned, she was her mother's only daughter. She wanted nothing else to do with Saphire and she was cutting all ties with her.

Saphire glared back at Gade. She was through with the pint-sized hussy. And to think she was considering giving Joe back to her. *Hmmph, not on my worst day,* she fumed silently. Gade didn't deserve a damned thing from her and if she had her way, she would cut her out of her wedding as well. But she knew not to play that card. Josey Michaels would have her hanging from a tree like a runaway slave.

Neither woman said a word as their eyes met. The only sound that could be heard came from the vacuum cleaner, which was still humming.

* * * * *

Clay tried Saphire's cell once more before he closed up shop for Mr. Bill. His Aunt Martha was coming for a visit from New York, and he wanted Saphire to meet her. Aunt Martha wasn't able to make it to the family picnic a few months back, due to Uncle Ray's diabetes. Now he was doing much better, and hopefully, they both would be able to attend the wedding in December. Yes, December 24th was the date Saphire chose. You would think most women would have picked a date in the summer, such as June or July, but that wasn't the case for Saphire. She was a dramatic woman and always at the center of attention. She was a handful at times, but he loved her dearly. That's why, not being able to contact her was driving him crazy.

Clay dialed her cell number again, and once again it went straight to voice mail. "Mmm, where the hell is she?" he swore under his breath. Her workday had ended long ago, and it was now after seven. Clay decided to call her home. After a few rings, Miss Josey picked up. "Hello Miss

Michaels, by any chance is Saphire home?" he asked anxiously.

Josey clutched the phone tightly. She was standing in her living room looking through the bay window. Saphire was getting out of an apple-red corvette. Some brown-skinned man who favored Samuel L. Jackson with a smooth baldhead sat behind the wheel. Saphire was carrying two bags from Macy's as she strutted up the walkway. The lookalike waved as he pulled away from the curb.

Josey stood on the porch as Saphire made her way up to the door. "Hello Momma," Saphire greeted her nervously as she attempted to go around her and into the house. Josey grabbed her by the arm and pulled her back. "Momma!" Saphire exclaimed as she gave her mother a quizzical look.

"Your fiancé is on this phone," Josey uttered through clenched teeth.

Saphire didn't even notice the phone in her mother's hand until now. Saphire grabbed the phone and proceeded to go inside. Josey followed her closely. She wanted to hear the lie she was going to give Clay, and she knew that whatever it was, Clay would swallow it whole. After she finished the call, Saphire headed upstairs, with Josey following. As Saphire entered her room, she placed the Macy's bags in her closet, closed the door, and then sat down on her bed, kicking off her three-inch black pumps.

"What's with the bags, Saphire? Guilt trip souvenirs?" Josey taunted.

"Momma, please don't start with me." Saphire exhaled as she looked up at her mother who was standing in her doorway. "I wasn't doing anything wrong, just hanging out with a friend," Saphire snapped.

"Yeah, I heard the story you gave Clay. Shopping with a friend, huh?" she questioned with a skeptical look. "So why didn't you mention that the friend was a male?" Josey asked.

"So what are you saying, Momma, I can't have male friends? Is it a crime for a man and a woman to just be friends?" she argued.

"If that's the truth, then why didn't you come clean with Clay and tell him who you were shopping with? Surely he would have understood that as well," Josey retorted with a raised brow.

"No, he wouldn't have, Momma. He would have reacted the same as you are doing right now. Looking at me as if I just came out of some cheap

motel."

"Well, did you?" Josey challenged.

"No, of course not," Saphire lied.

"Don't play on my intelligence, chile. Shopping wasn't the only thing you were doing with that man and you damned well know it. What is wrong with you, Saphire? You are about to be a married woman, or have you forgotten all about that?" Josey bellowed.

Saphire lowered her eyes from her mother's intense stare. She had her pegged. She and Bobby were at a hotel before he took her shopping, but she would never admit it to Josey. She'd rather rot in hell. "Of course I haven't forgotten that, Momma," Saphire muttered, looking down at the shimmering diamond she wore. "But I…was just having a little fun. He doesn't mean anything to me, and when I marry Clay, I will stop all of this. I promise you, Momma." Saphire held back the tears that were forming. Seeing the disappointment in Josey's eyes shook her.

"There will be no wedding if Clay finds out about your trifling ways, Saphire!" Josey said solemnly.

"He won't, Momma, I know what I'm doing, okay?" Saphire wheedled as she began to take off her clothes.

Josey stood shaking her head as she watched her daughter undress. "You are playing with fire, my chile," Josey exclaimed. "Clay is a good man, and with him, you will have a wonderful life. Don't mess it up by creeping in the streets." Josey came into the room and stood in front of her daughter. "I don't know what you are searching for, Saphire, being with so many different men," Josey said, holding Saphire's gaze. "Sometimes I think you are searching for the love you missed from your father when he walked out on us, baby. But you're not going to find it in the beds of different men. Your father was no good, Saphire, and I don't want you following in the same path."

"Oh, so you're telling me that I'm no good now, just like my father, huh? Don't you dare talk about us like that, Momma. My father was a good man and he took damned good care of us. You didn't have to work a day in your life when you were with him, so how can you say he wasn't

no good!" Saphire lashed out, feeling the years of buried pain coming to the surface.

Josey felt a sting of tears as her daughter spoke. She didn't know half the story, even though she thought she did.

"You are the one who ran him off, Momma," Saphire continued with a vengeance. "You stifled him, never letting him out of your sight. The man couldn't breathe with your smothering ways. I heard the arguments you two had about him going out. You wanted him right under your thumb like some wimpy ass man. Maybe if you would have loosened up the chains you had around him, he wouldn't have left us, Momma!" Saphire screamed as she stood up from the bed.

Josey's tears turned to anger now. How dare she blame her for her father leaving? "Let me enlighten you on what you think you know," Josey hissed as she stared into her daughter's fiery eyes. "I tried my damnedest to be a good wife to your father. I loved that man with all my heart." Josey choked. "I cooked and cleaned, ran his bath water when he came home, and tried to please him in every way that I could. Even in the bedroom, if you want to know the whole truth about it!" Josey's voice rose. "And he still cheated on me every chance he got. I wanted a happy, loving home and Russell…well, he just wanted the streets and every woman he could find there," Josey stammered.

"Well, Momma, maybe if you had backed off just a little, maybe he would have stopped. But you couldn't do that, now, could you?" Saphire shrieked accusingly. Shaking her head, Saphire pranced around the room. "Oh no, the almighty Josey had to have things her own way. What was it now, the same speech you gave to me and Gade, my way or the highway?" Saphire spewed as she glared at her mother.

"What should I have done, Saphire? Closed my eyes to it all and accepted the fact that my husband, the man I loved with all my being, was a dog?" Josey huffed with wide eyes.

"No Momma, yes, maybe…I don't know." Saphire struggled with the confusing emotions within her.

Josey lowered her head as memories of her husband's cheating filtered

through her mind. "I just couldn't take it no more!" Josey murmured with trembling lips. "I heard all the rumors around town. Women whispering behind my back, and the looks they gave me...it was pitiful." Josey swallowed hard. "And your own father confirmed those rumors without saying a word. Whenever he and I were together, his eyes would roam like crazy when a nice looking woman walked by."

With a slight whimper, Josey continued. "Your father was a fine yellow man, as you well know, Saphire." Looking at her daughter, Josey managed a small smile. "You're the spitting image of him," she said, touching Saphire's face with her thin fingers. "With the skin color of fresh corn, deep hazel eyes, and a solid build like your father." Saphire let out a low sigh.

"Women were drawn to your daddy like a magnet, and he loved it. Cheating on me with women I didn't know, Saphire, was one thing, but when he bedded my best friend Cherry, well, that was the straw that broke the camel's back." Josey's face was now wet with her tears. She quickly wiped them away. "So tell me, Saphire, are you following in his footsteps? Are you going to put poor Clay through the same turmoil your father did me?" Josey asked as she searched her daughter's troubled face.

Saphire held her tears, even though her throat felt like sandpaper as she saw the sadness in her mother's face. Was she her father's daughter in every sense of the word? Guilt shot through her as if it were a lightning bolt on a stormy day. She was so sorry for all the pain her father had put her mother through, but she loved him. And she wished he had never left them. Their lives would have been so different. Her heart ached deeply as her mind flashed back to the happy years of her childhood. Her father holding her in his big strong arms and telling her how pretty she was. A tear escaped her eye. As a young child, she saw only what she wanted to see. She'd blamed her mother because she was there, she could only curse her father in her dreams.

Saphire wanted to reach out, take her mother into her arms and rock the sorrow away. But she couldn't, her pride wouldn't let her. Instead, she murmured, "Momma, I'm sorry. And I will stop, just as I said earlier. As

soon as Clay and I are married, I will stop all of this, I promise you."

Tears clouded Josey's eyes and she started to speak but she held her tongue. She turned and walked over to the doorway. Josey looked back over her shoulder at her daughter. Sadly, she realized what she had known for years. Saphire was her father's daughter. How many times had she heard the same words coming out of Russell's mouth? *Josey, I will stop, I promise,* Russell swore.

"He never did stop and never will, Saphire."

A SECOND CHANCE

It was an unusually dark and dreary day in Southern California, but the day matched Gade's sullen mood as she sat in the dim light of the den. Looking outside, she listened to the sound of the falling rain. She laid her head against the back of the overstuffed recliner, and closed her eyes. A few weeks had passed since that fateful day she saw Lamonte and Chaniece together. Even more upsetting, he never returned the call she made to his house that night. She was certain Mr. Singletary had mentioned to him that she had called.

Gade resolved to accept the fact that Lamonte had moved on. To her surprise, after not hearing from Joe for the same number of weeks, he'd called her last night. He said he wanted to see her. In her anger, she hung up on him, but moments later, he called her back. Reluctantly, she agreed to meet with him later that night. Why not? It wasn't like she had guys knocking at her door. Hell, she didn't have anyone knocking at her door.

In a few hours, they were to meet in a place called Susie's. A small, but cozy little pub downtown that was well known for its tasty buffalo wings. A silent reminder of how she and Joe had met. Forty-five minutes and two drinks later, Joe was still missing in action. She'd had enough of waiting and she was preparing to leave. God only knows why he stood her up. Maybe he was playing her for the fool she was for agreeing to see him anyway, she thought as she slid out from under the table.

"Hey baby, leaving already?" Joe asked as she turned around to look into his gorgeous face. The man hadn't changed a bit. If anything, he was more handsome than she'd remembered. His very presence was setting her on fire.

Joe scanned Gade's petite figure in the shapely fitted jeans she was wearing. He could taste those soft supple lips, and oh man, how he missed

that little body. He gestured for her to sit back down. Gade slipped back into her seat as Joe sat across from her.

They stared at each other for another minute before speaking. "I know I owe you a hell of an explanation for disappearing on you the way that I did," Joe said as he took a sip of Gade's drink. "So I see you started without me." Joe smiled as he waited for her response.

"Yes, I've been doing a lot of things without you," she spat, showing the anger that still simmered within her.

"Ouch, that hurt." Joe grimaced. "But you have every right to be angry with me."

Joe was a free spirit and he went wherever the wind led him. He left no roots in his travels, only a string of faceless women who were a dime a dozen. He loved them and left them, as the lyrics from the Rick James song stated. He thought he could do the same thing with Gade. Unfortunately, the rules didn't apply to her. There was something so special about her. She touched him in a way no other woman ever had. Gade's love was like a dove, quiet and patient. Joe took in her beautiful face. So many women would have read him his rights and sent him off to prison by now.

He reached out his hand to touch hers, but she pulled away. "Gade, I know I've hurt you and I'm sorry. You see, I don't think I'm the right kind of man you need in your life. I was afraid of hurting you, so I backed off," Joe whispered as he leaned forward.

Gade's eyes filled with tears. "What am I supposed to do now, Joe? Act as if we never were?" she asked as her light brown eyes held his. "I was beginning to love you, Joe," she cried. "I even stopped seeing my boyfriend because of you…and you left me dangling." A tear fell down her cheek. "Now he's gone, and you're telling me that we have nothing. How do you think that makes me feel, Joe?" Gade choked.

Joe felt totally helpless as she continued. "I'll tell you how it makes me feel." Gade wept. "I feel like a fool. A complete and total fool," she said through clenched teeth. Lowering her eyes, she uttered, "You used me to get what you wanted and then you left me high and dry." Tears filled her eyes.

"It wasn't like that, Gade," Joe pleaded.

"Save it for someone who gives a damn!" Gade hissed, holding up her hand.

Joe shifted in his seat. Seeing the pain in her eyes chilled him.

"I should have listened to Saphire from the beginning," she continued. "She said you were no good, but I was too blind to see that. My sister was right about you all along. You're a user, Joe," Gade ground out, getting up to leave.

He couldn't believe Saphire had the audacity to say that he was no good when she was the one screwing around with him behind her sister's back. Now what did that say about her? As far as he was concerned, it was just a game he played, but blood was blood. What kind of woman would do that to her very own? He hated to admit it, but even he was feeling guilty about it all. That's the real reason he'd stopped seeing Gade. It was getting too complicated, heart-wise.

Gade had pierced his heart with her tender and loving ways. He couldn't continue to hurt her like that. When he confronted Saphire about calling off her wedding a few days ago and being with him, she'd flat out refused. Even after he admitted that he was falling in love with her. Love. That was a word he never used until he'd met the Michaels women. After Saphire made it clear that she was going through with her wedding, he pulled away and now here he sat with her sister. Strangely, he wanted to say the same words to her as well, because his heart was screaming it inside him.

"Wait a minute, Gade," Joe said, agitated, as he pulled her back into her seat.

He reached over and gave her the most tantalizing kiss. Gade was tense at first, but the heat from the kiss melted the ice that had formed around her heart. They left the restaurant together, rekindling the fire that had died between them.

* * * * *

"Ohh baby, that was out of this world," Clay swooned after a heated session of lovemaking. Saphire lay curled up in his arms. Yes, Clay could

be exhilarating when he wanted to be, she thought as she gave him a satisfied smile. Breaking their embrace, Clay sat up, reached over to the nightstand and retrieved his smokes. He lit up a Newport cigarette and took in a long drag, letting out a cloud of smoke that Saphire fanned away.

"You're smoking like a chimney," Saphire gasped as she sat up in bed. "I tell you one thing, Clay, that smoking in bed is going to cease once we are married and in our own house," she stated defiantly, looking him dead in the eye. "Once we are in our home, if you want to smoke, it will be out on the porch. Do you understand me?" she said, without breaking a smile.

"Come on, Sugar Plum, you don't really mean that?" He frowned.

"Do I look like I'm joking, Clay?" Saphire rebutted as she folded her arms across her big breasts.

"Are you going to be one of those bossy wives who rag all the time on their husbands?" Clay asked with a little mischief in his voice.

She loved the way his long lashes fluttered over his big brown eyes. She let out a small snicker at the boyish look on his face. Of all the men she'd ever been with, and there had been plenty, he was the only one she knew who really cared about her. He was real as they came. The man was hardworking, honest, loving and kind. He would give you the shirt off his back if you asked him to. Saphire knew she had a gem, and that gem loved her deeply. Her mother had been right about her. She wasn't any good. He deserved so much better.

Clay noticed the change in Saphire's demeanor. Where her face was once bright and cheery, a cloud suddenly took its place. "Oh baby, don't take me seriously," Clay muttered as he smashed the butt of the cigarette into the glass ashtray and pulled her into his strong arms. "If you don't want me smoking in the house, then so be it. I tell you what," he said, looking into her hazel eyes. "Before our wedding day, I will be smoke-free. I will quit it altogether, baby. I will do anything to keep a smile on that pretty face of yours." Clay was grinning. Tears began to travel down her cheeks. Taking his thumb, he gently wiped them away. "Why are you crying? I didn't mean to upset you."

Saphire licked the top of her lip, tasting the remnants of her own tears.

"It's not you, Clay," she answered softly. "Are you sure it's me you want to marry?"

Clay put his arms around her. "Sugar Plum, I can't see myself marrying anyone else. Your man is here for you always."

Saphire's tears continued as she contemplated her philandering ways.

* * * * *

Gade couldn't understand why Joe would not step foot in her mother's house. He made up all kinds of excuses about why he couldn't come over. Instead, they were meeting at restaurants, movies or parks and she was getting suspicious. "What's up with you, Joe? Are you afraid of Josey Michaels? Do you think she's going to come after you with a butcher knife and slice your head off?" She chuckled as she waited for a response.

Joe was certain if Gade's mother knew he was screwing both of her daughters, that's exactly what she'd do. Gade couldn't see his expression because they were talking on their cells.

"Joe, are you there?" she asked, at his silence.

"Yeah, baby, I'm still here," he finally responded.

"So, are we meeting at your place again tonight?" she quizzed.

"Yeah, and bring your appetite, you will be needing it in more ways than one," he crooned with a hint of lust in his voice. Gade let out a soft giggle as Saphire watched her. She was seething from across the room.

They were sitting in the family's den. The evening news was blaring from the wide screen TV, which Saphire had lost interest in. The event that held her attention was the expression on her sister's face. It was one of happiness as she cupped the phone in her slim hand. Saphire's mind wandered back to a few nights ago. The conversation she and Joe had was still fresh in her mind. He had enlightened her about the meeting between him and Gade at Susie's Pub a few nights ago. She knew what went down between them, and it sickened her. He had every intention of letting her down easy. He was supposed to give Gade one of those Dear Jane speeches, and call it a day. But when she mentioned that Saphire had called him no good, it made him very angry. So to get back at her, he made

up with her sister. Yes, it was a demented game they both were playing, but she couldn't give Joe up just yet. The man was too damned good between the sheets, not to mention the fact that Joe really wanted her.

He had begged her to call off her wedding to Clay and run off with him. And for a minute, she did consider it. But she couldn't hurt Clay like that. She could never live with herself if she had. The guilt alone would kill her. So having no other choice, she was going through with the wedding. And the good thing about it all, was that Clay's grandfather was loaded. The old man was well into his eighties. His only son had passed away years ago, and since then, Clay had been the center of his affection. He told him he was going to have their dream home built for a wedding present. Saphire could hardly wait. Clay had given her free rein as to how she wanted to decorate it. His exact words were, "Baby, do anything you want as long as we're together like two peas in a pod." Saphire thought that was a corny ass thing to say, but it worked for her, and working it was exactly what she was going to do.

Before his grandpa passed away, she was going to see what else Clay could get out of him. She had a feeling her future husband was in his grandpa's will as well. There was no way she was going to back out now. Even though Joe had money, Saphire knew Joe wasn't the settling type. Deep down inside, she wanted a loving home, and maybe one day a patter of feet, from children looking like her handsome husband.

"Joe is so sweet," Gade said, breaking into Saphire's thoughts. Placing the phone into its cradle, Gade smiled. "He invited me over to his place and we are going to have a very romantic evening," she purred like a kitten. "The man can't seem to get enough of me," she said, giving Saphire a catty stare.

Ignoring her gloating, Saphire huffed, "Are you ready?" as she hopped up and grabbed her Gucci purse from the small table in the foyer. "I want to get to the mall before the traffic gets crazy," she hissed.

The women sat in silence as Saphire drove. Traffic was already crazy, but in the City of Angels, it always was. Slowing to a snail's pace, they crept along the freeway. Cars were bumper-to- bumper now, and Saphire began to feel agitated. She took a long sip of the bottled water she had

brought along, hoping it would cool her down.

"You know, for a minute there, I thought we could get back to acting like sisters again," Gade stated. "After all, you invited me to go with you to the mall, and I thought we were over that stupid altercation we had the other day. At least that's what I'm trying to do." Gade waited for Saphire's response. She hoped it would be to call a truce between them.

"I invited you because I had no other choice in the matter. You are in my wedding, and we need the final and last measurements for your dress. If I could eliminate you, believe me, I would," Saphire said tightly.

Gade's feelings were hurt, and she blinked back a tear. She knew she and Saphire didn't always get along, but to hear her one and only sister say that she didn't want her in her wedding was devastating. "I never thought in a million years we would let a man come between us. This is what it's all about, now isn't it?" Gade asked with wild eyes. Saphire remained silent. "It's so pathetic. I mean, it's not like you're sleeping with my man, so why are we still at each other's throats?"

Saphire pondered her question. "So he is your man now," she repeated. Taking her eyes off the road, she peered over her sunglasses at Gade. She wanted to see her response.

"Of course he's my man, and he always was," Gade snapped.

"I thought just a few days ago, he was still missing in action, but now he is back and stepping into the role he left, huh?" Saphire huffed.

"We had some problems, but it's all worked out," Gade muttered, turning to look out her passenger side window. "I don't see why it should matter to you one way or the other," she said, looking back at her sister.

Saphire took in a deep breath to respond to her comment, but Gade interjected. "You are going to be a married woman with your own set of problems, or should I say, Clay is the one who is going to have the problems."

Saphire's head rolled in Gade's direction. "Well, if you think the relationship between you and Joe is going to end up in Happyville, then you are in for a rude awakening, my dear sister," she blasted.

It took all of her strength not to tell her sister that her man was screwing her every chance he got. But something inside of her wouldn't let her say

it. In spite of everything, she loved her baby sister and she couldn't hurt her like that. Saphire softened her voice. "Gade, men like Joe don't stay around. It's only a matter of time before he goes AWOL on you again. Please don't give him your heart, because you will get it back, broken."

Gade parted her lips, but never uttered a word. Once they reached the mall, Gade got out of Saphire's Lexus and slammed the door as hard as she could, not waiting for her sister to catch up. If she wasn't mistaken, Gade thought she saw something in Saphire's eyes that told her she knew Joe better than she did.

* * * * *

Lamonte rolled over in his bed and glanced at the digital clock. It read 6:00 a.m. Another day at the plant. He hated every minute of being there, slaving away for the almighty dollar. He wanted his own business so bad he could taste it. He wanted to run things the way he wanted to without "The Man" constantly looking over his shoulder. Lamonte studied the skyscraper he'd made out of Legos years ago. His mother had kept it all this time. She had found a spot for it on the corner of his tall oak dresser.

She told him that he started playing with Legos on Christmas when he was just three years old. He would sit on the floor for hours, building and rebuilding creations as tall as he could get them. He completely ignored all of his other toys, which consisted of Tonka trucks, soldier men and airplanes. Now, as a grown man, the fever for building things still ran hot in his blood. This was what he wanted to do, so why wasn't he doing it? Lamonte sat straight up in bed. He wasn't going to work today.

In fact, he just quit his job. He jumped out of bed and dipped into the shower, turning the water on full blast. Today, his mind was made up. He knew what he wanted to do and now was the time to do it. Once dressed, Lamonte headed out the door. It was early as he sat in the parking lot of Bank of America on La Brea Avenue. In the cool of the morning he sat with his window slightly down as he listened to the soft music that played on his radio. He would be their first customer of the day, marking the beginning of his new life as an entrepreneur.

SINGING THE BLUES

Joe was seated at the bar in Bernie's Grill on Fifth Avenue. It was Friday night, and a freaky one. It has been ages since Joe Burrels had no plans. Usually, he would have been freaking with one chick after another, but tonight he sat alone nursing the only friend he ever had, his drink, a double Martini. Gade had been all caught up in her sister, Saphire's wedding. That's where she was tonight, at some rehearsal dinner. Of course, she'd invited him, but he had to be a no show at this affair. Since being with Gade, he hadn't even looked at another woman. "Well, except Saphire." Joe chuckled under his breath.

Shaking his head, Joe couldn't believe what a trip he was on. He thought about the day he called Gade at home and her mother picked up. He'd said, "Hi babe," before he realized he was talking to Josey instead of Gade. Their voices were so similar; it was eerie. Josey had reprimanded him for not coming over to her house. He had to make up a tall order of excuses, and he seemed to have smoothed things over for now.

The bartender sat another shot in front of him and Joe downed it all at once. He felt like he was losing his grip. He'd never in all of his game, been attached to anyone, as he was with the Michaels sisters. They were the reason he was drowning himself in alcohol. He needed someone to talk to about his true feelings. He was in love with Saphire and had strong feelings for Gade. Damn, how screwed up could he get? His cell vibrated on his hip. He retrieved it and read the number.

He debated answering it. It was his little brother calling. He hadn't spoken to him in months. They didn't have the typical brotherly relationship. They were never really close, even though they were raised in the same household. He was much older than his brother, and that made it a lot harder to form a close bond. Joe's father had left his mother for a

younger woman when he was ten. It left his mother a basket case and Joe's father ended up getting custody of him. A year later, he was presented with a baby brother from his new step-mom, whom he hated with a passion. He blamed her for taking away his real family, and he made her life a living hell. As soon as he turned seventeen, he was out of their house. He moved to South Carolina where his mother resided with her family. Joe never looked back.

He kept in touch with his baby brother as the years went by. He made appearances for some holidays, and he never forgot his birthday. After all, the same blood ran through his baby brother's veins as his, both coming from their father. His father tried for years for all of them to be one big happy family, but it never worked. No matter how much Irene tried to treat him as her own, he would find some way of rebelling. She would never be his mother. It was all a farce, anyway. From the very first day he laid eyes on her, he knew she didn't like him much. He looked too much like his mother, the woman both Irene and his father had betrayed. As far as his baby brother was concerned, he loved him, even though a part of him resented him as well. He was the product of his father's love affair. He tried keeping his distance, but his baby brother always found a way to reach him.

He brought the phone up to his ear and answered. "Hello Lamonte, what's up, my brother?" Joe greeted him with reserve.

"It's about time you answered that cell of yours. I was about to hang up." Lamonte chuckled. "You haven't called me in a while. What's up, you lost my digits?" Lamonte asked guardedly.

"No man, I've just been busy, that's all."

"So how's everything in South Carolina?" Lamonte asked. Lamonte wasn't aware that Joe was in Los Angeles. Joe never told him he was coming. Another part of keeping to himself. If Lamonte knew he was here, the man would be all up in his space. Joe was a loner and he planned to keep it that way.

"Just striving and surviving, man."

"Well, let me run something by you, big brother," Lamonte started, as

Joe held on. His heart jumped at Lamonte's calling him his big brother.

"Go ahead man, I'm listening." Joe set his elbow on the bar.

"You know I always wanted my own business, right? Today I did it, man," Lamonte stated excitedly.

"Did what?" Joe quizzed, hearing the joy in Lamonte's voice. "I quit my job at the plant, went to the bank, and got myself a business loan. I'm going to do it, man. I'm going to start my own construction company, so what do you think?"

Joe could tell Lamonte was beaming with excitement. "Oh man, that's great! From what you just told me, sounds like you are well on your way. Now all you have to do is get your staff in place, and your crew, of course. And don't forget to get yourself a lawyer and good insurance for all your workers," Joe rambled. "Take care of all the business aspects and everything else will fall into place," he finished.

Lamonte knew he could count on Joe for his business advice. Joe was a savvy businessman in his own right, and Lamonte wanted him on his team.

"Have you thought about a name?" Joe asked as he motioned the bartender for another drink. "

Lamonte chuckled again. "That was the easiest thing I had to do, bro. The Brothers Construction Company, and Joe, I want you as my partner." Joe's heart took another flip. Here it was again, no matter how much he tried to stay away from his little brother, he always found a way to pull him in. Before Joe could answer his brother's proposition, Lamonte began speaking again. "I've already found a great spot for the business, bro. It's in the middle of downtown, a great location, I think. If only you could come and see it, man," Lamonte sputtered all in one breath.

Joe stared into the fresh drink the bartender had sat before him. If only his brother knew that he was already in town. Been in town for months now, just never contacted Lamonte or their own father. He wanted to lay low, avoid them all. It was best that way, he figured. No feelings to hurt, no bad memories to relive. And now here it was, his baby brother wanted him to be a partner in his business. He couldn't get out of it, Joe thought as he

heard Lamonte calling his name.

"Are you there, man?"

"Yeah, yeah, I'm here," he muttered.

"Where are you anyway? Don't tell me I interrupted the player of plays. Are you with one of your honeys?" Lamonte quipped, remembering his brother's healthy appetite.

"Nah man, it's nothing like that. Let me hit you back, I need some time to think about all this," Joe answered, pushing the empty shot glass away. He had gone way past his limit, and if he was going to drive home without anyone noticing he was drunk, he'd better stop now.

"Joe, I don't expect for you to drop everything you got going on in South Carolina on a whim. You got your own thing going, but please give it some thought. With your business skills and my creative mind, I know we can make a name for ourselves here in LA," Lamonte continued eagerly.

"I'll give you a call in a few days, man. You can count on it."

"Okay, oh, and Joe," Lamonte said, catching him before he hung up. "I'm not giving up on us either, man. You are my big brother, my blood, and I love you, man."

If Joe didn't hang up now he would be crying like a child wanting his mother. He felt hot tears brimming in his eyes. "Later, man," was all he could manage as his voice broke.

A KISS IN THE DARK

Saphire turned off her computer. Another workday had been completed and she was looking forward to going home and taking a long hot bath. Saphire thought back to the altercation between her and her mother. She was determined to play it straight—well, almost. She severed all ties to the other men she kept on the side, but there was one she couldn't get rid of just yet. Joe gave her something none of the others could hold a candle to. With Joe, it was like being on a roller coaster ride. The thrills he gave her were exhilarating and she loved every minute of it. She was addicted to the high Joe gave her and she just couldn't let him go. As she picked up her purse and turned off the office light, someone pushed her back inside. A huge lump formed in her throat and Saphire's heart took off at high speed.

"It's me," Joe whispered in her ear as he held her close.

Joe's firm hands found their way down to the gray pencil skirt she was wearing and pulled it up. His fingers toyed with her pink lace panties. Saphire moaned quietly as she clutched his broad shoulders. Her purse fell from her fingers as Joe entered her. He rocked her body slowly, and then faster, getting into rhythm as they rode the waves of heated desire. Minutes later, they both exploded, their sexual appetite wet with satisfaction once again.

Saphire rested her head on his chest as she listened to his rapid heartbeat.

"I missed you like crazy," Joe uttered, as beads of sweat rolled off his face.

Saphire pulled away, straightening her skirt as she struggled to compose herself.

"It's been a couple of weeks since…the last time." Joe's voice faltered.

"Joe, as much as I love you, we have to let this thing go," Saphire stated.

She couldn't believe what she was saying, but it was true. She realized having her candy and eating it too would soon come to an end. An end that might not be as sweet.

Joe straightened up and focused on Saphire's face. There were slivers of light coming from the office blinds. He could see the outline of her beautiful round face staring at him. "It was you who said we could continue this," Joe reminded her.

"But Joe, you know the circumstances. It's getting harder and harder for me to look Clay in the eye. And my sister..." Saphire's throat tightened as tears gripped her. Shaking her head as if to clear it, she added, "We just can't keep on like this."

Joe pulled her into his arms again. "I'm in love with you, Saphire. Come with me. We can start all over again, in another city, hell, country, if you like," Joe muttered as he kissed the tip of her nose then the nape of her neck.

Electricity ran through her veins at Joe's touch. Saphire's shoulders slumped and she found her body growing weaker. Willing a strength she didn't have, she shook her head from side to side and gently pushed him away. "No Joe, I can't. My wedding is in a few weeks and I won't up and leave Clay hanging like that. I would never forgive myself, and neither would my family." Saphire let out a low breath. A brief silence fell between them. Breaking it, Saphire said, "You know my mama would kill me with her bare hands." She gulped, wiping the tears from her face.

"You're doing this for all the wrong reasons," Joe whispered.

Saphire closed her tear-filled eyes. She felt as if the weight of the world rested on her shoulders. Here she stood in front of a man she had come to love. She loved him more than Clay, a secret she had to keep. Yes, she had run from one man's arms to another's, but not anymore. She was through with running. It all would stop today.

As if he read her mind, Joe said, "You don't love Clay as much as you think you do. You're just trying to prove to your mother that you are not like your father."

Saphire knew in her heart Joe was right. She had a hard time admitting that to herself. And she certainly wasn't going to admit it to him now.

"Stop it, Joe. I do love Clay, and I want to…am going to marry him," she confirmed as she struggled for the words.

"Clay doesn't give you that spark of fire like I do," Joe hissed.

"And what about my sister, Joe? Does she give you that spark of fire as well?" Saphire challenged. "You never stopped seeing her, so you must have feelings for her as well. I saw the way you kissed her the other night in front of our house," Saphire lamented with her voice rising. "You never came inside, but I saw you two in the driveway under the glow of the street light. You looked every bit a man in love." Saphire's voice broke again. With narrowed eyes, she spat, "In spite of myself, I wanted to come down the stairs and rip your lips away from hers."

Joe grimaced as he stared into her twisted face. "The only reason I'm with her, Saphire, is because I can't have you." Reaching out and touching her smooth cheek, he muttered, "I never told Gade I loved her. Sure, I played around with words. But I'm telling you here and now, that I love you, Saphire Michaels. It's you I really want. It's you I need in my life. I know that more now than ever." Joe attempted to pull her back into his arms.

Saphire's cell rang. She stepped away from him and turned to answer it. She didn't bother to look at the number. She already knew who it was. She answered in the sweet voice she always used. "Hello Clay. Yes, baby, I'm on my way home now. I got…tied up with a report I had to finish. See you soon. Yes, I love you, too," she whispered as she closed her cell.

"Obligations," Joe mumbled as he walked out the door.

MOVIN' ON

Lamonte spent his days wading through paperwork, looking at office sites and interviewing potential employees for his upcoming business. And in turn, spending less and less time with Chaniece. However, Lamonte did find the time to do a lot of soul searching. Deep down inside, he never got over losing Gade. Dating Chaniece was like a safety net for him. He was afraid of being alone. But now, he realized that his feelings for Gade were just as strong as ever. No woman could replace her in his heart. He had run into Gade at Office Depot. He was there purchasing office supplies for his future office. Lamonte still couldn't come to grips with the knowledge that his business was about to become a reality. As he came down the aisle with his cart, he looked up and there she stood. She looked like an angel. Her smooth skin and sparkling eyes captured his heart all over again. All he wanted to do was hold her in his arms. They both just stared at each other for a brief moment before speaking.

Gade broke the silence with a warm smile. "Hello Lamonte."

"Hello," he mumbled. The palms of his hands broke out in a cold sweat as he realized just how much he loved the woman who stood before him. How could he have been so stupid as to let her go?

"What's up with all the stuff you got there?" Gade asked, peering into his full cart.

"Um, I'm starting my own business," he answered proudly.

"Really?" Gade asked, returning Lamonte's bright smile.

"Yes, I decided I had enough of working for the man, I want to do my own thing. You remember we talked about me doing this for quite some time. The thing about it was, that's all I did–talk. But now, everything has been put into play. I've secured a business loan from the bank, and already checked out a couple of sites for my office. In fact, I think I've found one."

Lamonte smiled broadly. "It's right in the middle of downtown, not far from Crenshaw. It's not the best-looking place, but with a little paint and curb appeal, I think it will attract customers." Realizing he was doing all of the talking, he said, "And how are you these days?"

"Um fine, just fine. I'm still in school and working part time at the hospital." Gade gave him another warm smile. "Oh, before I forget, Saphire's getting married," she announced.

"You got to be kidding me?" Lamonte responded as he and Gade moved closer together as another couple went by.

"So Clay has finally tamed the tiger," Lamonte shook his head in laughter.

"Well, I hope so," Gade qualified. "My sister is a wild child, and I hope he will be able to hang onto her." Gade smiled weakly, gazing into Lamonte's handsome face.

"Yeah, I wish I had done the same," he confessed as he returned her smile. His feelings were spilling over. Gade meant the world to him and he wanted her back.

She cleared her throat. "Lamonte, I'd better be going, I just stopped in to get a couple of—"

Before she could finish, Lamonte pulled her into his arms, and gave her the most sensual kiss she'd felt in a long time. Old feelings began to stir as the familiarity of being in his arms comforted her. She felt as if she was home again, right where she belonged.

Just as fast as he pulled her into his arms, he let her go. "I'm sorry...I had no right to do that," he stuttered.

Gade didn't respond, instead she gave him a quizzical look and hurriedly made her way down the aisle.

Lamonte stood as he watched the woman he loved disappear.

As Lamonte pulled his SUV into the parking space of his apartment complex, he knew what he had to do. He wanted Gade back, and just like his business, he was going to go after her with everything he had. He knew Gade still loved him, he felt it in her kiss, and that was all the evidence he needed.

BREAKFAST IS READY

Gade and her mother, Josey, sat at the round glass breakfast table enjoying their Sunday morning breakfast. Josey went all out this morning. She'd prepared sausage, grits, eggs and hash browns along with fresh brewed coffee that filled the air with its rich aroma. On the table sat a pitcher of fresh-squeezed orange juice. "Momma, I don't know why you go to the trouble of cooking all of this stuff," Gade exclaimed with a mouth full of food.

"Well, I see you sure are enjoying it." Josey chuckled as she watched her daughter wipe the corner of her mouth with a napkin.

"I didn't say it wasn't delicious, Momma. I'm just saying, it's only the three of us, and I think Saphire and I are old enough to grab something to stuff down our throats."

"I love cooking for my girls. Always have and I always will." Josey smiled, patting Gade on her hand.

This was the time Gade enjoyed the most. Josey wasn't only her mother, but her best friend as well. They shared so much, and she'd been there for her so many times when she was teased about her size. Josey listened intensely while Gade confided her inferior feelings when people compared her with her sister. She had the ugly duckling complex, but her mother always assured her that she was just as pretty, and a whole lot smarter than Saphire. She remembered her saying that she used her mind, whereas Saphire used, well, whatever to get ahead. Gade always giggled at that point, because her mother would never say what exactly Saphire had used.

Saphire strutted into the kitchen, impeccably dressed in a two-piece periwinkle suit, matching pumps and cream-colored pearls with matching earrings. Her auburn weave rested flawlessly around her shoulders.

Saphire was looking like Monique's cousin for real this morning. Gade had to admit her sister was a beautiful full-figured woman who carried herself well.

"Wow, we're sure looking mighty fine today," Josey proclaimed as she took in the sight of her oldest daughter.

Saphire sat down at the table, poured herself a cup of coffee, and proceeded to dip a serving of eggs, grits and sausage onto her plate. "I'm going to church with Clay this morning," Saphire announced.

It was unusual for Saphire to attend church without a brimstone sermon from their mother. Gade remembered many dragged-out fights in their younger years on Sunday mornings. "You gave your behind to the devil last night, and you're going to give your soul to the Lord this morning, Saphire Michaels!" Josey would yell as she pulled the covers off Saphire's sleeping form.

Now here she sat before them with serenity on her face and her black leather bible in her hand, which she placed on the breakfast table. Gade and her mother exchanged knowing looks. There was something up with this. Saphire had another agenda besides seeking the Lord. "I know what you two are thinking," Saphire said as she took another bite of her food. "Like I told you a few days ago, Momma, I am changing my ways. I am going to be a good wife to Clay and make him very happy." Saphire smiled as she poured herself a glass of juice.

"Yeah, right, and dogs will fly, won't they?" Gade smirked.

Saphire's face grew dark as she looked over at Gade.

Josey saw the anger rising in Saphire's eyes. "Nip it right there, Gade Michaels. There won't be a repeat of what happened here before," Josey warned. "Now apologize to your sister," Josey ordered.

Gade twisted in her seat and mumbled, "Sorry."

"I accept," Saphire said with a crooked grin, knowing full well Gade didn't mean it. Just as she didn't mean she accepted it either. It was all for their mother's benefit.

"Why are you two not dressed for church this morning?" Saphire asked on a lighter note.

"I've been in revival all this week, chile, and to tell you the truth, I'm just plain tired. I'm staying home today with Lifetime as my companion." Josey sighed, getting up from the table with her empty plate.

"And you?" Saphire asked Gade. "Don't tell me, your boyfriend did another disappearing act and now you got to go find him?" Saphire added mischievously.

Gade was about to let Saphire have it. Her eyes were on the full glass of orange juice that Saphire just poured. She wondered what it would look like over that pretty periwinkle suit.

Josey turned around just in time to see the anger on Gade's face. "Stop it, both of you. Jeez, I can't turn my back for a second without you two getting in each other's face. I'm beginning to think that Joe is the whole problem here," Josey stated with her hands on her hips.

Both sisters became silent as the air thickened around them. "Am I right? Does all this bickering between the two of you have to do with Joe Burrels?" Josey quizzed as she waited for an answer.

"Momma, I don't know what the problem is with Saphire. From the very first day I met Joe, I could see it in her lustful eyes that she wanted him too. Why do you always have to go after my men? Lord knows you got enough of your own!" she spat. Gade couldn't hold it in. It seemed as if Saphire got off on taking her men and she was just sick and tired of it.

"Is this true, Saphire? Have you been chasing after your sister's boy-friend?" Josey silently prayed that it wasn't true, but from looking into Saphires's smug face, she knew her prayer wasn't answered. Just like her father, the evidence was there. However, Saphire lied with a straight face.

"Gade is trippin' again, Momma. I was just trying to be the protective sister and watch out for her. I know all about men like Joe Burrels. Their type never forms a lasting relationship with no woman, and I don't want her to get hurt, that's all." She smirked as she scooped up more eggs and placed them on her plate.

Gade sucked her teeth and rolled her eyes at her sister. "Another perfect performance. Somebody give her a hand," Gade said, clapping.

"But as you can see, Momma, she thinks I want him." Saphire turned

her attention to Gade. "And for your information, I never took any of your men. They had eyes, I can't help it if they were for me," she gloated.

Josey's face burned with anger. She didn't realize how shallow Saphire could be.

Before Josey or Gade could respond, Saphire blurted, "Don't take it as an insult, please." Saphire continued in a satisfied tone. "I'm marrying the man I want, Lil' Sis, so you don't have to worry about me taking your so-called man." Saphire stood and grabbed her bible. "I think I need to get out of here before I get jumped like a mugger in the street." She chuckled. "I will say a prayer for you, Gade," she added with a smirk on her face. "And I will pray for you, too, Momma!" Saphire hollered over her shoulder as she headed out the door. She stopped abruptly as she opened the door. "Momma, you don't have to cook a whole lot today, I'm having dinner with Clay's family. His aunt Martha is down from New York along with his grandfather."

"Well, have a good time!" Josey called out in relief as Saphire closed the door.

Saphire's eyes stung with tears as she drove over to Clay's church. She couldn't believe how she lied so straight forwardly to her mother and Gade. In all of her lies, there was one she could not hide from and that was the almighty God. He knew all of her secrets. Oh, how she hated the attraction she felt for Joe Burrels, but just as much as she hated it, she loved it. Her whole body ached for him, craved his loving touch, and it was only just yesterday they had made love–yet again.

ARE YOU IN?

Lamonte kept checking his cell for messages from his brother. He hoped Joe would give some serious thought to his proposition. He also hoped he had gotten through to him, not only about the business, but about how much he meant to him as well. Joe didn't sound like himself. Even though they could go months without talking, he knew when something wasn't right with his brother. He also knew that eighty percent of the time, it was him reaching out to Joe. His mother, Irene, got on his case about that. His mind wandered as he plopped down on his brown sofa and clicked on the flat screen TV. Irene had made her feelings for Joe perfectly clear. From his understanding, she and Joe had never gotten along, and it caused a hell of a lot of problems between his parents.

When he was old enough to understand the real reason behind it all, Joe was about to graduate from high school. Lamonte had just returned from a scrimmage football game when he walked into their home and found his mother, father and Joe hurling nasty accusations at each other. They were going at it so heatedly, they didn't hear him come in. He heard the words home wrecker, bitch, and a few other choice words directed at his mom from the mouth of his big brother.

He remembered yelling, "Stop it, just stop it!" when they all turned around and looked towards him. He threw his football helmet down and went full force out the back screen door. He remembered running, the wind whizzing by his ears, his eyes not seeing where his feet were taking him. He just had to get away and breathe, because he felt as if he was suffocating.

He fell to the ground, flat on his face. The smell of the grass intoxicated him, the soft blades on his face. His cheeks were wet with tears, but he didn't care, not one damned bit. His heart was crushed as if it had been run

over by a bulldozer. Then he felt the strong arms of someone picking him up. He began to fight. When he opened his eyes, he looked into the face of his big brother, Joe, who held him firmly in his grip. On deaf ears, he was telling him over and over again how sorry he was, and how much he loved him. When he cooled down, they sat on the velvet grass. His tears dried and his thoughts cleared. Joe explained to him why he said those awful words to his mother, Irene. He explained how he blamed her for breaking up his father's marriage to his mother.

"But what about Dad? Don't you have to blame him as well?" he remembered asking Joe, but he never got an answer. In Joe's mind it was Irene's fault and her fault alone.

Over the years, Lamonte had tried to look at things through Joe's eyes. Here it was, his mother who ended up marrying their father, and then he came into the picture. A world torn apart, and a new one thrust upon him. That was a lot for a little kid to swallow, but Irene was his mother and he loved her dearly. Joe was his half-brother and he loved him as well. Even in the midst of this dysfunctional family, their father tried his best to hold everything together because he loved his sons. He tried to create a normal family. But as hard as his father tried, Irene and Joe would constantly bump heads. He knew it was a relief to their father when Joe finally graduated and moved down south with his mother.

Lamonte missed his brother terribly. Joe had protected him through school. The bullies knew not to mess with him because he was Joe Burrels' baby brother, and Joe Burrels kicked ass. Joe was quite a handful, even in high school. But he was also smart and driven. Whatever he went after, he got, and with that spirit, he knew he and his brother would make a mark in the construction business.

Lamonte's land phone rang and he hopped up to answer it. "Hi Mom, how are you?" he said, smiling.

"I'm fine, son, but since you got your new place, I hardly see you anymore," Irene chimed. "I almost forgot what you look like," she continued, making Lamonte chuckle.

"Now come on, Mom, it hasn't been that long." Lamonte said, warmly.

"I just saw you, Mom."

"Mmm, I think it's been about three weeks now, son." She sighed.

"Well, I guess it has been a while, huh? But I still love you.

"I love you, too, Lamonte. So can your dad and I expect you over for Sunday dinner? I'm cooking your favorite, pot roast and garlic creamed potatoes."

"Oh, that sounds so delicious. You're making me hungry already, Mom. Yeah, I'll be there, you can count on it."

"Are you going to bring that pretty little girl with you?" she asked cheerfully.

"Oh, you mean Gade?" he said without thinking.

"Gade? I thought you and Gade were history?" Irene replied, puzzled.

"We are, but I've been thinking about her a lot lately. I think I moved away from her a little too soon. I still love her, Mom," Lamonte stammered.

"Well, if you want to know the truth, Lamonte, I think Chaniece would be a better choice for you. I don't know the Michaels girls that well, but I've heard rumors about the older one."

"Oh, so you're picking my women for me now?" Lamonte said, a little agitated.

If only she knew, he didn't have a smidgen of love for Chaniece. Sure, he liked her, and they had fun whenever they were together, but she wasn't the woman he wanted to spend the rest of his life with. "Let's just change the subject, Mom," Lamonte muttered, stretching out his long legs. "I've found the perfect spot for my office and I want you and Dad to come down to see it real soon."

"Well, isn't that great, son! Can I help decorate?" she asked with excitement.

"You certainly can. I know you've got a flare for that sort of thing."

"Lamonte, I'm really happy for you, and I know everything is going to work out, son," Irene assured him.

"To tell you the truth, Mom, I would have a heck of a better chance if I had a good partner."

"Have you thought about running an ad in the local newspaper?"

"Yes, but I want someone I know I can trust, not someone I have to build trust in. I want my business to be a family owned business, Mom." He exhaled.

"Well, what about your cousin Calvin? I know he is just as tired of working at that plant as you were."

"I already have Calvin on board. He's going to be one of my crew members. But I need somebody with office brains, a real go-getter." Lamonte sighed.

"And who would that be, Lamonte?" Irene asked with a sigh of her own.

"My brother Joe. I know if he joined in with me, we can take this business to the top."

"That man doesn't give you the time of day, so how in the world is he going to help you in a business?" Irene retorted.

Before Lamonte could respond, Irene ranted, "All those years I wasted trying to love him and all he ever did was cause me and your father so much grief."

"Wait a minute, Mom, I don't want to take a trip back in time," Lamonte interjected. "I believe if we'd just forget about the past and concentrate on the here and now, we would all be a lot better off," he said, sitting up straight on the sofa.

"But son—" Irene attempted to speak, but Lamonte cut her off.

"Mom, Joe is a grown man now, and so am I. We can't go back and change the past. We can only make the future better for the both of us," Lamonte reasoned.

"Well, if that's the way you want to look at it, Lamonte, then you just go right ahead. But for me, I wouldn't mind if I never laid eyes on him again."

"Lay eyes on who, honey?" James asked, kissing his wife on the cheek.

"Oh baby, I didn't hear you come in. I was talking to Lamonte," she crooned. "He's coming over for dinner on Sunday," she said, looking up at James. "Lamonte, your father's home now. I'll tell him you said hello and we will see you on Sunday. We love you, son," Irene said hurriedly as she hung up the phone.

Lamonte knew why she hung up so quickly. Talking about Joe was like swallowing a spoonful of poison. Dangerous. Lamonte let out a low sigh. Even if his mother didn't agree with him, he still wanted Joe on board.

Lamonte stretched back out on the sofa and closed his eyes. He slowly drifted off to sleep. The ringing of his cell woke him up. Lamonte didn't recognize the number, but he answered it anyway.

"Hey, little brother," Joe greeted.

Lamonte sat straight up and rubbed his eyes. "Joe, man, it's good to hear your voice. I thought you had forgotten all about me."

"Nah man, I just been doing some things." He laughed.

"Yeah, I see you're calling from a different number. Is this one of your women's cells you're calling from? I know you are an undercover brother." Lamonte chuckled. "You are still a character, man." Lamonte was happy his brother sounded like himself this time around. "So tell me, did you think about my proposal?" Lamonte held his breath as he waited for his response.

"Yeah man, I gave it some serious thought."

"And?" Lamonte asked anxiously.

There was a brief pause before Joe spoke.

"I guess I can help you get started."

"Oh man, yes! yes!" Lamonte stood up, shouting. "I knew you wouldn't let me down man, I just knew it."

The excitement Joe heard in Lamonte's voice made his heart swell. He couldn't let his baby brother down no matter what the circumstances. After all, he was his blood.

"Now Lamonte, I said I would help you get started, and then I'm leaving. You know I don't put down roots, so let's get that in my contract, all right?"

Lamonte was only half listening to anything else Joe was saying. The only words he clung to were that The Brother's Construction Company would soon be a reality, and he couldn't wait. "So how soon can you get here, man? I'll pick you up from the airport, just tell me when."

"Um, no, I don't want to put you out like that, bro. I'll just call you

when I get to the hotel. I'll see you in a few days," he said, and hung up. Joe couldn't tell Lamonte he was already in LA, and neither could he let him down.

WAITING AND WAITING

Gade sat quietly in the front pew of Peaceful Baptist Church as everyone waited for the Queen Saphire to make her glorious appearance. The bridal party was beginning to whisper now as the time got later and later. The groom, the best man, and the rest of the bridal party sat anxiously as their eyes kept staring at the front door of the huge church. Rev. Burch and Josey were standing near the podium with their heads together as if they were sharing some secret. This was Saphire and Clay's wedding rehearsal, and she should have been there with bells on.

If she can't be on time for her own wedding rehearsal, I wonder what time she'll arrive for the actual wedding? Or will she arrive at all, Gade mused as she shifted in her seat. Her eyes focused on her future brother-in-law's handsome face. He had worry lines creasing his forehead. Clay was such a sweet guy. So loving, caring and trusting. Qualities Saphire would use and abuse, she thought and sighed.

So many times, she'd wanted to tell Clay to run like hell and never look back. Her sister wasn't half the woman he thought she was. But knowing Clay, and that he was head over heels in love with Saphire, he probably wouldn't have listened to a word she said. And if by chance, he would have believed her, how could she have given him the answers to the questions he surely would ask?

If only he would take off the blinders and see for himself. Surely, tonight should spark some suspicion in him, she thought as her eyes caught those of her mother, Josey. Josey trekked over to where Gade was sitting and plunked down next to her. She was fanning herself like crazy with a Martin Luther King face-shaped fan. Gade saw the beads of sweat on her mother's forehead.

"Where is that sister of yours, Gade? People are starting to whisper. My

God, this is so embarrassing," Josey muttered tightly.

"Momma, why don't we do Clay a big ole favor and tell him the truth," she said, turning to face her mother.

"And what truth is that, Gade?" Josey asked, becoming agitated.

"The woman is a sleaze bag, liar, and a cheat. She's probably just rolling out of bed with her latest conquest," Gade answered.

Josey's eyes grew wide and her voice dipped to a low tone as she spoke to her youngest daughter. "Shut your mouth. How dare you say such evil things about your very own sister?" Gade looked at her mother as if she was staring at a stranger. "Your sister could have gotten sick or, God forbid, might have been involved in an accident or mugged and you're talking about her like this!" Josey flared.

Disregarding her mother's concern, Gade spewed, "Momma, do you really believe Saphire has changed her ways? All that talking she did about being a faithful wife to Clay was a bunch of..." she remembered that she was seated in the house of the Lord, "...crap," she finished.

Josey just shook her head, not bothering to respond to Gade's observations. She wanted to believe in her firstborn. She loved her so, and she wanted to believe that she had gotten through to her that day they both revealed a piece of themselves to each other.

Gade peered into her mother's tired eyes. Josey was a beautiful woman, and she looked much younger than her fifty years. But now, with the lines that creased her eyes and her tight expression, Josey looked as if she'd aged ten years. Worrying about that trifling Saphire had not been favorable to her. Well, Josey might have been truly worried, but Gade wasn't. She would bet her whole paycheck that Saphire was just as fine as wine. And sure enough, they heard some commotion coming from the back of the church.

As they both turned their heads, lo and behold, Saphire Michaels came strutting down the aisle, making her grand entrance and looking like a breath of fresh air. She greeted Clay with a long kiss that made the ring bearer and the flower girl giggle. Saphire's arm was in a sling, though, making her mother's theory factual, and it made Gade feel guilty—a little.

Saphire gave everyone a detailed description of what happened.

Saphire's explanation to them all was, she had rushed around all day, attending to the final details for the wedding. The last stop was the bakery, and as she ran out the door, her three-inch heel got snagged on the carpet and she fell, injuring her arm. The store owners felt so badly about it, and possibly fearing a lawsuit, offered to take her to the hospital, pay all her expenses, plus giving her compensation for her pain and suffering. So there it was. All cut and dried. She had just left the emergency room of Mercy Hospital and assured everyone her arm wasn't broken, just sprained. There were a lot of oohs and ahs as everyone sympathized with the bride-to-be. And Clay, well, he just held Saphire in his arms like the doting husband-to-be that he was. Somehow, Gade just didn't buy into it, so she took it all in with a grain of salt–and so did Josey.

SOMETHING IS NOT RIGHT

Joe pulled Gade back into his arms, and as he did, he noticed a slight hesitation. Gade had come over to his place for another romantic evening, but something weird was going on. Gade couldn't wrap her mind around what it was, but deep down inside, she felt as sure as she was standing in front of Joe in the middle of his living room, something just wasn't right.

"Babe, what's wrong? Are you feeling well?" he asked, peering down into her round face.

This was Gade's fifth time being in Joe's apartment. You would think after becoming his girlfriend, she would have been there more often, but that wasn't the case, and it was because of Joe. He was a very private person, almost downright secretive. Sometimes Gade felt as if Joe was hiding something major. Like, maybe he was a fugitive. Scenes of America's Most Wanted played in the back of her mind. Could she be loving a killer, or perhaps a rapist or maybe a bank robber? She nearly jumped out of her skin at the touch of his fingers.

"Baby, you're trembling," he said, reaching for her again.

This time she let him hold her. The man smelled so good, and it felt like heaven in his arms. He never did anything to make her feel threatened. He always was a gentleman with her, very protective, but there was just something…

Joe let go of her and they both sat down on his black and gray sofa. Joe had a nice bachelor's pad that he kept immaculately clean. His apartment decor was masculine, yet warm, in gray and black tones. His entertainment center consisted of the most modern equipment, and the 52-inch wide screen TV had the sound turned down low as Gade watched the characters in motion. He handed her a drink, she sipped on her red wine slowly. Joe's

bedroom was done in the typical manly tiger print, with gold and brown tones. The gold-colored satin sheets the couple had just made love on were silky, but none of that mattered now.

It was what she had found on the floor of his bedroom that weighed heaviest on her mind. Gade had found a pear-shaped diamond earring hidden underneath the walnut nightstand. She saw it there when she accidently knocked over a glass of juice sitting on the nightstand. Joe threw her a small towel to sponge up the liquid and there it was, shimmering in the glow of the lamp. Gade circled her fingers around it and picked it up. Holding it in the palm of her hand, she felt it sting like fire. She had seen this earring before. Her mind searched as to where, and then it dawned on her. It was the day she and Saphire went to the mall. After being measured for their dresses, they went shopping. Saphire brought a set of earrings just like the one she held.

Gade's heart began to flutter. Was Joe sleeping with her sister? No, he just couldn't be. But if it wasn't Saphire's, and she hoped like hell it wasn't, the fact remained that he was sleeping with someone. She held the evidence right in the palm of her hand.

"Talk to me, baby. What's going on in that pretty little head of yours," he asked, touching her cheek with his fingertip. She didn't respond. Instead, she reached into the pocket of the pink nightie shorts she was wearing and placed the diamond earring into the palm of his hand. Joe's expression went from bright to dark like an unexpected thunderstorm on a sunny day as he peered down at the sparkling earring. "Where did this come from?" Joe questioned, finally finding his voice.

"Your bedroom, on the floor near the nightstand, to be exact," Gade hissed as anger played in her voice. "Is there something you need to tell me, Joe?" Gade asked, crossing her arms.

"Um, no, there isn't," he sputtered. "I mean, you found an earring, so what? It could belong to any one of my exes or even my housekeeper, Meredith," he rambled.

"So you mean to tell me that it's just now making an appearance after all this time?" she spat, standing up.

"Come on, Gade, don't do this. I don't know where it came from, but I do know that you've been my only lady…in a long time. Don't make such a big deal about this," Joe pleaded.

"Finding a diamond earring beside my man's bed that doesn't belong to me is no big deal? Yeah, right." Gade made her way into the bedroom and took off her nightie. She proceeded to get dressed, slipping on her mint green pantsuit and sliding her petite feet into the matching pumps.

"Baby, I thought we were spending the night together," Joe moaned.

"Yeah, I thought so too, but thanks to the mysterious earring, I don't think I'm interested." Gade brushed past Joe, heading for the door.

"Gade, I told you I don't know who that earring belongs to, I honestly don't." Joe had a hint of anger in his voice. "We are not teenagers here, and you are not my first, baby," he huffed.

Gade gave him the stare of a black panther. Sensual, but ready to pounce. "Thank you for reminding me of the fact. Knowing you, I am probably your hundredth, but in my case, you are my last."

"What's that supposed to mean?" Joe asked with a blank expression.

"It's over, Joe. I'm outta here," she mumbled as she walked out the door.

"Gade, wait!" Joe called out as he watched her run to her car. His pleas fell on deaf ears as she jumped into her car and sped away.

She had to get out of Joe's apartment. As much as she wanted to believe him, something deep down inside just wouldn't let her. He was a player, she'd known it from the start, but he swore to her things would be different between them. He told her she was unlike any other woman he had ever met. She thought she had tamed the tiger, but the tiger just took a bite out of her heart.

UNSETTLING REVELATION

Saphire stood in front of her bathroom mirror, admiring her new hair weave. She decided to tone it down a bit. The light auburn hair she once wore was now dark brown with golden highlights. She was about to be a married woman; in just two weeks she would become Mrs. Clay Matthews. Butterflies fluttered in the pit of her stomach. Time had flown as she and Clay waited for the finishing touches to be put on their new home. The split-level home had five bedrooms, three baths, living room, den, family room and a beautiful large stainless steel-equipped kitchen, which Saphire adored.

Clay's grandfather had kept his promise. Their wedding present was the best ever, and just like Clay had agreed, he let her make all the decisions on the decor in the stylish home. Saphire truly felt like a queen as she thought about the good times she and Clay would have entertaining their family and friends. She loved to see the drool from the lips of her envious friends. Clay's family was good to her. Her husband-to-be had come from good stock. Now, if only she could hold her antics to a minimum. Saphire slipped on her shower cap and eased her voluptuous body into her sweet-scented bubble-filled tub.

The garden tub in her mother's home was fine, but she couldn't wait to get into the Jacuzzi in the master bedroom of her new home. Saphire smiled to herself. Everything was progressing beautifully, except for one little rumor she'd heard a couple of days ago from Judy Benton, a nosy busybody at her law firm.

They were all hanging out at King's, an after-hour spot on Figueroa Boulevard. It was a hangout for people to go to unwind after a hard day of work. Judy knew everything about everybody. Saphire thought she would make a good host for Inside Edition. As she sat at the small smoke-filled

table with Mia, another co-worker and friend from the office, Judy came over to her yet again to congratulate her on her upcoming nuptials. Judy's short haircut was boyish, but it framed her oval face well. Her big eyes were set far apart, with perfectly applied mascara. It made her look as if she was an upcoming model.

Saphire, I hope you and Clay will be very happy," Judy slurred, obviously over her drinking limit.

"Why, thanks again, Judy," Saphire murmured, turning back to face Mia who was telling her about her latest boyfriend.

Judy continued to stare at them both as if they had forgotten their manners. She was hoping for an invite to join them, but when none came, she leaned in and whispered to Saphire, "If I were you, I would be very careful, love. Cruising around town in a red corvette with a handsome young man could do a whole lot of damage for a woman who is a few days away from saying I do, don't you think?"

With that, Judy walked unsteadily away and vanished into the crowd. Thinking about that night gave Saphire goose bumps, even though she was in a hot tub of water. Nothing could go wrong in the coming weeks, Saphire reasoned. She was behaving herself. She'd had no conquests since the night of the rehearsal. Thinking back to that night, Saphire remembered arriving late, thanks to Bobby, who just had to see her one more time, he declared. Bobby sounded like such a baby over the phone when he had called her earlier in the day. He told her that soon she would be married and he wanted them to have one last fling. Picturing how good Bobby was in bed, she let her desires lure her into saying yes. After a tantalizing session of lovemaking at The Holiday Inn, they both fell into a deep sleep, and when she awoke, she realized she was going to be late for her rehearsal. Not just a few minutes, but almost an hour late would be more like it.

She'd hurriedly gotten dressed. She had to come up with a believable excuse, and when her eyes fell on the sling Bobby had in his car, left there by one of his nephews, an idea popped into her head. Her excuse was framed like a picture, and everyone bought into it. Saved once again, Saphire mused as she slipped farther down into the water. But now, her

risk-taking had to stop. Clay was a wonderful man and he deserved a good woman to make him happy. She intended to be just that.

And that included staying away from Joe Burrels as well. They had supposedly ended things weeks ago, but somehow they always found themselves creeping back into each other's arms. A lump formed in her throat as she thought about the day Joe had phoned her at the office. He told her all about Gade finding her pear-shaped diamond earring in his bedroom. Saphire had searched all over the place for that diamond earring and it never dawned on her that she had lost it at Joe's apartment. She hoped for God's sake, Gade didn't remember her buying those earrings when they were together at the mall. Who was she kidding? Gade's little steel-trap mind probably zoomed right into it, but so far, she hadn't said a word.

Gade was only giving her coy looks when she thought she wasn't looking. Then another episode played in Saphire's mind as she closed her eyes. The scene that put the icing on the cake. It happened just a couple of nights ago. Yet again, she and her friends were hanging out at another famous spot in town. Malcome's Crib was known not only for their good food, but their hefty supply of fine ass men as well. Women flocked to the club in their designer best, looking for either a husband, or someone else's husband, with deep pockets.

Clay had worked extra hard that day and phoned to tell her he was staying in for the night. Well, that was just music to her ears. Since becoming engaged, they'd spent almost every single minute of their free time with each other. So when Mia invited her to a girl's night out at Malcome's, she eagerly accepted. It felt so good being out without the stigma of sneaking around. LaShon was always the life of the party, and she had Saphire and Mia laughing hysterically at a joke she ran by them. LaShon stopped laughing abruptly as she recognized a familiar face. Her eyes focused across the room on a handsome man dressed elegantly in a two-piece olive-colored suit; a diamond stud glimmered in his ear as his head tilted. The man was looking like he had just stepped out of an Ebony Mag.

LaShon gave Saphire a nudge in her side with her elbow. "Saphire,

isn't that your sister's man over there?" she quizzed as Saphire and Mia's eyes followed her stare.

The man was dripping with finesse as he stood chatting with some broad who surely wanted him in her pants. The way she was hanging onto his arm, you would have thought they were glued together. Saphire's girlfriends had never met Joe, but they recognized him from the one and only photo Saphire had shown them that was taken at Venice Beach. Another lie she glazed over with the women, saying it was Gade who had taken the picture when she knew full well Gade wasn't even in the equation.

They looked like a happily married couple standing together with his arms thrown casually around her shoulders, their smiles beaming. The memory of the day she took the picture was etched deeply in her mind because it had been such a special day. She had called in sick at work and she met Joe at his apartment. She took off her office attire, and replaced it with a lavender top and matching shorts. Saphire's office pumps were tossed aside as she slipped her feet into soft leather sandals.

They had packed a picnic basket, and throwing caution to the wind, they headed for the beach. They had such a good time, and their lovemaking at the hotel was intense, yet satisfying. Now staring at Joe and the hoochie who had her cleavage all up in her juice was making her steam like a freight train.

"Who is that bimbo all over my man?" Saphire found herself saying as LaShon and Mia stared at her as if she had just lost her mind.

"Your man? Did you just say your man?" Mia questioned with her eyes growing big as saucers.

Saphire didn't care what her friends thought at the moment. Her territory was being threatened, and like a lioness, she was ready to attack.

She shot up from her seat and proceeded across the room, walking like the queen she was. The girls watched with open mouths. Joe was surprised to see Saphire as she approached them. But not as surprised as the nameless woman when Saphire pushed her out of Joe's arms.

"Take your slutty hands off him!" Saphire steamed as Joe looked on.

"Who the hell are you, bitch?" the woman screamed, stepping up to Saphire and staring her down.

Saphire reached out to grab the woman when Joe intercepted. Some of the club patrons noticed a fight was brewing and a small audience began to gather. Joe wasn't one for making a scene, so he took Saphire firmly by the arm and led her out of the club. Saphire couldn't understand for the life of her what had gotten into her head. She was an engaged woman who would be walking down the aisle in a matter of weeks, so why was she in a club getting ready to throw down over some man that wasn't even hers–or was he?

Joe took her to his SUV, which was parked across the street from the club, and slid her into the passenger seat. Once Joe closed the driver's side door, he pulled her into his arms, and kissed her deeply. She couldn't help but respond to his sensual kisses. The connection they shared was so strong and binding, that she wanted him to be hers always. If there ever was a question about it before, the evidence was clear now. As much as they tried to stay apart, something kept drawing them back together. They let go of each other, both catching their breath as their heartbeats slowed. Before either could speak, a knock on the vehicle window startled them.

Joe pressed the electric button. The dark-tinted window eased down as he saw Clay's puzzled face staring into his. Saphire almost pissed in her black lace panties as Clay's eyes caught the sight of her. Needless to say, her brain went into overdrive as her mouth tried to form words that would justify her being in Joe's SUV. Never saying a word, she did what most women would have done in her situation, she started to cry. Thank God, Joe's head was more stable than hers. He'd cleared his throat as he stepped out of the SUV. Giving Clay a serious look, he motioned for him to step away from the vehicle. Clay followed and stood inches from Joe. Clay knew who Joe was. He remembered him from the picnic a few months back and knew he was seeing Saphire's sister, Gade.

Clay had many questions, and the most important one was why in the hell was Saphire sitting in Joe's SUV. Even though they'd stepped away, Saphire could still hear them as they spoke. She listened as smooth lies

rolled from Joe's lips that even she believed. Joe had explained to Clay that he heard a commotion at the front of the club while he was sitting down at the bar. As the crowd gathered, he pushed his way through and saw what was causing the ruckus.

A bimbo in the club had gotten into Saphire's face for some unknown reason. Being that Saphire was his girl's sister, he'd stepped in, defusing the situation, and he'd taken Saphire outside to cool her down. He explained to Clay how difficult that was to do as he may well know, Saphire being the kind of woman she was and all. The explanation of her sitting in the vehicle? He was about to take her home, of course.

"Bravo, Joe," Saphire whispered to herself as she opened the passenger side door and got out. She ran to Clay's arms with fresh tears still falling down her cheeks. Joe did the show well, now it was up to her to close it down. She wrapped her arms around Clay as they walked away. She never turned around to look back at Joe. Instead, she silently whispered words of thanks to the almighty.

Saphire's mind snapped back to the present. Too many close calls. If she kept it up, one day her luck may just run out. Looking up, she asked God to help her to be the kind of wife Clay would be proud of. Loving, kind, and faithful.

TRUST

Gade had done a lot of soul searching since the incident in Joe's apartment. Coming to the conclusion that if you can't trust the man you're sleeping with, there was no point of being in the relationship. To add insult to injury, Joe hadn't done a damned thing to convince her that he cared one way or the other. Their relationship was like a plane falling from the sky–it had crashed and burned. Gade was finished, it was time for her to move on.

"Move on to what?" she murmured, getting out of bed and heading into the bathroom.

Gade studied her reflection in the mirror. Dark circles had formed under her eyes. She looked tired, drained, and pissed. Saphire's wedding was just around the corner, and the woman ran around the house like a ball of sunshine. Not to mention, it was Christmas. There was so much joy going around, but it seemed as if all of it was passing Gade by. There was no Christmas cheer in her world anymore, only emptiness.

Gade came out of the bathroom and lay back down on her bed. She was wearing her favorite Santa Claus pajamas. She wore them every year. She looked down at the jolly Santa Claus faces, smiling with glee as silver bells dotted the green background on the cotton print. Usually, it made her feel like a little girl waiting to open up the many presents she knew were under the tree. Gade remembered the comment Saphire would make as well when she laid eyes on her. *You need to take that mess off, Gade, you look like an overgrown kid parading around the house.*

Gade sucked her teeth. "Who gives a damn what Saphire thinks," she mumbled, sitting up and curling her legs under her.

Her mind reflected back to the diamond earring she had found in Joe's apartment. Could it have belonged to Saphire? She refused to wrap her

mind around that observation, for if she did, then that would have meant they both were.…. Gade closed her eyes tightly at the thought. As much as she and Saphire argued and fought, she was certain her sister would never have betrayed her in such an evil way. After all, just like her mother had said before, they were blood, and blood would never do that, or would it?

Gade jumped off her bed and ran into Saphire's room. She searched for the gold box containing the earrings Saphire had purchased at the mall. She rummaged through Saphire's dresser drawers, trying not to disturb anything along the way. Her fingers searched through underwear, bras and pantyhose.

She went through blouses and camis, finding nothing. Gade was out of breath as she stood up and looked at the vanity table by Saphire's bedside. She walked over to it, her eyes flickering over the many elegant perfume bottles in different shapes, sizes, and colors. Her eyes settled on the object of her massive search, what she had feared finding. Tucked behind a bottle of cologne by Patti Labelle was the gold box. Gade opened it as if it contained a valuable gift. Gade let out a slow breath as her eyes focused on the pair of diamond-shaped earrings. Yes, it was the pair of diamond earrings. They both were there, but somehow she didn't feel as relieved as she thought she would. Enough time had passed, she reasoned. Joe could have easily given the missing earring back to Saphire. Gade placed the box back on the vanity table and slowly went out of her sister's room and back into her own.

She lowered herself onto her bed. Around her neck, her fingertips touched the thin sterling silver chain. Sliding her fingers down, she felt it. A half-heart pendant Lamonte had purchased for her just before he went on his last assignment. He told her no matter what happened, she would always have a piece of his heart. A salty tear slid down her cheek as she revisited that day. They kissed long and passionately before he boarded the plane with his squadron. Gade thought about all the good times they'd shared. Lamonte was full of life and he could make any dark day bright. Just hearing his laughter made her smile.

She remembered all the dreams he had. One of them was of owning his

own business and making a good life for him and his future family. Seeing him the other day proved to her Lamonte was more than a dreamer. How proud she was of him when he shared his plans with her that day in their chance meeting. Gade touched her lips as she remembered the warm kiss he'd placed upon her lips. Her body begged to respond; oh, how much she wished things could go back to the way they used to be. Gade let out a soft moan. How could a solid relationship fall apart so suddenly? Gade placed her head on her pillow and closed her tear-stained eyes.

She must have dozed off, because the ringing of her cell startled her. Gade fumbled around the nightstand, curling her hand around the phone. Groggy, she answered, "Hello."

No one said a word for a brief moment, then she heard the sultry voice of Lamonte.

"Hello, Gade, Merry Christmas," Lamonte murmured softly.

"This is quite a surprise," Gade managed to say as she held on.

"I know, I know," Lamonte uttered, then he exhaled. "Gade, after seeing you a few days ago, I…just…can't get you out of my mind. I don't know what happened to us…but I do know I miss you so much," Lamonte struggled to say. Something magical washed over her. Miracles do happen, because what she was hearing from Lamonte was just what she'd longed to hear deep within her heart. All the hurt and pain she was feeling these past few days had dissipated, leaving her filled with joy, hope, and love. Fresh tears found their way down her cheeks.

"I've missed you for so long, Lamonte," she choked.

"Don't cry, baby, please don't cry," he said, feeling a stab of pain shoot through his own heart. He wanted to wrap his arms around her and hold her forever.

"Gade baby, go out with me tonight. I want to take you to Sweetie's," Lamonte said.

A small smile curved Gade's lips at the mention of Sweetie's. It was the place where she and Lamonte had their first date. Sweetie's was a Southern hospitality restaurant that specialized in home-cooked meals. Southern fried chicken, collard greens and buttermilk cornbread were her

favorites when she dined there.

"Okay," Gade relented as she wiped her eyes.

"Great, baby, I'll pick you up around seven," Lamonte responded with excitement in his voice.

"No, Lamonte, let me meet you there," Gade interjected quickly. She heard Lamonte's breath catch but he didn't protest. Instead, he said, "Gade."

"Yes, Lamonte?" Gade waited for his next words.

"Don't speed, you know you have a lead foot." Lamonte chuckled.

Gade also laughed. Lamonte still had his sense of humor. Now Gade couldn't go back to sleep if she wanted to. She couldn't wait to see Lamonte again.

Gade thought about Lamonte's offer of picking her up. There was no way in hell she was going to let him come to her house. Her mother would be on him like a private investigator on a new case. Josey had already graced her with her opinion of Lamonte. *He's a nice boy, Gade, but those soldier boys are so unsettled and immature. You need an older man who's mellowed and secure.*

Like Joe possessed those qualities. Joe might have been slightly more handsome than Lamonte, but they had similar features. And what was more important to Gade, was that Lamonte held qualities Joe didn't. She just didn't know why it took her so long to see that.

BUSINESS IN THE MAKING

Things were going slower than Lamonte expected, but he wasn't worried. Contracts were coming together, and so was his relationship with Gade. After their meeting at Sweetie's, they agreed to become friends all over again, taking their relationship to a deeper and more stable level than ever before. Personally, he didn't need the 'friend' title, he wanted Gade as his lover and someday, "My wife. Wow!" he'd said it. His mind and heart knew it deep down inside, but now he'd voiced it out loud, and the word, wife, felt good, damned good. Lamonte smiled as he stood on the ladder, using up the last coat of vanilla crème-colored paint.

His mother, Irene, was busy with the movers. Giving orders was second nature to Irene. The lady only stood a little over five feet, but her boisterous voice made up for her short stature. Lamonte had a beautiful mother; her dark brown curly hair framed her oval face like an African doll. Her chestnut-brown eyes sat deep in her oval face, a feature Lamonte had inherited.

Lamonte climbed down the ladder and placed the paintbrush next to the empty can of paint. He grabbed the thick white towel from the floor and wiped his hands. Just as he did, the movers came in with a large mahogany desk followed by Irene, who was right on their heels.

"Mother, why don't you give the movers a break and come have lunch with me?" Lamonte suggested.

"But honey, I want to make sure they put things exactly where we want them to go," Irene retorted with a firm expression.

"Mother, this is an office, not a mansion in Bel Air. It's not hard to figure out, believe me." Lamonte chuckled and took her by the hand. "Come on, Mom, I think we both could use a break." They headed out the door.

Before getting into his mother's pearl-white Lincoln Town Car,

Lamonte stared at the sign hanging in front of the building. The Brother's Construction Company stood out in big black bold letters and a smaller banner hanging below it stated, 'Coming Soon'. Lamonte's heart swelled with pride. It was soon to be a reality. His dream was finally coming true.

After lunch, he convinced his mother to go home and relax. She had done enough for today. Surprisingly, she didn't give him a hard time. Lamonte returned to his office and was taken aback. The movers did a great job of placing the furniture in the right places. The huge mahogany desk was front and center. The gray steel file cabinets were situated near the corner of the office.

"Knock, knock," a deep voice said from the doorway.

Lamonte turned and his eyes widened at the sight of his big brother, Joe. He almost leaped into his arms. The men hugged for a brief moment, letting go as they each gave the other a once-over.

"Man, you haven't changed a bit," Joe bellowed, looking down at Lamonte. Joe had him by two inches.

"You haven't either, bro. Maybe a tad bit uglier, but other than that, you are still the same," Lamonte joked.

Joe playfully punched him on the shoulder. "Yeah right, man, don't hate on my looks. I can't help it if father nature been good to me," Joe responded, smiling.

"You've always been an arrogant brother, haven't you?" Lamonte chuckled.

"It's so good to see you, bro." Joe sat on the corner of the huge desk.

"Nah man, that's my desk, you got to get up off of that." Lamonte snickered.

"And where am I going to sit? I don't see any chairs here," Joe asked, looking around.

"The chairs are in the back, I haven't brought them out yet." Lamonte replied with a mischievous smile.

"Well, what the hell are you waiting on?" Joe boomed, standing.

"You." Lamonte chuckled. "We are partners, remember? You got to pull your own weight around here, son." Lamonte grinned.

Joe gave Lamonte a 'you got me' look.

"So how is everything down south?" Lamonte asked after Joe returned with a chair.

Joe leaned back and put his hands behind his head. Joe contemplated what he was going to tell his brother. There was little Lamonte knew, and he intended to keep it that way.

Lamonte watched his brother's expression. It was the same expression Joe formed whenever he inquired about Joe's other life.

"Things have been going a little slow, but that's the South for you. And as far as my mom's concerned, she is fine," Joe said, vacantly.

Lamonte exhaled, he was surprised Joe offered that piece of information. Usually he wouldn't even mention his mother.

"I hope I didn't inconvenience you. I mean, you came out so quickly."

"Don't worry about it, everything is under control," Joe said firmly.

There was that fence again. Lamonte could feel it in Joe's tone. His brother didn't share anything concerning his life in the South. All he knew was that after graduation, he flew down there. Got a job with some advertising company and looked after his mother. And as far as he knew, Joe didn't have a steady girlfriend. He told him he never met anyone he wanted to stick with long enough to have a relationship.

Joe's voice interrupted Lamonte's thoughts. "What we need to be talking about is getting this place up and running."

"Yeah, I know, but...let's get serious for a moment." Lamonte confessed, "There is something I must get off my chest. You are my brother, Joe, and I love you, man."

Joe sucked in his breath. He knew when Lamonte mentioned his feelings towards him it would be an intense conversation.

"I don't know anything about you, really," Lamonte continued, shaking his head. "I mean, we grew up in the same house, shared the same meals, slept in the same room for a minute but...I don't know you," Lamonte said, earnestly.

Joe stood up and placed his hands in his blue jean pockets. He didn't want to go there. He knew how it would end. Joe attempted to speak, but

Lamonte cut him off. "Let me get this out of my system, man," Lamonte stated. "I can't help what happened between my mother and our father. All I know is that people have fallen in and out of love since the beginning of time. Sometimes the reasons are not clear, and almost always, the victims are the children who are caught up in the mix. Even though we aren't children anymore, Joe, we still carry the scars." Lamonte sighed and cocked his head, never taking his eyes off his big brother. "Hell, I wasn't even born at the time when all this mess went down, so why do I feel like I'm being punished, Joe?"

Joe's eyes grew dark like a brewing storm. "Who said you are being punished?" again his voice boomed.

With a startled look, Lamonte responded, "It has been said many times that actions speak louder than words, and from the way you treat me, Joe, you are the one who is punishing me!" Lamonte ran his fingers over his freshly cut fade. "It wasn't my fault, Joe. I had no control over Pops and him leaving your mother. I had no control of him fathering me with my mother. All of that is their doing. It had nothing to do with us. You couldn't help what went down and neither could I. All we can do now is to accept what happened, move on and love each other," Lamonte pleaded as he took a deep breath and stared into his brother's eyes. "Be it right or be it wrong, man, we are in this thing together. We can't go back and change a damned thing," Lamonte said as he felt close to tears. The years of hurt and pain stabbed at his heart. "You left me, brother," he grimaced with his voice breaking. "I thought for a long time you hated my guts."

Joe felt tears of his own coming to the surface. "I…didn't…leave you, Lamonte, don't you see?" Joe stammered painfully. "I had to get the hell away from it all. Your mom acted like it was no big thing that she had torn my world apart. Parading around like what she had done to us didn't matter. Pops and my mom were very happy, I know they were. We did so many things together as a family." Joe choked, staring out the small office window. He looked as if he could see into the past. "Pops always made Mom and me laugh. I remember him coming home from a long day at work and taking us out for dinner. We would stay up late on Saturday

nights sitting in our small den watching old movies on TV, and then come Sunday morning, we would attend church as a God-fearing family." Joe exhaled. "And then…and then…Pops was gone, just like that," he mumbled, snapping his fingers. "He left us…my mother and I, hanging like loose tree limbs. Pops acted as if she—we—were never a part of his life."

Shaking his head, Joe continued. "My mother didn't understand, she was hurt beyond repair." A deep frown appeared on Joe's honey-colored face. "My mother was so good to him. She had taken very good care of Pops and I, and he…just left us–for her," Joe spat this out bitterly.

As he stared at Lamonte, Lamonte knew exactly who Joe was talking about. He rarely called his mom by her name.

"Your mother came along and snatched my world right out from under me," Joe spewed as anger raged in him. "I still remember the day Pops came and got me from school. He said there was someone he wanted me to meet. Someone who would be a part of my life," Joe continued as the fire burned in his eyes. "He took me over to her apartment. She stood in the doorway all dolled up, holding her arms open for me to run to her like I was her child. I wanted to spit in her damned face," Joe snapped. "How could she steal my world away from me and expect me to run into her waiting arms?" Joe hissed as the veins in his neck protruded.

Now it was Lamonte's turn to get angry. He felt Joe's pain, and even sympathized with him to a certain extent, but it was his mother he was talking about. "I understand your pain, my brother, but you got to realize that it wasn't all of her fault. My mother couldn't have separated them if our father didn't allow her to. Our Pops was a willing partner in this thing. Why can't you see that?" Lamonte asked, holding Joe's stormy gaze.

Joe closed his eyes and exhaled. He turned away from Lamonte and continued to stare out the window.

"From what I was told, our Pops fell out of love with your mother and in love with mine," Lamonte almost whispered, realizing the depth of his words and the truth that he didn't want to hurt his brother even more.

Those words made Joe's eyes blaze, right along with his anger. With a

quick turn, Joe was facing him again. "What am I hearing, Lamonte? Do you think your mother was better than mine?" Joe asked wildly. Before Lamonte could respond, Joe lashed out again. "What did she have that my mother didn't?" Joe yelled violently. "Was it the temptation of her younger body and beauty, or the fact that she never had a child? Or maybe because she hadn't an ounce of morality in her. What was it, Lamonte?" Joe's voice filled the room.

Lamonte took a step back. He had never seen Joe react this way before, and it startled him. But Lamonte stood his ground. "That's enough, Joe, remember, you are talkin' about my mother, man," Lamonte spouted. "Pops' marriage to your mother was shaky for a very long time, they just didn't want you to know it," Lamonte fumed.

"Liar!" Joe shouted. "Like you said, Lamonte, you weren't there so you don't know a damned thing. Those were lies your mother filled your head with."

Lamonte shook his head. "Oh, so you think Pops told you the God's truth. What did he do, Joe? Took you fishing and spilled his guts. A grown man telling his ten-year-old son all about his screwed up marriage. Don't take me for a fool," Lamonte lamented as his eyes stayed glued to Joe's face.

Joe balled his fists, he wanted to strike out, and Lamonte's face would be the designated target.

Lamonte noticed Joe's hands curled up into tight fists. Was his brother going to actually hit him? Well, if it had to be this way, Lamont was ready. "Go ahead, my brother, take your best shot. Beat the hell out of me, if that will make you feel any better," he taunted. Both men stood like boxers preparing for a duel each wanted to win. Lamonte's chest heaved as he and his brother locked stares. "Joe, love happens to people, it's not our fault," Lamonte muttered, trying to make his brother see through his pain.

Joe fought for control as he spoke. "My mother loved Pops with her whole being. Why did you think she ended up in the nut house? I'll tell you why, Lamonte," Joe ground out, stepping up to him. "Because your mother put her there, and for that, I will never, do you hear me? I will never

forgive her for that!" Joe shouted as he bolted out the door, knocking over the iron chair in his path.

Lamonte stood staring at the chair. He realized Joe had complicated issues that he couldn't begin to reach. But he hoped someday he would find somebody who could.

DINING OUT

L amonte leaned back in his seat. He couldn't get another bite down if he wanted to; he was stuffed. "Baby, I can't move," Lamonte muttered as he rubbed his belly.

Gade peered into Lamonte's plate, make that second plate, and shook her head. "How many hot wings did you have, sweetheart?" Gade asked as she stared at the dozens of chicken bones lined up by Lamonte's plate.

"Too many to count, but boy, were they good," he answered. "You can't even trip on me, Gade." There was only meager evidence left from what Gade had. Fried chicken, rice with brown gravy, mac-n- cheese, string beans seasoned with pork, all was reduced down to beggar's crumbs on her plate. Even her tall glass of lemon ice tea was finished, leaving remnants of melted ice in the glass. The restaurant they had chosen tonight was elegant, but not overly expensive. The atmosphere was warm and cozy as soft music played in the background.

Staring at Lamonte's handsome face was sending naughty messages to Gade's sex-starved body. It had been weeks since she had any. She declared herself celibate until she was in a good, solid relationship again. Lamonte touched the tips of Gade's fingers, rubbing them lightly before grasping her hand. Just his touch sent chills through her body. It felt like old times, but there was something different about it as well. Lamonte gave her that heart-stopping smile of his she loved so much, but then the question he asked made her feel as if someone had just kicked her in her guts.

"Gade, what happened to us?" Lamonte whispered.

Gade's mouth went dry as the paper napkin she was holding. She struggled for the answers she knew he deserved.

"Was it something I've done or haven't done to cause you to turn away from me?" he asked sincerely.

Gade lowered her eyes from his stare. How could she tell him that she had gotten caught up in a sexual fantasy with an older man.

Lamonte saw her struggle. "Look, never mind. It's water under the bridge now. The important thing is we are here together now. I have you back in my life, and for that, I'm forever grateful." Lamonte smiled.

"Yeah me too, Lamonte. In the midst of it all, I never stopped loving you. Not for one single moment of time," she whispered, feeling her eyes swell with tears as she held his gaze. "Maybe our separation was a way for God to make us see just how much we really loved each other." Gade quivered.

Lamonte's eyes misted as he watched Gade's soft expression. He cleared his throat. "You know even when I was with Chaniece, sometimes I would pretend she was you." With a crooked smile, he continued, "Now that is something a man wouldn't dare to admit to a woman he's trying to get back."

"I know, Lamonte, but remember, you are not most men," Gade said with a smile.

Lamonte leaned in and gave Gade a warm and lingering kiss.

BELLS WILL BE RINGING

Saphire's wedding day had arrived. Peaceful Baptist Church was beautifully decorated in hunter green and burgundy. Saphire's bridesmaids glowed in their satiny low-cut gowns that matched the colors of the church. The ushers were just as handsome in their black tuxes with hunter green and burgundy cummerbunds. And of course, the woman of the hour, Saphire Michaels, was absolutely stunning in her satin wedding gown sprinkled with simulated diamonds that sparkled with each step she took as she sauntered down the long aisle. Walking her down the aisle, however, was an unexpected guest. Someone whom Gade and her mother Josey never thought they would ever lay eyes on again.

Russell Michaels looked so handsome in his black Giorgio Armani tux, holding onto his daughter's arm as his heart beat wildly in his broad chest. Savoring the moment, he blinked back tears as they made their way to the minister.

Clay awaited his bride, beaming. Saphire would be his wife in a matter of minutes, and he thought his heart would burst from the love he felt inside.

Gade stood as maid of honor. She was proud that her sister had made it to this day. Her eyes flickered over the congregation. The huge church was filled to capacity. Gade caught a glimpse of her mother, Josey, who looked stunning in her own right. Her burgundy-colored fishtail dress shaped her petite body perfectly, and the matching satin three-inch pumps added height to her short stature. Her mother's friend, Mr. Stan, stood right beside her. Mr. Stan was such a good man. He was a few years older than Josey, but they looked like the perfect couple. With skin the color of cream coffee, dark eyes, and short but wavy cropped hair, Stan was a good-looking catch. He chased after Josey for years before she finally accepted him as

more than a friend.

Gade took in her father's face as he strolled down the aisle with Saphire on his arm. No one knew, except Saphire, that Russell was even coming, let alone a part of Saphire's wedding. Josey damn near had a fit when Saphire enlightened them with the grand news. Gade's mind reflected back to the scene that transpired between all of them yesterday morning.

Josey looked as if she had seen a ghost as she stared at the two people who had caused her the most pain in her life." A range of emotions raced across her face as her eyes shifted from her former best friend, Cherry Wilson, to her ex-husband, Russell Michaels, back to her former best friend Cherry Wilson. It was obvious that even after all this time, she was still affected by the sight of Russell.

"Now Josey, I know this is kind of awkward, but Saphire is my daughter too, and she asked me to be in her wedding. How could I turn my oldest daughter down on such a special day of her life?" Russell asked as his eyes traveled to the smiling face of Saphire.

Josey gave Saphire an evil stare before planting her eyes back on Russell. Josey then cleared her throat and spoke directly to Saphire, who was looking like the cat who swallowed the canary. "I can't believe you have been in contact with your father all of this time without me knowing about it," Josey fumed as she glared at her daughter.

"Momma, I knew how you felt about Daddy. And I knew what you would have said if I confided in you that he was coming to my wedding. He is just as much a part of me as you are, Momma, and I wanted him here to be a member of my wedding party and I don't see a damned thing wrong with that," Saphire huffed.

Josey's eyes were filled with hurt and anger. "You are certainly right about that, Saphire, he is a part of you, isn't he? And you both have the same trait hidden in your genes—deceit," Josey hissed before she ran up the stairs, leaving Gade to entertain her father and Cherry, her mother's once best friend, alone.

What a screwed up situation, Gade thought as she shifted the weight from her left foot to her right. Those satin spike heels were killing her and

she couldn't wait to take them off. In fact, she couldn't wait for this whole affair to be over and done with.

Gade thought about her own feelings towards her father. She loved him, of course. After all, he was part of the reason she was breathing. As for running off with her mother's best friend, well, that was certainly a big pill to swallow. Seeing the years of hurt her mother had to endure because of him and his cheating ways made Gade sick. Gade was civil to him, but that was about all she could do.

Saphire, on the other hand, acted like the man didn't do a damned thing wrong. She even gave Gade her sordid explanation of her father's reason for leaving them. *Love was a funny thing. It controls you, not the other way around. Daddy couldn't help it if he fell in love with Cherry. He didn't plan it that way, it was just something that happened.*

"Yeah, right," Gade sighed under her breath. What about them? Where was his love for his own family? Wasn't his love for them just as important as his lust for another woman? She would never forgive him for what he had done to them. Unlike Saphire, who seemed to have forgotten all the pain he caused. But then again, Gade thought, the two were so much alike when it came to love and commitment. In their lives, those were interchangeable. Russell apologized to her relentlessly and she accepted it, but she would never totally forgive him as long as the reason for his leaving was still by his side.

Gade's eyes continued to roam over the congregation as the minister began speaking to the young couple. Gade found Lamonte's handsome face and she gave him a warm smile. He mouthed the words I love you to her and Gade felt a chill run down her spine. She thought of how close she had come to losing the man she truly loved. Gade's attention was brought back to the blissful couple when she heard Rev. Burch ask Saphire the ultimate question.

"Do you, Saphire Alicia Michaels, take Clay Anthony Matthews to be your lawfully wedded husband in sickness and in health, forsaking all others till death do you part?" Saphire held her breath for a brief moment. Perspiration blanketed her face like a mask. She wanted to answer that

question with the most sincere and honest conviction she could muster.

Saphire vowed days ago to stay away from Joe Burrels and cling only to her husband once they said their wedding vows and that ring was placed on her finger. Now the time was here and she was determined to keep her promise.

No matter what may come, from this day forward, she would be faithful. With conviction and the utmost love in her heart, Saphire uttered the word yes firmly with tears in her eyes as she returned Clay's happy stare. Gade felt her own tears making their way down her light brown cheeks. In spite of everything that went down between her and her sister, she was happy for her and wished her all the love they both could ever hold.

Gade made a solemn promise of her own that special day as well. She was blessed to have Lamonte back in her life, and she wasn't going to let anyone come between them ever again. On that day, both women made promises they planned to keep as each remembered the love of one man they just couldn't get out of their system: Joe Burrels.

LET'S HAVE SOME PEACE

A couple of weeks had gone by since that explosive argument between Lamonte and his brother Joe. They called a truce, agreeing to keep things on a business level only. They never spoke again about their private lives. Even though things were strained between them, the business began to flourish. Contracts were coming in from all over town. Lamonte had to hire a couple of extra men to keep up with the demand, and he couldn't have been more pleased.

Now, if only things would go the same way in his personal life, he mused as he pulled the black velvet box out of his desk drawer. Lamonte slowly opened the box and watched the diamond solitaire ring sparkle in the sunlight. He'd already made dinner reservations at The Pink Lady, a fine dining restaurant famous for their Caribbean meals. Lamonte closed the velvet box and tucked it in his Roca wear jean pocket.

Tonight, he was going to ask Gade to be his wife. Lamonte closed his office and made a mad dash across town to his small apartment. He had to hurry and dress. He couldn't wait to see the look on Gade's face when he slipped the diamond on her finger. Lamonte turned his radio to his favorite station and joined in with the melody booming through his system. Feeling an emotional high, Lamonte was grinning ear-to-ear.

As he turned into his apartment complex, his emotional high took a dive. He was looking at Chaniece's car parked where his should be. Once inside his apartment, Lamonte stared into the face of the girl he knew had fallen in love with him.

"What's up, Lamonte?" she asked, posed seductively on the sofa.

Her silky hair flowed over her shoulders. The sheer baby blue dress she was wearing left little to the imagination. Lamonte's eyes focused on the center of her cleavage. He remembered tasting those breasts of hers and it

sent a heated thrill to his manhood.

Clearing his throat, Lamonte tore his eyes away. "Chaniece, we need to talk," he began, throwing his keys on the coffee table.

"Talk about what, baby?" she crooned, standing up and wrapping her arms around him. The girl felt so good. Lamonte took in a deep breath and pushed her away from him.

"Why are you acting so silly, Lamonte?" Chaniece asked with a puzzled stare.

"Look, Chaniece, there is no simple way to say this, so I guess I'll just spit it out. Gade and I are back together. I'm sorry," he mumbled.

"You're right about your sorryness, Lamonte Singletary. You are one sorry ass brother to have led me on all these months," she answered with her eyes on fire.

"Chaniece, you knew how I felt about Gade from the start."

"Yeah, and you told me you were getting over her, too," Chaniece finished.

"Um, I thought I was…but I love her and I'm going to ask her to marry me."

He could have kicked himself for letting that bit of information slip, but he was feeling so good about it. Chaniece strode over to him and slapped him squarely on the cheek, leaving him feeling as if he had been stung. Lamonte flinched at the pain.

"Have a happy damned life!" Chaniece shouted as she grabbed her purse and sailed out the door.

* * * * *

As the months flew by, Saphire settled into her married life. Her role as Clay's wife was secure and happy, for the most part. Decorating her beautiful huge home was very satisfying. She and Clay spent a pretty penny on the solid oak furniture that filled the huge rooms in their magnificent home. The colors in the living room were sandalwood and burnt toast. The dining room decor was done in mauve and cream. The five bedrooms sported different colors, sunshine yellow, periwinkle blue, pink rose, ecru,

and lavender, with curtains to match. Lavender was the color of the master bedroom. Clay was awestruck as he stood and scratched his head. At first, he really didn't think he would like it, from a man's point of view.

"Sugar Plum, most people wouldn't have chosen this color for their bedroom," he stated.

"Well, I'm not most people, now, am I?" Saphire crooned as she strutted across the room to Clay, in her pink robe, and gave him a sensual kiss. She tugged at the silk black boxers he was wearing. Her long manicured fingers began to pull at the elastic.

"Sugar Plum, let's take a chill pill for the rest of the night," Clay groaned, stepping away from her. "We've been at it like rabbits since we said our I dos." Clay chuckled as he kissed the tip of her nose.

Saphire gave him a bewildered look and sighed.

"Be reasonable now, it's getting late and I got a long day ahead of me tomorrow. Business seems to be picking up," Clay explained, falling into bed. Saphire was planted in the same spot Clay had left her in as she stared at him.

She'd never had a man turn her down for sex, and it had really thrown her for a loop. Surely he must be trippin', she mused as she watched Clay stretch out his long muscular legs.

"Bring your sexy self over here," Clay said, patting the empty space on the king-size bed. "I want us to fall asleep in each other's arms." He smiled widely.

Watching the warmth in his eyes, Saphire let go of the anger brewing inside as his sensual smile touched her heart. They'd made love numerous times during the day, and maybe she did wear him out, she concluded as she joined her husband in bed. Saphire snuggled up against his broad smooth chest as Clay kissed the tip of her nose. "I love you so much, Saphire," he murmured.

"I love you too, Clay," she whispered as he held her close. Clay closed his eyes and was asleep within minutes.

Saphire lay wide awake, staring at the brass ceiling fan as its blades turned. She still had an itch that needed to be scratched. The only man who

could satisfy her needs was the man she swore to stay away from. A vision of Joe Burrels entered her mind.

KEEPING HIS DISTANCE

Joe kept his distance from his family. He had learned long ago, his absence was the best medicine for everyone. The friction he caused was like a storm. Now, after agreeing to his partnership with Lamonte, he'd begun to regret that decision more and more each day. It had been over six months since the door to The Brothers Construction was opened, and he had to admit, for a new business, they were climbing pretty quickly. In fact, they had just landed one of the biggest contracts in the city. Even though the money was rolling in, things were still touchy between him and his baby brother.

Joe was in his office at the rear of the building. He leaned back in his black leather office chair after picking up the gold-trimmed invitation Lamonte had left on his desk. He turned the invitation over and over again as his mind reflected back to the conversation between him and Lamonte a few days ago. Lamonte had made an effort to make things right between them by inviting him over to their parents' home for Sunday dinner. How could Lamonte expect him to sit down at a table with Irene and gulp down her poisonous meal? He'd rather eat with dogs on the street before lowering himself to dine in the presence of that woman, so he'd flat out refused. He wanted so much for things to be peaceful between him and his baby brother and he would like to share his life with Lamonte. After all, he knew nothing of his brother's private life.

Joe let out a long sigh as he continued to analyze their relationship. They spent ten to twelve hours each day cooped up in this small office building, never sharing lunch together or even a beer after work, like most people would do after a long hard day. Looking down at his brother's name written in gold letters on the invite to Lamonte's engagement party, a feeling of guilt passed through him. He was honored that even though

things were rocky as hell between them, Lamonte's love for him still shined through.

The problem was the other name on the card, the one that freaked him out. The name Gade Michaels was linked to Lamonte's. A name he knew so well and in so many ways. His heart began to accelerate through his crisp white Armani shirt as memories surfaced. The beautiful petite young woman he'd met months ago who had captured his heart like no other was now marrying his baby brother? Maybe this was another woman sharing the same name. It had to be, Joe rationalized as he stood up from his desk. Surely, Lamonte had a picture of this woman in his office; after all, this was his future wife, Joe thought as his long legs reached Lamonte's office.

His eyes roamed over Lamonte's huge desk. Mounds of papers and files crowded the surface, but no pictures were in sight. The walls were scattered with diplomas and army certificates, but not one picture of the face he so desperately searched for.

"Damn!" he swore as he slowly turned around. He was about to leave the office when Lamonte walked in.

"Hey man, what are you doing in my office? Is there something you need?" Lamonte asked in a sober tone.

Their latest conversation had left him with a bitter taste in his mouth. Joe didn't answer as he watched Lamonte's eyes travel from his face to the card he held in his right hand. "Oh, I see you got your invitation. Is there a slim possibility that the only brother I have in this world will honor me with his presence?" he hissed as he brushed past Joe and took a seat behind his mahogany desk.

Lamonte shuffled through the papers on his desk as he watched his brother's reaction.

"Uh…I…don't know, man," Joe stammered.

"Save the lame excuses, Joe, I don't want to hear it," he spat as he placed some folders into the gray file cabinet. He let out a slow breath. "You know, I'm beginning to think Mom was right about you after all. You don't give a damn about me. I can't for the life of me understand why you accepted my proposal to be partners in this business. What was it, Joe? Did

the monkey of guilt jump on your back?" Lamonte sneered.

Joe let out a deep sigh. "I did it because I love you, dammit!" Joe bellowed.

Just then, two crew members appeared in the doorway. The weather was gruesome. It was almost a hundred degrees outside, and the men's bright red faces showed it. The shorter man with a thin build spoke out as he took off the white hardhat he was wearing.

"We're having some problems, boss," he said, looking at Lamonte and then at Joe.

"It's the McBee Property," the other man added, approaching Lamonte's desk and spreading out a map. He pointed to the place with his chubby finger. "See here, boss, this is where the line's supposed to be, but we've been diggin' for hours and can't seem to find it," the man uttered in exasperation.

Joe began to saunter away from the men, but before he could reach the doorway Lamonte's voice boomed out.

"Joe, you never said what you wanted."

"Nothing, man, nothing at all," Joe mumbled as he made his way back to his office.

REALITY CHECK

That night in his apartment, Joe loaded the dishwasher, wiped down the wood grain countertops and placed the pitcher of ice tea he'd just made into the black stainless steel fridge. Joe was a fanatic about keeping things clean and in order. His mother had taught him well. A smile crept across his lips as he thought of his mother, Roewena, and her dazzling smile. She was a beautiful woman with a heart of gold.

A brief memory flashed through Joe's mind. They were in his mother's kitchen. Her soft hazel brown eyes twinkled as she spoke to him after he had finished helping her wash the dishes. Joe remembered her saying, "You did such a great job, son, how about we go out for our favorite, banana splits?" She smiled as she gave him a warm hug. He took the glass of ice tea he poured for himself and made his way into the living room.

Taking a seat on the brown leather recliner, he grabbed the remote from the adjacent coffee table and clicked on the wide screen TV. His favorite football game was on, but his mind kept returning to his mother. He had spoken with her only a couple of days ago. Even though he kept his distance, he didn't let too many days go by without hearing Roewena's sweet voice. Once she'd gotten through the nervous breakdown, her life slowly returned to normal. She'd even remarried after a few years, a fact Joe found upsetting at first. But then he realized that if his father had found happiness elsewhere, then why shouldn't his mother do the same? Jerry seemed to be the best thing that could have happened to his mother and they were living happily in Charleston, South Carolina.

Roewena was now a marketing associate for LMD Laser Medical Dignostic. She and Jerry shared a ranch-style home out in the suburbs. Roewena was happy with her life. If only he could move on with his as well. Joe couldn't count the times she'd begged him to get on with his life,

but how could he? The damage goes too deep, and hurt way too much. So many good and happy years wasted. Joe sighed as he downed the last of his iced tea.

"Stop holding grudges, Joe, life is too short," his mother told him in the conversation they'd had the other day. Joe sat the empty glass on a coaster. Hmph, how could his mother so easily forgive a woman that not only tore her marriage to shreds, but was instrumental in her landing in a mental ward in the process. Joe stared at the golden invitation on the coffee table. The end to his quest to find out if it was the same Gade Michaels had come unexpectedly. He'd overheard Lamonte talking to someone over the phone one afternoon just before closing time.

Lamonte told the person jokingly to tell Saphire not to upstage his engagement party with her presence. The party was about her baby sister and not her. Lamonte grinned as he held the phone to his ear. There was only one Saphire and one Gade that he knew of and they were sisters for sure, so the writing was not only on the wall, but on the ceiling as well.

It was the same Lamonte Gade had mentioned in the beginning of their relationship, his very own brother. Deep down inside, he'd always known it, but in reality, he just didn't give a damn. Why should he? This sort of thing had never bothered him before. He slept with married women, his bosses' wives, his coworkers' girlfriends and their friends—and he slept like a baby every night. So what was so different now? He tried to convince himself that it was nothing. Just another day in Joe's neighborhood.

"Damn," was all he could mutter. Joe leaned back in his chair. All of this time he was sharing his brother's girlfriend. He guessed that old saying was true, 'It's a small world'. Joe closed his eyes as he thought about his situation. He wanted to be in his brother's wedding, but how could he? Irene would be there with bells on acting as if she had morals. The morals of an alley cat, he thought. Irene was the least of his problems, though. All eyes would be glued on him as tongues wagged with questions. Neither sister knew he was Lamonte's brother.

After he turned eighteen, he changed his name to his mother's maiden name of Burrels. He didn't want to have any ties to his father. He wanted a

clean break and he got just that. A new identity and a new life. Now looking back, he realized it was another way he hurt his father for what he had done to him and his mother. Bitterness lingered within him in spite of the years that had gone by. Lamonte was wrong when he said he held his father blameless. He blamed the hell out of him, but there was a difference in the way he chose to blame him. Men were weak when it came to women like Irene. She was a Jezebel. Women like that set their claws out for married men, preying on them, using lust like bait.

Irene had caught his father in a moment of weakness and wouldn't let him go. Joe tried to focus back on the game, but his mind was restless with memories. Saphire's face appeared before him. How he missed their wild lovemaking. Saphire had shut down that part of their relationship since she married that Clay dude. She told him in no uncertain terms that she was going to be the faithful little wife Clay deserved. A chuckle came from his throat as he remembered the serious expression on her face. Saphire reminded him of a Girl Scout taking her pledge. Joe knew it was just a matter of time before the Girl Scout would be on his doorstep with her box of cookies.

And as far as Gade was concerned, she too was addicted to his loving. Even though he had been dumped by two sisters, Joe kept his bragging rights. Two sisters as different as night and day, but they both had one common interest–him; he smiled as he leaned back. They both had Joe Burrels deep in their system, and the urge to taste his tan, muscular body would surface again and he would be there waiting. Only a matter of time, he decided, as he focused back on his game.

JOSEY'S BIRTHDAY BASH

Josey spread the red-and-white checkered tablecloth on the picnic table in her backyard. It was her forty-ninth birthday, and it was supposed to be a surprise birthday party taking place for her today. Her daughters tried to keep it from her, but, as always, she'd found out. She didn't know how many times she drilled into their heads that she just didn't like surprises. Usually they came with a price tag, and sometimes it was too high to pay. As with the case involving Saphire's father, Russell, coming out of nowhere after all these years. She still had a trace of anger at Saphire for bringing him back into their lives.

Behind closed doors, the man acted like he couldn't keep his hands off of her. Did he not get what he wanted when he ran off with his lover? Or was it like the old saying, the grass always looks greener on the other side? Too bad he found out it was really brown. Josey smiled broadly at the thought. She watched Saphire carrying a big bowl of homemade chili. She was headed her way wearing a sunshine smile.

"Hey Momma, is the table ready for the food?"

Josey placed a vase of fresh-cut daisies on the table. With a satisfied smile, she uttered, "Bring it on, chile," as she saw her beau coming out of the back door of her home.

Stan kissed Josey lightly on the cheek. "Happy birthday, Baby." Stan grinned, giving her an intimate look.

She and Stan had their own private birthday celebration last night in her bedroom. The man had Josey singing like a bird at the beginning of spring. Josey worried a little, with him being a few years younger than she is, and asked herself how long he would stick around. Since Russell walked out, Josey just couldn't trust a man, no matter how good he was to her. But the way Stan was looking at her now with his dreamy dark eyes made all of

her insecurities melt like ice cubes in the sun.

Josey smiled at him and glanced over at Saphire who had her thick arms wrapped around Clay. They shared a laugh, and then he kissed her gently on the lips. Just looking at them made Josey smile, but it also left her wondering if it was for real or only a Kodak moment. Josey just couldn't shake the feeling she had about Saphire. The woman was slick as oil, and the stunt she pulled by bringing Russell and Cherry to her wedding was a trick for the books. Josey shook her head as she continued to stare at the happy couple. As sad as it was to say, she would never trust her daughter again, or her ex-husband, or even her ex- best friend. With friends like them, who needed enemies?

Gade bounced over to the table with food in hand. She placed the platter of crispy fried chicken and the big bowl of potato salad down on the red-and-white checked tablecloth. Gade had skills when it came to carrying food, thanks to her stint as a waitress last summer at Ray's Bar and Grill. Lamonte came over to her wearing a big grin.

"I came to help you, babe, but I see you got it under control. I just wanted to make sure you didn't drop Miss Josey's southern fried chicken. KFC ain't got nothing on her," Lamonte quipped as everyone laughed.

That Lamonte is such a character, Josey thought. Maybe she was wrong about him after all. His business was getting off the ground quite nicely. The man was making some crazy money, and Josey knew her daughter, Gade, would be well taken care of. But still, she thought Joe Burrels would have been a better catch.

He seemed to have been more worldly, and from what Gade had told her early on, the man had done some extensive traveling. Josey's mind drifted back to her younger days. She had wanted the same thing for herself at one time. To be totally free, no strings attached. She would have had it, if…if she hadn't met Russell Michaels, and given up on her dreams to settle for a man who left her with two babies to raise alone. That Russell was quite the man, though. He went on to get his engineering degree, and now he and Cherry lived in some high-rise condo out there in Texas. Josey felt a tear touch the corner of her eye. Yes, even after all these years, it still

hurt like hell.

A strong arm encircled her waist. As she turned, she looked into the handsome face of Stan. He held her firmly and whispered the words "I love you," in her ear. Life wasn't bad after all for Josey. She smiled as the girls brought out her birthday cake and began singing Happy Birthday.

* * * * *

The next day, Gade sat at Lamonte's small kitchen table with a pen and pad. "Lamonte, this list is getting longer and longer." She sighed. "I'm thinking maybe we should just place an invitation in the newspaper and invite everyone in the city."

Lamonte took the pen from her hand and pulled her onto the couch. He kissed her deeply as his fingers caressed her. "Don't worry about it. Baby, as long as you, me, and the preacher man are there, I don't care about anybody else," he crooned as he kissed her again.

Gade gently pushed Lamonte off and sat up on the couch. "I knew we forgot someone important!" Gade almost shouted.

"Who?" Lamonte sat up straight alongside her.

"Your brother, dummy, Joe Nathan," Gade said, popping Lamonte on his forehead.

"Uh…well…I don't think he can make it," Lamonte mumbled in a strange tone.

"He can't make it? "What are you talking about, Lamonte? Of course he can make it to his own brother's wedding. I don't know what the man even looks like, and I'm going to be his sister-in-law. Don't you think it's about time for me to meet him?" Gade asked standing up now, with her hands on her hips.

Lamonte shook his head. "He's not coming, babe. The man wouldn't stop his life for one moment to come to our engagement party, so what makes you think he is coming to our wedding?"

Gade let out a long breath. "I don't know what's up with you and that brother of yours. Are you sure he's not wanted by the FBI or something?" Gade grimaced. Lamonte fell silent as he grappled with the situation,

searching for an explanation. Before he could come up with one Gade interjected. "Lord knows I thought Saphire and I had issues, but you and your brother make us look like bosom buddies." She chuckled lightly.

Lamonte stood up and wrapped his arms around her. "The man is an island unto himself and that's where he wants to stay, baby. I have come to accept that and you will have to as well."

"But Lamonte, you work with the man every day and he won't even try to socialize with you or your family. What is his problem? You know what, I've got a good mind to go to your office and give him a piece of my mind."

"Naw baby, the last thing I need is drama at the workplace," Lamonte chided. "Just leave it alone, baby. You will be a part of my family. I don't need him as validation. My parents'love you and their opinion is all I care about."

"I just don't see how you do it." Gade sighed as she dropped back down on the couch.

"Business is business, baby, and plus, by the time we are married, he'll probably be long gone again, anyway," Lamonte mumbled, grabbing the car keys. "I'm going to get us something to eat," he announced over his shoulder. "Chinese okay?" he yelled.

"That's fine baby." Gade said, picking up her list again.

MEETING WITH AN OLD FRIEND

Since Saphire's wedding the previous year, she and Gade had grown a little closer. She'd really surprised Gade and her mother. She kept her promise of not cheating on Clay, but that didn't mean temptation hadn't knocked on her door several times. Saphire ran into old flames that fanned their fires at her, but she was able to put those flames out; that is, until she ran into Joe. It was at the end of summer and she had taken Clay's niece, Bonnie, and nephew, Jaydon, to the park. It was the same park where Clay's family reunion was held. They were sweet little kids. Bonnie was five and Jaydon, three. Clay was hoping that by her spending more time with the children, the motherly instinct would somehow rub off on her, making her want kids of her own. *Not a snowball in hell could convince me of that,* Saphire thought, as she ran behind Jaydon, who managed to get away from her. The little booger could run like he was in an Olympic race.

By the time Saphire caught up with him, she was spent. Bonnie with her big brown eyes was a nosy little thing. She could easily become a news reporter, because she didn't miss a thing. Several guys spoke to Saphire as the children played in the park, and Bonnie wanted to know who each man was and why they were talking to Saphire. Finally, Saphire made it to the swings. She placed each kid on a swing and began pushing them.

Saphire looked over at the basketball court. A few guys had already gathered in anticipation of playing a game. As they started, Saphire watched them. Glistening muscles wet with sweat, a variety of colors, mocha, chocolate and crème vanilla bounced on the pavement as the ball swished in the basketball net. Saphire found herself getting aroused. Nothing turned her on more than a sweaty muscular male. Saphire licked her lips as if she could taste the salty sweat on their bodies.

"Well hello, stranger," a deep voice said, breaking her out of her fantasy.

When she turned around, she sucked in a big gulp of air. In true form stood the man she had been dreaming about for months. The tan specimen appeared before her like the sweet Hershey bar he was.

"Joe?" Saphire managed to utter as she fought to regain her composure. She turned away quickly to give Jaydon another push, with a little more force this time. "This is totally a surprise," Saphire said.

"It most certainly is. Married life has been good to you I see," he responded as his eyes roamed her perfectly shaped body.

"Why, thank you." Saphire grinned as she glanced over at Bonnie, who had her big brown eyes glued to Joe's face. She had stopped swinging and now stood right beside Saphire. "I…thought you had left town. I mean…I haven't seen you in months," Saphire managed to say. Taking in Joe's handsome face was making her insides melt like a strawberry sundae on a hot day.

Before Joe could answer, Bonnie began her interrogation. "Aunt Saphire, is this your friend? Does he like you, Aunt Saphire?" This little girl was getting on Saphire's last nerve.

Joe couldn't help but stare at the pink low-cut blouse Saphire was wearing. Memories of his face buried deep in her bosom were making his nature rise. What he wouldn't give to go down memory lane once again.

Saphire knew she had it going on, dressed in her pink Gucci shorts outfit with her pink wedges and, for an innocent look, she wore a pink ribbon tied around her braided ponytail. Her vibrant appearance brought her many stares from the men on the basketball court. Clay tried to get her to tone it down some, since she was after all, a married woman now. Saphire just scoffed at him. She informed Clay that she had dressed like this when they first met, and by no means was she going to dress any other way. She also reminded him that it was he whom she came home to every night, and that seemed to calm his fears.

Saphire leaned over and gave little Jaydon another push. "Hold on sweetie," she instructed as the swing went back and forth. Inquisitive Bonnie was staring a hole into Joe. "Bonnie, why don't you go back to your swing. We will be leaving soon," Saphire said, giving the little girl a firm look. She

toddled over to her swing, glancing back several times before climbing on.

"So you must be babysitting?" Joe inquired as he watched the children.

"Yes, just for a while. These are Clay's sister's children," she informed him. "I think he's trying to bring out my maternal instincts," Saphire joked.

"Well, is it working?" Joe asked with a crooked grin. Before Saphire could respond, Bonnie had gotten off her swing and made her way back over to the couple.

"Who are you and why are you talking to my Auntie Saphire?" Bonnie asked with a serious expression on her little pecan-colored face.

"Bonnie, this is an old friend of mine, now you run along and play," Saphire informed her in a parental tone of voice. Saphire must have been speaking in Spanish because Bonnie didn't move an inch.

Instead, she folded her little arms across her chest and with a big voice she said, "Auntie Saphire, I'm tired and I'm ready to go."

"Well, young lady, I'm not ready, therefore you are not ready. Now why don't you take Jaydon over to the monkey bars and play," Saphire instructed as she took Bonnie by her little shoulders and pointed her in that direction. "Grab Jaydon by the hand and watch him closely, you hear me?" she yelled out as she watched them run off. Saphire could have sworn her mother Josey was standing right next to her, for she sounded just like her. "Kids," she said, and shook her head as she walked back to join Joe.

"You didn't answer my question before, but I can tell from your expression that you are not ready for the motherly role yet," Joe stated.

"You are so right about that." Saphire chuckled. "Don't get me wrong, I love kids, but I don't want any of my own for a very long time." She sighed. Saphire couldn't help but notice Joe's muscular physique. The man was built like a god, and all the memories she tried to suppress came flooding through her mind. She wanted him with everything in her.

When Joe met her stare, Saphire lowered her eyes. Joe could feel the electricity flowing between them and he was enjoying every minute of it.

"Will you be here later? I should be getting the kids back to their mother." Saphire hesitated.

"Do you want me to be here?" Joe asked her directly, moving into her

personal space. He was so close to her, she could almost feel the heat of his breath.

Saphire shifted on her feet with nervousness. Joe was taking away the fence she always put up when it came to temptation. She took a step back and cleared her throat. "Where have you been keeping yourself anyway?" she asked, trying to regain her composure.

"My plans were to leave town, but something came up. A business venture I wanted to pursue," Joe answered as he danced around Saphire's question.

"And did you?" Saphire asked soaking in his bedroom eyes.

"Yes, and I'm happy to say it's doing quite well."

"So what now?" Saphire asked, not wanting this man to leave her sight again.

The memories of their hot lovemaking, his large hands all over her body, caressing her in places he knew drove her wild, caused Saphire to let out a short breath of air. *Get a grip, girlfriend,* Saphire scolded herself. After all, she had a husband at home now, she didn't need this man to satisfy her, or did she? Joe leaned in and gave Saphire a kiss that set her soul ablaze. Heat filled her body. She wanted this man, needed this man.

"Meet me later at my apartment, I'll be waiting," Joe whispered in her ear before he quickly walked away.

Saphire exhaled as she felt a tug on her shorts. Bonnie was staring up at her with her big brown eyes.

"Auntie Saphire, why did that man kiss you?"

"Damn," Saphire swore under her breath. This little heifer didn't miss a trick. She stared into her little round face. The child was pretty as an angel dressed in her yellow lace shorts set with yellow bows on her two long brown ponytails. "Bonnie, listen to Aunt Saphire and listen good. That was just a friendly kiss that most adults share when they haven't seen one another in a long time. Now promise me that we will keep this to ourselves," Saphire ordered in a stern, yet gentle tone of voice.

"Um, I promise if I can get some ice cream," Bonnie sang out.

"All right, Bonnie, now go get your brother." Saphire exhaled as she

watched the little girl trot over to the monkey bars and grab Jaydon by the hand. Saphire realized she had just been blackmailed by a five- year-old.

A LITTLE INDISCRETION

Saphire took a long warm bath in her huge black garden porcelain tub. Afterwards, she prepared Clay's favorite meal, roast beef, cream potatoes, and garden salad, with buttercream pound cake for dessert. Saturday wasn't usually a work day for Clay, but since the owner of the mechanics shop retired and sold Clay the business, he had been putting in a little overtime. Clay gave the shop a whole new look along with a new name, Matthews' Body Shop and Repairs. Saphire was so proud of her husband. A new marriage, a magnificent new home, and now a new business as well. Life was good to them both. Saphire felt blessed, so why couldn't she be content? She wondered as she floated around her new home with her plans for the night fresh in her mind. Meeting Joe would be her little secret, and she was going to do it just once, she promised herself. The lie she conjured was well rehearsed as she heard Clay's key in the sunburst door.

Clay walked in and began to peel away his oily uniform. Saphire would not allow him an inch farther until he discarded his soiled clothing and boots in the foyer. She always placed a robe in the hall closet he would slip on upon entering the living room area. Clay sauntered over to Saphire who greeted him with a kiss and a cold glass of lemonade. Clay took the kiss first, then washed it down with the delicious drink. "Sugar Plum, I sure love coming home to you." Clay smiled giving his wife another warm kiss.

"Welcome home, baby, I missed you so much today," Saphire crooned as she held onto his firm arm.

"I missed you too, Sugar Plum," he said staring down into her eyes.

"I cooked your favorite meal, and your bath water is ready and waiting." Saphire smiled.

"Why all the special treatment?" Clay asked as his suspicion rose.

"Because I love you, Clay." Saphire announced as she headed for their master bedroom. He followed closely behind her and cupped her buttocks once they reached their king-size bed.

"How about a quickie before dinner?" he asked in a husky voice as he crushed her into him.

Saphire allowed him to kiss her for several minutes before pulling away. "Clay, we can't right now. I've got to…go out for an hour or so," she stuttered.

Clay looked at her with a blank expression. "Go out, where to?" he asked with a furrowed brow.

"Baby, Mia called me right before you got in. She and Mike had a big fight, from what I could understand. She was crying so much I could barely understand what she was saying. Mike pushed her around and messed up their apartment in his childish rage. The girl is all shook up and I promised her I would come over. I won't be gone long." Saphire feigned concern.

Clay gave her a skeptical look then he smiled. "Girl support, huh?" he mumbled.

"Yes, baby, you know how it is. I mean, I am her best friend and she would be there for me if I needed her."

"All right, but don't you be gone too long." Clay sighed. "And I want my lovin' when you get back," he said playfully as he slapped Saphire on her firm behind.

"You will get it, baby, I promise." Saphire gave Clay another long hot kiss. Then she grabbed the keys to her Lexus and headed out the door.

Thank God, Clay didn't say anything about the outfit she was wearing. The low-cut tangerine sheer dress hugged her figure nicely. The matching stilettos showed off her shimmering legs. Saphire wasn't worried about the story she gave Clay. Mia knew all about her plans with Joe, and if Clay decided to call Mia to verify, she was prepared to answer as a battered wife. If Clay wanted to talk to her, the story would be she had gone out to get Mia some aspirin for the splitting headache Mike had given her. Saphire's back was covered and now it was time to play. She smiled as she popped a mint into her mouth.

Fifteen minutes later, she was in Joe's bed as naked as the day she was born. The man was taking her places she never thought possible as his tongue did delicious things to her heated body. Surely, she had died and gone to the pearly gates. One thing for sure, like the lyrics to the song by Keith Sweat, "Nobody," nobody could do it like Joe Burrels, NOBODY. Saphire thought, as she smiled to herself.

ANOTHER SET OF BELLS

Six months later, Gade and Lamonte jumped the broom in their old-fashioned wedding. Gade wanted her theme totally different from her sister's. She wanted to make her own statement to the world and she had done it in country style, thanks to the help of her great-aunt Aggie, who'd had a similar wedding years and years ago. Family and friends watched as the couple said their I dos most in the audience had tears of joy for the couple, while a particular person, Chaniece-Half- Breed, had an ugly scowl plastered on her almost white face. She certainly didn't get an invitation, but that didn't stop her from showing up.

Chaniece kept her eyes glued on Lamonte, who was looking like the singer Chris Brown in his white Armani tux as the cameras flashed. The happy couple shared a lingering kiss and it sent Chaniece into a frenzy. Gade managed to give her a diva look as she reached for Lamonte's face again, giving him an even more sensual kiss while the audience moaned with oohs and ahs. At the very back of the church stood a tall man wearing a designer hat and dark designer shades. He kept his distance from the wedding party and their families as he shadowed the ceremony. He wanted to be as inconspicuous as possible. He toyed with the idea of not showing up at all, but how could he miss his baby brother's wedding? He turned him down flat when Lamonte asked him about being his best man. There was no way in hell he could have done that, even as bad as he wanted to, it would never work.

One thing for sure, his brother was marrying the woman of his dreams and he wasn't going to do anything to mess that up for him, no matter how he felt about Gade. His mind floated back to the time they shared last summer. Gade was a good woman and Lamonte was lucky to have her.

Joe's eyes scanned the room through his dark shades. His eyes settled on

Saphire, who was looking stunning as ever. The memories of the steaming hot sex they had a few nights ago filtered through his mind. Saphire was addicted to him like a suburban housewife on pain pills. She couldn't get enough of him.

Joe stared at Saphire's husband, Clay. He had his arms draped over Saphire as if he was shielding her from the world. Wonder what he would say if he could have seen all the positions he had his wife in a few nights ago? As Joe looked on from a distance, Lamonte placed the white lace garter on Gade's shapely butter crème thigh. Joe winced as a jolt of envy hit his veins. He had no reason to feel as he did, because there was another secret he would have to keep from his baby brother. A secret concerning his wife that he would never understand, and perhaps never forgive.

His mind traveled back to a week ago when he ran into Gade. Her car had broken down on the freeway. He had just left the office, and was on his way to see a new site for an upcoming building project.

Lamonte was swamped with paperwork at the office, and had asked him to go check it out for him. Tensions still ran high between them, but at least they were civil towards each other. Joe seized the opportunity to leave the office and get some fresh air. He had his slow jam music playing on the radio in his SUV as he cruised down the freeway. When the music ended, Michael Baisden came on with the topic of the day. Cheaters. Joe let out a low chuckle. What a great topic, he thought as he stared out into traffic. Different voices offered their opinions about cheaters as Michael interviewed them.

"If you are a cheater, my man, play the game well. Don't let the game play you." Joe laughed out loud, as he had his own opinion. As he passed slower moving cars, he noticed a familiar vehicle on the side of the road with flashing lights.

As he got closer to it, he realized it was Gade's car and he saw her bending over and peering into the engine. Joe drove to the next exit and turned around. It took him a few minutes before he finally reached Gade and her broken-down car. He pulled up behind her and hopped out of his SUV.

"What seems to be the problem?" he asked as Gade turned around with a stunned expression.

Joe looked down into the engine and played around with a few things. The sunny day was slowly turning gray as Joe worked on the engine.

"I don't know what happened, it just started acting funny, and then when I pulled over, it died," Gade explained as she watched Joe trying to start the car again. No luck, the car didn't even whimper.

"Looks like you may be needing the services of a tow," Joe concluded as he looked down into Gade's beautiful face. A face he missed seeing, a body he missed holding as his eyes traveled over her shapely petite frame.

"Where have you been, Joe?" Gade found herself asking. She realized she had no right to ask the question; after all, it wasn't any business of hers. They had broken up and she was assured he had moved on, just as she had. Before Joe could respond, Gade said, "That's no concern of mine. I guess I'd better call my towing service." Gade stumbled, reaching into her car and retrieving her cell. Joe watched her as she spoke.

Everything about Gade was turning him on, and he wanted her. The sky turned a dark gray, and within minutes, rain began to pour. Joe closed the hood of Gade's car, grabbed her by the hand and led her to his SUV. They both hopped in, but to no avail, they both were soaking wet. Joe remembered he had a towel in the back. He reached over and grabbed the multi-colored towel, and gave it to Gade.

"Thanks," Gade whispered as she dried her face. Her new hairdo was ruined. The white poplin blouse was now matted to her Victoria Secret black lace bra, showing the full shape of her medium-sized breasts. Gade's eyes focused on Joe's handsome face. He was even more good-looking than she remembered. His white business shirt was rolled up at the sleeves showing the veins in his muscular arms. His dark gray slacks fit his masculine body like a GQ model, sending lustful thoughts racing through her mind. Gade let out a slow breath. What was she doing? Her wedding was days away, and here she was lusting after the man that broke her heart months ago. Joe broke the vibes that were sparking between them.

"Did you get the towing service on the phone?" Joe asked, never taking his eyes off her.

"Yes, they said it may be a while before they come, but they assured me someone was on the way," Gade replied as she placed the now damp towel across her lap. She noticed her baby blue short pencil skirt had inched its way up, exposing her butter crème thighs, after stepping into Joe's SUV.

A streak of lightning hit the sky and shook Gade to the core. She jumped into Joe's lap. She'd been afraid of lightning since childhood. Joe held her tightly as he took in the fresh scent of her hair. She felt so good in his arms.

"I can't believe how fast and hard this storm came," Gade mused as she inched her way out of Joe's arms.

Joe wasn't thinking about the weather at all. His mind was strictly on Gade's body, and, given the chance, he knew he could make her come just as fast and just as hard. Without a moment's notice, Joe pulled her back into his arms, and gave her a throaty kiss. At first, Gade pulled away, but Joe's kiss made feelings rise in her body she thought she had long forgotten. Gade let her body go limp in his arms. The sky turned black as the rain and wind battered the truck, making it sway.

Was a tornado brewing? Neither one cared, because as far as they were concerned, the tornado was already inside, as they made thundering love to each other.

Joe shook his head as he came out of his trance. Taking one more look at the blushing bride and groom, he turned and left the church.

Even in the disguise he was wearing, Saphire noticed Joe from across the room. She went around to the side door of the church and into the church parking lot just in time to see Joe's gold SUV drive away. Saphire heard the music begin to play, and then Clay's voice as she turned around to enter the church.

"Sugar Plum, what on earth are you doing out here?" he asked, giving her a puzzled look.

"I just needed some air," she mumbled as they both went back inside and joined the happy crowd.

FAST FORWARD

As Gade lay in her husband's arms, her mind replayed the rainy day she slept with Joe Burrels. Part of her felt guilty as hell, while the other part savored the memories of Joe's touch. Gade wanted to erase that day from her mind and get on with her life. Her eyes settled on Lamonte's sleeping face. She loved the way his lips curled as he slept, reminding her of the expression a newborn would make.

Speaking of a newborn, Lamonte's hand rested gently upon her protruding belly. Gade was almost seven months pregnant with their son. Lamonte couldn't wait for the boy to make his entrance into the world, and neither could she. She and Lamonte were very happy as they awaited the birth of their first child. Lamonte spent his weekends painting the nursery. Before they knew it was a boy, they painted the nursery yellow and blue. "Neutral colors," Lamonte concluded, grinning as he held up the paint brush the day Gade walked into the nursery from a day out shopping with Saphire and their mother. They laughed in unison as Lamonte took her in his arms and kissed her lovingly.

Gade slipped her fingers through her short, curly hair. She hoped her son would inherit her grade of hair, and not her husband's thick as a cornfield hair. For a boy, it really wouldn't matter, haircuts were easy. But if it miraculously turned out to be a girl, a good relaxer kit would be next to the nursery rhyme books, she decided and giggled softly.

Lamonte stirred at the sound of her voice and opened his dark caramel-colored eyes. "I see you are awake. What's the matter, baby, you couldn't sleep?" Lamonte asked, scooting up in the bed.

"You know, this booger keeps me up at night with his gymnastics." Gade chuckled. She propped herself up on her elbows and exhaled. "I can't wait to get my body back, I feel like a cruise ship," Gade complained.

"A beautiful cruise ship, may I add," Lamonte muttered, giving Gade a soft kiss. "Now you just relax." He smiled as he jumped out of bed.

"Where are you going?" Gade questioned.

"Downstairs to make my wife a scrumptious breakfast," he yelled as he grabbed the black robe that hung by the door. "Close those pretty eyes of yours, baby, and relax. I'll be right back," Lamonte hollered over his shoulder as he went out the door. Gade did exactly as she was told, and repositioned the fluffy pillow under her head. Her mind was now filled with happy thoughts of her new family and the wonderful life they had ahead of them as she dozed off.

* * * * *

Life went on for the sisters. Saphire quit her job and opened up her own beauty salon, which she named Styles & More by Saphire. Business was great, thanks to her marketing skills. She not only offered the latest hairstyles, but she went a step further. She had nail technicians as well as masseuses under the same roof. A woman could come in, get her body toned and her hair and nails done, all in one day. Saphire had so many clients, she had to hire extra personnel just to keep up with the demand.

One Friday afternoon as Saphire took a break, she was summoned to the front. Taz, a Korean girl who was one of her best nail technicians, knocked on her office door.

"You have a visitor, Mrs. Matthews." Taz smiled.

Saphire walked out of her elegant office. She almost passed out as her eyes met the tall frame of a woman. Sandy had actually walked into her salon. Sandy of Hollywood Hair Salon was still in business, but her clientele was slowly dwindling. *I can't imagine why,* she thought with a sly grin.

"I'm here for a women's retreat. I think that's what you call it," Sandy mumbled as she averted her glance from Saphire's curious eyes. Saphire couldn't help but smirk as she looked around for her spa director, Dell.

She saw her talking to another customer and she got her attention. "Dell, when you finish with her, will you please take Miss Sandy here to

our spa room?"

Dell immediately came over and showed Sandy the way to the big open room that mirrored a vacation brochure. It was decorated with artificial palm trees and ocean murals on the wall, giving the room a relaxing ambiance. Saphire let out a hearty laugh as she remembered the day Sandy threatened to throw her out of that little ol' shop of hers after she and Chaniece had choice words. Maybe she should return the favor, she wagered. Naw, she was well past all of that. She was a businesswoman now, and truth be known, Sandy was the reason she'd opened her own salon in the first place. Seeing how Sandy handled her shop and the customers she had filtering in, made Saphire believe she could do the same—and she did. Only she had done it better.

Sapphire walked over to the pink princess phone on the marble countertop. Saphire phoned the spa room and Dell answered on the third ring. "Dell, let Miss Sandy know her retreat will be on the house today." Saphire hung up, grinning.

Gade decided to pay her sister a visit at her salon. It had been a while since she'd visited the place, and she wanted to see how things were going. Gade had just left the doctor's office with Brice for his well-baby checkup. He was almost a year old now, and he was his father's pride and joy. Gade pushed the stroller into her sister's beautiful and modern salon. Gade was very proud of what her big sister had accomplished. Since they both were now married women, their relationship was closer than ever. Both marriages were going well, and so were their lives. Clay's auto shop business was booming and Saphire's salon was doing great. Gade had her LPN license now and was working at The Good Samaritan Hospital. Lamonte's construction business was well known around the city and thriving, even after that low-budget brother of his just up and jumped.

Yes, life was blessed for the sisters, and it showed on the women's faces as they greeted each other. The women in the salon stopped what they were doing and surrounded the baby. The beauticians filled the salon with their cooing. "Gade, he is gorgeous," one woman with golden braids said.

"He most certainly is," another, who reminded Gade of Regine from

the sitcom Living Single, agreed.

Saphire smiled broadly. "He's just like his daddy, drawing women like a magnet," Saphire quipped, looking over at Gade.

Gade wasn't so sure she liked the remark, but hey, that was Saphire, so she let it slide.

"So what brings you by, Lil Sis?" Saphire asked.

"Last time I checked, this was a beauty salon, and maybe a girl wants her hair done, or even a retreat." Gade chuckled as she eyed her sister.

"Looks to me like you're overdue for both," Saphire snickered as she picked up Brice and tickled his belly with her nose.

"Now don't you start nothin', Saphire. Momma's not here to take me off of you," Gade sneered. The women stopped talking and gave each other questioning stares.

"Take care of my sister, girls," Saphire ordered as she walked away with Brice. "We will be in my office when you're done, Lil' Sis," Saphire said over her shoulder as she disappeared into the back with her baby nephew.

For sure, no matter how much junk they talked to each other, Saphire loved that little boy. Just knowing that made Gade smile as she followed the Regine woman over to her chair.

BREAKING FREE

Joe decided about a month after his brother's marriage to Gade, that he had to leave town. Even though he never ran into Gade or saw Saphire, he knew it was only a matter of time before things would come to a combustible head. Gade almost saw him one day when she came to the office to surprise Lamonte with a picnic basket. He damn near had to hide in the office closet. When Lamonte called out his name, he didn't answer. He was relieved that he'd loaned his SUV to Miguel, who went out to buy lunch for them, so Lamonte assumed he'd already left for lunch. The very next day, he left his resignation on Lamonte's desk, and within a week he was gone. Lamonte phoned him, trying to get him to change his mind.

"Lamonte, I told you from the beginning, I don't put down roots, man."

"Yeah, but I thought after you went down south and returned, you'd realized what a good thing we got going here," Lamonte argued.

Going down south was another lie Joe had told Lamonte during the time of his wedding. He sputtered off a story to him about his mother's being on the verge of another breakdown, which was a boldfaced lie. His mother was doing better than ever, but he knew Lamonte would not question him on the subject.

"How can you just up and leave me like this?" Lamonte asked with hurt in his voice.

Joe felt his brother's pain, but he knew the little pain he was feeling now couldn't compare to the pain he would endure if he found out he had known his wife as he did.

"This is for the best, Lamonte, trust me, man. We will stay in touch, I promise," and with that, Joe hung up.

His eyes filled with tears as he sat in his apartment in South Carolina. Joe went over the relationships he had with the Michaels sisters. Gade's

face smiled at him in his mind's eye, and so did Saphire's. Why did he let things go so far? Why didn't he come clean with Gade that day in his SUV? God knows he'd wanted to. He thought about it, but he just couldn't do it. His selfishness overruled any common sense he should have had. And what about Saphire? He wanted her as well, but he knew she would never leave Clay. Centering on Gade, Joe thought she could have been his wife instead of his brother's.

"God!" he cried out.

What was wrong with him? For the first time, Joe realized he needed help to deal with his errant emotions. And now, more than ever, he was determined to get it. Joe finished off the bottle of Hennessey and fell into a deep sleep.

LIFE GOES ON

Days turned into weeks, and the weeks turned into years as life went on. Gade was now working in her chosen field of pediatrics. She loved children, and couldn't wait to have another one of her own, since Brice was turning five. Gade and Lamonte had tried everything from the practical to old wives' tales, trying to get pregnant. She kept up with her ovulation and made sure Lamonte was at her disposal during those times, but nothing seemed to be working, and it was making Gade a little nervous. Maybe something was wrong with her. Surely if it were, her doctor would have told her when Brice was born. His delivery was perfect. She had a normal birth, and was back to work six weeks later.

Lamonte kept telling her it would happen sooner or later, but she was beginning to worry. After six months and still no baby, she finally got Lamonte to agree to go with her to a fertility doctor. Now, weeks later, as she sat in front of specialist Dr. Cathy Wicker, a good friend of hers as well, Gade's world fell apart. Holding the results of Lamonte's test, she just couldn't believe what she'd read. The word sterile was written in red letters.

"This has to be a mistake, Cathy!" Gade almost shouted as her eyes remained glued to the paper.

"There is no mistake, Gade, I ran it twice," Cathy confirmed in response to the bewildered look on Gade's face.

"Well, something is definitely wrong here," Gade exclaimed. "Lamonte and I have a son, so how could he be sterile?" she asked, her voice now strained.

"Maybe Lamonte is not his father," Cathy uttered barely above a whisper as she studied her friend.

That's when it all came crashing down. The buried memory revisited

Gade's mind like a nightmare. Gade fell back into the soft leather chair and began to sob.

Cathy quickly came around her desk and sat beside her. She pulled her into her arms and began to soothe her. "Gade, what is it? I'm sorry, I didn't mean to imply anything."

Gade remembered that day Joe stopped to help her on the freeway. Visions of them going at it like dogs in heat filled her mind. Joe was her son's father. She knew it with everything in her, now. The way Brice smiled sometimes reminded her of Joe, but she thought it was all in her head. Just a residual memory, prompted by her missing him.

Cathy retrieved a couple of Kleenex from her desk and handed them to Gade. Gade wiped her tears and took a deep breath. "Cathy, I need a huge favor from you," Gade choked. Her chest felt as if a monster truck had fallen on it, making it difficult for her to breathe.

"What, Gade? Just name it," Cathy said with concerned eyes.

"I don't want Lamonte to know about this."

Cathy's eyes widened. "But Gade, he has every right to know," she protested.

"Please, Cathy, I beg of you. If my husband ever finds out that he is sterile and our son is not his, my marriage and my life will be completely over!" Gade shrieked. Her sobs had returned, heavier than before.

"Calm down, Gade," Cathy urged, putting her arms around her.

Gade's tears continued as she rocked back and forth. "Please, Cathy, promise me this will stay between us?" she cried.

Cathy looked long and hard at Gade before she spoke. "Tell me one thing, Gade," Cathy said as she held her gaze. "Do you know who Brice's father is?"

"Yes, yes I do," Gade whispered. Her throat was dry as shingles on a hot tin roof.

"Are you going to tell him about Brice?"

Gade's face grew dark. In a husky voice she answered, "He will never know, Cathy, he will never ever know."

Cathy took the paper out of Gade's trembling hands. "You know I

could be in a whole lot of trouble if this ever got out. Serious trouble," she said sternly.

"It won't, Cathy. I promise you, I will take this to my grave. You have nothing to worry about, I swear," Gade pleaded with Cathy.

Cathy placed the paper into the office paper shredder and turned it on. Gade winced at the grinding sound of the machine.

As she drove home that night in the pouring rain, memories filled her head as the vision of Joe's face came into play. She hadn't seen him in years, and now she carried the knowledge that they shared a son. How did her life end up like this? The rain came down in torrents, as silver streaks sliced through the sky like a reminder of years ago, taunting her over the conception of her son. Gade wondered what the forecast for her life would be. Would sunshine ever grace her life again?

* * * * *

Gade almost jumped out of her skin when she heard the phone ring. It had been over a week since she'd learned the paternity of her son. She felt as if she was encased in a deep fog, and it was driving Lamonte up the wall. Gade answered the phone with a small hello.

"Gade, baby, what's the matter?" Josey asked with concern after hearing her daughter's hollow voice.

Gade fought back tears as she tried to regain her composure. "Are you pregnant, Gade? That must be it because you haven't been to work all this week and you don't miss work for nobody," Josey rambled on.

"Momma...Momma, stop, all right?" Gade commanded, bringing a halt to Josey's chatter. "Momma, how did you know I wasn't at work? Did you call my job?"

"Well, of course, chile. How else can I keep up with you? Since you and Saphire got married, I hardly see you these days."

"Now, Momma, you know that's not the truth. We all just had dinner together two weeks ago."

"Yes, baby, two whole weeks ago, that's a long time for a woman my age." Josey sighed.

"Momma, you are in your middle fifties, and that's not old." Gade rebuked her assertion.

"My age is not what I called to talk about. So tell me, baby, how far along are you?" Josey asked with a smile.

"Momma, I'm not pregnant and will never…" Gade's voice faded.

"What did you say, Gade?" Josey questioned.

Gade cleared her throat. "Momma, I'm not pregnant, I think I came down with a virus, that's all. I will be back at work tomorrow."

"Oh," Josey said a little uneasily. "Well, don't worry, baby. As much as you and that husband of yours stay in bed, you will be pregnant in no time."

"Momma, I got to go now. Brice will be here soon," Gade said hurriedly before hanging up. Hearing Josey talk about her and Lamonte's love life made her cringe.

Gade went back to bed and fell in, then glanced up at the clock. Brice would be here in another forty-five minutes. Good. She could sleep for another thirty minutes at least. Sleeping soothed her pain, for when she was asleep, she didn't think about Joe. But the conscience can sometimes play mean tricks. Upon awakening, Gade could have sworn Joe was standing in her bedroom holding Brice in his arms with a big smile on that handsome face of his.

* * * * *

Clay was irking the hell out of Saphire again. She remembered how he hounded her about marrying him, and now he was singing another song. This time it was lullabies and nursery rhymes. Since they were coming up on six years of marriage, Clay swore they were about to be senior citizens.

"Baby, we are still young, we have plenty of time for a child. Plus, we have Brice over here half of the time anyway. To tell you the truth, he feels almost like mine." Saphire chuckled.

Clay plopped down on the bed with a scowl on his face. "Yeah, but he isn't, now, is he?" he spat.

Saphire stifled a scream as she shampooed her hair. To think, as an

owner of a flourishing salon, she shouldn't have to worry about such tasks, but she enjoyed doing her own hair. After blow drying it, she then applied hair lotion and pulled it into a loose pony tail.

"You're not going to church this morning?" Clay quizzed as he slipped on his black and gray Stacy Adams.

Shaking her head no, she answered, "I'm going to sit this one out."

Clay's lips formed a tight ball as he grabbed the jacket to his black Armani suit and headed downstairs. Their arguments about babies always ended this way. He would run away, pissed off with her, and not speak to her for days.

Saphire couldn't help but notice how fine her husband was. Even after six years, Clay had kept his muscular body well-toned. His short haircut and trimmed mustache gave him a very sexy look. She knew the women's eyes roamed over her man's body, leaving them gawking in heat, but Saphire wasn't worried, not one damned bit. Clay belonged to her, mind, body and soul.

Saphire ran down the stairs as Clay made it to the front door. "Clay, don't be mad at me, please, baby. I can't stand it when we argue like this," she begged, batting her long eyelashes at him. Clay didn't respond. He just kept right on walking towards the door. "I know you want a child, but Clay, don't you enjoy our freedom? I mean, we can pick up and go when we want without the worry of a babysitter."

Stopping, he said, "Your sister manages just fine. In fact, she and Lamonte just came back from the Virgin Islands not too long ago. And Saphire, we are not poor. We can afford a babysitter any time we need one." Clay exhaled. His dark eyes scanned Saphire's face. Saphire's shoulders slumped. "Face it, Saphire, you just don't want kids, or maybe you just don't want me," Clay spewed at her.

Now where in the hell did that come from? Saphire thought as her eyes grew wide. "Are you crazy, Clay? Of course I want you. I wouldn't have married you if I didn't."

"Sometimes I wonder about that," Clay murmured, stepping around her. "You keep giving me these damned excuses, and it's making me feel

as if there is something else out there you want."

Saphire shook her head as she pulled her husband back from the door. "Stop this foolishness, Clay," she demanded quickly as she placed her thick arms around her husband and kissed him fully on the lips. Clay was a sucker for Saphire's affection. "I love you, honey, and if a baby will help you see that I do, then so be it. We will start tonight. Okay?" Saphire crooned with a sly smile.

Clay pulled her into his broad chest and squeezed her tight. "Do you really mean that, Sugar Plum?"

"I most certainly do," Saphire whispered as Clay gazed down into her eyes.

"I love you so much," he said with moist eyes.

"I love you too, honey," Saphire replied, wondering how in the hell she'd talked her way into this.

After Clay was gone, Saphire retrieved the Sunday paper from the front door and made her way to the breakfast table. She spread the paper over the glass tabletop, pulled out all the sales sheets and began to look them over. Saphire's mind wandered back to her and Clay's conversation this morning. It wasn't like she never wanted a baby, but she thought the timing just wasn't right. Actually, that wasn't the truth at all. The real reason she was so dead set against it was because a baby would slow her down considerably. How could she dart out on her secret sexcapades with a baby in tow? Speaking of sexcapade, she had one to attend to in a couple of hours.

Bobby had invited her out for brunch and she'd accepted. She and Bobby had run into each other a few weeks ago. The man still looked as good as the first day she met him all those years earlier at the gas station. After a brief talk about their lives over the years, they decided to get together and finish catching up. Saphire knew the catching up part would yield more than just talking, and she couldn't wait. Bobby wasn't as good as Joe in bed, but he came in second, easily.

A couple of hours and a quickie later, Saphire found herself in a hotel room with Bobby. The man hadn't lost his touch. Bobby turned over and

kissed her lightly on the lips.

"Damn, woman, I missed you so much," Bobby gasped as he gazed down at her.

Saphire smiled at Bobby's confession. "Yeah, it has been a while, hasn't it?" She snickered as she pulled the sheet away from her sweaty body and stood up.

"Where are you going?" Bobby called out.

"I've got to get going, Bobby. Clay will be back from church soon, and I must be home by the time he gets there," she answered as she stepped into the shower.

Afterward, toweling down, Saphire walked out of the bathroom and right into Bobby, who had failed to get dressed. The man was standing in front of her in the nude, sending more chills down her spine than cold air on a winter day.

"Is there any way I can change your mind? I want you, Saphire," Bobby whispered as he reached for her.

Saphire moved aside. She was tempted to fall into Bobby's arms again, but her obligations wouldn't let her. Her marriage, believe it or not, was the most important thing in her life, and she wasn't about to get stupid. "Sorry, Bobby, but I got to go now." She dressed quickly.

As she was about to walk out the door Bobby asked, "When can we do this again?"

"Soon," she whispered as she shut the hotel room door behind her.

On her way home, she decided to make a detour. She hadn't spoken to her sister Gade in a few days, and she needed to see her baby sister. Gade's home wasn't as extravagant as hers, but it was very nice and in the West Gate subdivision, which boasted well-manicured lawns and homes with pools in back. Saphire pulled in behind Gade's pearl-white Expedition. She got out and walked up the stone driveway.

As she reached the porch with two white columns standing tall, Saphire realized she and her sister were truly blessed. Josey had done a damned good job in raising them by herself. Images of how they could have been on the system, raising two or three babies in the projects, floated across

Saphire's mind.

Lamonte opened the door with a wide smile. "Hello, sister-in- law, what a surprise," he said, stepping aside and letting her in. "Good seeing you," Lamonte continued as he closed the door.

"Good seeing you, too, Lamonte, I hope I'm not interrupting anything. I just took a chance that you two would be home, it being Sunday and all."

"Yeah, well, usually we would have been in church, but Gade hasn't been feeling well lately."

Saphire's heart did a flip. "Tell me, Lamonte, she's not sick, is she?" Saphire asked with concern.

"No, not physically, but she has been kind of down. This baby thing is getting to her. You know we have been trying for months now, and so far she is not pregnant. I think she feels as if she may never be," Lamonte said sadly.

Just then, Brice came flying down the wrought iron spiral stairs. "Aunt Saphire!" he yelled, running into her arms.

"Hey there, buddy," Saphire said, reaching down and giving him a warm hug.

"Did you bring me something, Aunt Saphire?" he asked breathlessly.

"Brice, watch your manners, young man. Your aunt is not obligated to bring you things every time she sees you," Lamonte chastised.

"It's all right, Lamonte, my buddy knows I'm always thinking about him." Saphire smiled genuinely as she reached into her large Gucci bag. She pulled out a bag containing a Spiderman coloring book along with crayons and a Spiderman figure she'd purchased days ago, but never got around to giving him.

Gade heard the commotion as she made her way into the living room. "My, my, what brings you here, sis?" Gade asked, giving Saphire a peculiar look.

"Am I not allowed to visit my family?" Saphire smiled.

"Well, I'm going to leave you two alone," Lamonte laughed, taking Brice by the hand. "Come on, my boy, let's go do some coloring." He chuckled as he and Brice headed up the stairs.

Gade moved over to the ecru plush couch and sat, folding her legs up under her. Saphire joined her and crossed her legs.

"Now what's the real reason for this visit?" Gade questioned as she stared into her sister's eyes.

"Lamonte told me you weren't feeling well, but that hasn't damaged your keen insight, I see," Saphire sneered.

Gade let out a cool breath. "I feel fine, it's just…"

"Yeah, I know, the baby thing," Saphire finished. "I'm having the same problem, sort of." Saphire sighed.

Gade took in Saphire's serious expression. "Are you and Clay trying to have a baby?" Gade asked in surprise.

"No, well, I guess…I don't know," Saphire said, frustrated. "Clay wants a baby like yesterday, but as for me, I'm not so sure." Saphire chewed on her bottom lip as she waited on Gade for an answer.

"Saphire, you and Clay have been married a long time now. Most couples have their first child within a year or two of marriage. It has been…"

"Yeah, yeah, I know, six years. Clay reminds me of the fact almost every day," Saphire said, shifting in her seat. "Now he thinks I don't love him because I won't give him a child."

"You do love him, don't you?" Gade asked cautiously.

"What kind of question is that?" Saphire huffed. "Of course I love my husband."

"I'm sorry, Saphire, I know you do," Gade responded quickly. She just wasn't so sure because she knew in her heart of hearts, Saphire had never stopped cheating on the man.

After all these years, she just couldn't shake the feeling that something happened between Saphire and Joe. The remembrance of the diamond earring she found in Joe's bedroom never left her mind, even after all these years. That earring belonged to Saphire, but there was no way she could prove it.

Saphire snapped her fingers. "Gade, where are you?"

"Huh? Oh, I'm sorry, Saphire, I guess I zoned out for a moment,"

Gade stammered. "I've just got a lot on my mind," she murmured as she repositioned the cushions. "Let's get back to what you have done now."

"Who said I've done anything?"

"Oh, um, what were we talking about then? Oh yeah…children," Gade stuttered. "Clay wants a baby? I don't see a problem here, Saphire. You knew from the beginning Clay loved kids and he wanted them, so give the man a baby."

"It's easy for you to say. You are a gem at motherhood. I just wish it was as easy for me," Saphire choked out.

"Just think about it, Saphire…" Gade's voice faded then she cleared her throat. "You got a damned good husband who loves you very much. The man has shown you that for years. Nothing you ever wanted, Clay hasn't provided. Now all he's asking you for is a child. A precious child you both could love and nurture. A child is so precious, Saphire. All the money in the world can't compare to the love of a child." Gade's voice quivered, and for a brief moment, a disturbed look crossed her face. "My God, Saphire, don't you think he deserves the opportunity to be a father?"

Saphire stared at her sister as if she had two heads. "Yes, but not now!" Saphire spat.

"If not now, then when? A woman only has a certain amount of time before her clock stops ticking," Gade said with her voice rising. Shaking her head, she added, "Oh, how naive of me. Giving your husband a child would ruin your little sexcapades," Gade fumed while Saphire gasped. "You're still cheating on your husband, aren't you?" Gade asked point blank.

Saphire's face burned with shame. "How did you know?"

"I knew you were," Gade said, jumping up from her seat. "Saphire, what the hell is wrong with you? You are going to end up ruining your marriage with your trifling ass ways!" she shouted.

"It's not like that, Gade."

"So what is it like? Tell me. Help me to understand this thing that keeps you hopping in bed with different men?"

Saphire shot up. "I can't talk about this right now, I've got to go. Clay

will be home from church soon," she stated, picking up her designer bag.

"We are so not finished with this conversation, Saphire." Gade warned.

"I know, I will call you later, Lil' Sis," Saphire murmured as she bolted for the door.

Gade ran after her and stopped Saphire in the doorway. "Listen, Saphire, we've both made big mistakes in the past. But we've got good men now, who love us. Our marriages are worth holding on to. Think about that before you ruin yours, please think about that." Gade had fresh tears in her eyes.

As Saphire walked down the driveway she wondered who Gade was really talking to. Was it her or was she responding to some secret demons of her own?

* * * * *

Life returned to normal, or as normal as it could be for Gade. Seeing Lamonte and Brice rolling around in the grass, laughter and joy in their voices, tugged at Gade's heart as she sat on the deck. It was a beautiful, but typical Saturday afternoon, and they had just finished eating hot dogs and fries. It was Brice's favorite meal other than pizza. Gade thought back to the conversation she'd had with Lamonte a few days after finding out the status of his fertility test. She turned the whole thing around. She told Lamonte the test results showed it was she who had the so-called problem, and not him. Her tubes were blocked, she lied evenly. Lamonte grimaced, pulled her into his arms and cried right along with her. He assured her of his love, saying that as long as he had her and Brice in his life, they were all he needed to be happy. A silent tear fell down her cheek as she laid the romance novel she was reading on the wicker table after hearing Brice call out to her.

"Mommy, Mommy, look at me!" Lamonte had him seated on his shoulders and Brice had his arms outstretched. "Mommy, I'm the tallest boy in the whole world!" he yelled, staring at the clear blue sky. Lamonte turned him around and around and then they both fell to the ground, dizzy.

"Who loves you, kid?" Lamonte chuckled, holding Brice tightly.

"My daddy!" Brice sang out, giggling as Gade's heart skipped a beat.

COMING BACK TO MY ROOTS

Joe Nathan was on the plane, heading to Los Angeles, California. It had been five years and three months since he'd stepped foot in the city of angels. Joe had been in treatment for the past two of those five years. He had a lot of feelings to sort through. His parents' marriage breaking up, the hate he held inside for his father's mistress, his mother's breakdown, and the birth of his baby brother Lamonte was quite a lot for an eleven-year-old boy to digest, according to his therapist. He said Joe took on the blame of his parents' divorce.

In rebellion, he let his emotions grow out of control, harboring hate, and distrust. His therapist concluded that the way he treated women came from the emotional detachment he felt due to the abandonment of his family. He had been hurt deeply, and in return, he would not let anyone into his space, fearing the rejection that doing so would bring.

As far as his baby brother was concerned, he loved him. No matter how much hatred he held in his heart, Lamonte was the cushion that soaked up his love in spite of everything else. A childhood memory crossed his mind. It was Halloween, and Irene was taking Lamonte trick or treating along with a couple of the neighborhood kids. Lamonte was dressed as a cowboy. The vision of him in that outfit brought a smile to Joe's face. Irene had asked if he wanted to come along. He was a teenager then, and he felt like he was too old for that. He answered her, with a cold voice, "No." So they left. His father was still at work, so he had the house all to himself. Joe went upstairs and turned his boom box on full blast.

About an hour later, Lamonte came banging on his door with tears streaming down his face. Some neighborhood bullies had stolen his big bag of candy. Through his tears, Lamonte described the bullies to him. Joe was furious. He ran past Lamonte and Irene, who had just come up the

stairs.

"Joe Nathan, leave it alone!" he heard Irene yell after him as he headed out the door, but he did not stop.

He searched the neighborhood until he found them hassling a couple of kids on a corner lot five blocks from where Joe lived.

Joe Nathan punched both of the boys in the face, retrieved Lamonte's bag of candy, and gave the other two kids back the candy the bullies had taken from them. When he came home, Lamonte was sitting down at the kitchen table with a sad look on his face. But when he saw him, his eyes lit up like the sun. Joe Nathan gave him back his candy and Lamonte shouted in his little voice, "See, Mommy, I told you my big brother would get my candy back!" Lamonte ran over to him and wrapped his small arms around his waist.

Tears stung Joe Nathan's eyes as he heard the flight attendant giving instructions. The plane was about to land. As he stared out the window, taking in the twinkling lights of the city, Joe contemplated his decision to return home, and he hoped like hell he'd made the right one.

* * * * *

After Joe left town a few years back, Lamonte had accepted the truth that he would never enjoy the kind of relationship he had wanted with him all of his life. He tried so hard to see things Joe's way. He imagined what he would have done or how he would have felt if he'd had to walk in Joe's shoes. He knew the weight he carried, but he loved him, and so did their father. Why wasn't their love enough for him? Thinking about how Joe missed out on so many important events in his life made him sad. The family get-togethers they'd had over the years, his wedding, and the birth of his only nephew.

Even though he felt the sadness, the feelings of anger would always surface. How could a man hurt his family that way? He was a selfish bastard. Why couldn't he think of someone else other than his damned self? He picked up the paper cup, crushed it and then threw it in the trash can. It was lunch time, and he was preparing to leave. He needed to take

a drive, clear his head, he thought as he went out the office door. The Brother's Construction had grown tremendously. They had moved a year ago from the cramped office downtown into a huge building that offered a modern cafeteria with Southern meals prepared daily for the workers. His mother ran the show in that department. Since retiring from her job, the cafeteria kept her busy.

"Hey, Boss, where are you heading?" Billy asked as he looked up from his plate of fried chicken and mac-n-cheese.

"Looks like you will soon be going to Weight Watchers if you keep eating like that!" Lamonte joked as he clapped Billy on the shoulder.

Billy, a short stocky man with reddish-brown hair, was a good employee. He worked very hard, and Lamonte appreciated him. In fact, Billy had stepped into Joe's position since he'd left. Billy was smart, but no one could take the place of Joe.

"Right, man, right," Billy chuckled, placing his fork onto his half-finished meal. He placed his pale hands on his big belly and exclaimed, "You have to blame all of this on your mother. The lady can burn, man," Billy crooned as the three other men seated with him began to laugh.

"Boss, you got a phone call in your office," Gina said, breathlessly as she ran to catch up with him.

Gina Torres was his new secretary. She was fresh out of college and smart as a whip. She kept his company running as smooth as a well-oiled machine, and most of the time, he thought he was lucky to have her. But at other times, he wasn't so sure.

Gina was a blond-haired, blue-eyed bombshell. Beautiful failed to describe her. The guys ragged on him all the time for hiring such a beauty queen. Weighing the pros and cons, Lamonte figured a pretty face brought in more business, and it was evident that he was right. Clients hung around a little longer just to drool over Gina.

"Thanks, Gin," he said as he made his way back to his office, which was double the size of his old one. Lamonte pressed the red button flashing on the office phone. "Lamonte Singletary," he answered.

"Hello, baby brother, remember me?" Joe Nathan bellowed.

"Barely," Lamonte murmured as he pushed his office door shut. He didn't want his employees to overhear his conversation, in case he ended up cursing his brother out.

"What do you want, Joe, and make it quick. I was on my way out the door," Lamonte grumbled into the phone.

"I want to...apologize...for everything," Joe Nathan said brokenly.

"You're apologizing to me?" Lamonte asked, wide-eyed. "Are you in jail with a life sentence hanging over your head? And by the way, did you find Jesus there, like most convicts?" Lamonte sneered.

"Hell, no, I'm not in jail, and I don't need jail to find Jesus. Jesus may have found me, have you ever thought about that?" Joe Nathan returned.

"So are you a Buddhist now or a Jehovah's Witness?" Lamonte laughed bitterly.

"Come on, brother, I am serious about this. I want to make amends for how I treated you and your mom all these years. I'm sorry, man, truly I am." Something about the way Joe's voice sounded made Lamonte realize his brother was serious.

"Joe," Lamonte said as he ran his hand over his forehead.

"Wait, man, let me finish. I love you, Lamonte, and I want to be the kind of brother I should have been to you...if you'll give me the chance."

Lamonte slumped down in his black leather office chair and exhaled. "Listen, man, don't play with me. Don't come back into my life, only to leave me hanging again. I'm through with your yo-yo kind of life."

Joe Nathan interjected, "No man, I'm tired of running. What I've been running from all these years was really myself. I can't hide from the man in the mirror, even though I tried." After a slight pause, Joe confessed, "Believe it or not, I've been in treatment for the last two years. My head is on straight now, man, and I want to be a part of my family. All I'm asking for is a second chance. You do believe in second chances, don't you?"

Lamonte closed his eyes and lowered his head. How long had he waited to hear those words coming from Joe? It felt like a lifetime. Taking a long breath, he replied, "Yeah, I guess I do. So when are you coming back to LA?"

"I'm already in LA, Lamonte," Joe revealed.

Surprised, but relieved, Lamonte said, "Okay, that's great, man. Um, I want to see you, brother. Come over for dinner tonight. I want you to meet your sister-in-law. You will love her," Lamonte rambled.

Joe paused. *I already have, many times.*

"And your nephew, Brice. He is five years old now. I can hardly believe it. And the little guy doesn't even know you," Lamonte continued.

"Whoa, man, let's do this another time."

"I knew you were faking me out," Lamonte quickly returned.

"No man, I'm not ready for all of that yet. Just give me a little more time. There are things I need to talk to you about before I meet the rest of the family. Let me make things right between us first," Joe pleaded.

Lamonte inhaled. "Okay, if that's what you want."

"I'm going to get settled, and we will meet at the end of the week," Joe said earnestly.

"Don't disappear on me," Lamonte warned.

"Lamonte, listen to me, man. No matter what happens between us from here on out, I'm in it for you, and I'm not going anywhere," Joe said firmly. "Now let me ask you a question."

"Shoot, man."

"Can I have my old job back?"

Lamonte ran his hand over his short military-style haircut as a broad smile creased his lips. "Your job was always here, Joe. It was you who was absent," he finished as tears stung his eyes.

Lamonte stopped by his parents' home after work. He knew his mother Irene couldn't care less about the news he had to tell them, but he was sure his father would be elated. Since Joe left, he had only contacted their father twice a year, on their father's birthday, and Christmas. Now maybe with Joe back in town, they could all sit down and resolve the ill feelings that had been plaguing the family for years. Lamonte pulled in the driveway and bounced up the stairs to the two- story stucco home he grew up in. So many memories flooded his mind, both good and bad. He knocked lightly on the door before entering. He always used his own key when he came

to his parents' home. He let out a small chuckle as he remembered his momma threatening to take it away from him. She said one day he might walk into a scene with her and his daddy getting busy. Now that was a sight he definitely wasn't interested in seeing.

"Anybody home?" he yelled out.

"I'm in the kitchen," his mother answered.

"Where's Pops?" Lamonte asked as he gave his mother, Irene, a kiss on the cheek.

"Where he always is, in the garage with that old car of his," Irene quipped. His dad was the proud owner of a 1987 red Chevy he kept in mint condition. The young men around town bombarded his father with offers to buy the car, but he turned them all down. Irene walked over to the screen door leading down to the garage. "James, Lamonte's here!" she yelled down. She came back inside and found her son peering into the fridge, taking out leftovers. "Some things never change," Irene said, crossing her arms over her pink-and-white lounge dress as she smiled at her son. "Give it here," Irene instructed, taking the food out of his hand and making her way over to the microwave. She began to warm it up for him. Looking over her shoulder, she asked, "You're sure this won't spoil your appetite? I don't want Gade calling here blessing me out for feeding her husband." She laughed.

"Momma, Gade will have no problem with me eating over here, trust me," Lamonte assured her as he sat down at the round glass kitchen table.

Just then, Lamonte's father entered the kitchen. James was a tall man, well over six feet with balding hair and thick eyebrows. He was ruggedly handsome like a lumberjack. He carried Musky, a small brown Terrier with black eyes that he'd picked up a few months ago from the pound.

After greeting each other, the men turned their conversation to the dog and Irene felt completely left out. "Uh, can we talk human for a change?" she said with discernible irritation in her voice.

"Your momma thinks I done threw her away since I got Musky." James laughed deeply.

Irene pursed her lips. "I'm sure Lamonte didn't come all the way out

here to talk about that dog of yours, James." Irene smirked as she sat beside her son.

"Well, son, what's going on?" James asked, joining them.

"I don't know exactly where to begin," Lamonte started uneasily. Lamonte turned to his father who had just let Musky go. The dog ran under the table with his tail wagging.

"That's his favorite hiding spot." James laughed.

Lamonte smiled and then turned his attention back to his parents' waiting faces. "Pops, when was the last time you heard from Joe Nathan?"

Irene grimaced but said nothing.

"Let's see, about a couple of months ago. Why, son, is anything wrong?" he asked, leaning forward as a worry line creased his brow.

"Relax, Pops, Joe Nathan is fine. In fact, I just spoke with him a few hours ago."

James let out a breath while Irene sucked one in. She drew back her lips at the mention of that man's name. He had been trouble since the first day she laid eyes on him. "Well, what did he want?" Irene scoffed as she stared into Lamonte's eyes.

"He's here, Momma, in LA. Not only that, but he's coming back to our business."

"Say what?" James bellowed.

"Yes, Pops. We had a long talk, and while it's a long road we have to travel, we decided to start acting like the brothers we should have been years ago."

Lamonte could see a tear form in his father's dark eyes. "That's all I ever wanted, son," James mumbled, leaning back in his chair.

Irene clapped her hands together. "Good performance, James, and hats off to you, Lamonte." With a stern expression she growled, "If you two believe that crap Joe Nathan dished out, both of you need some help."

Lamonte knew from the start, convincing his mother that his brother had changed wasn't going to be easy. "Momma, Joe is a different man. He apologized for all the hurt he has caused and he wants all of us to be a real family now. That's why he came back, to set things straight with all of us."

"Bull crap!" Irene yelled out. "You may have bought into his lies, but I haven't and I'm not going to. I know that evil twisted mind of his and believe me, he hasn't changed one damned bit."

"Irene, you don't know that!" James shouted.

"Don't be so gullible, James," Irene shouted back.

"Stop it, you two!" Lamonte ordered. "I didn't come here to start an all-out war. I want this family to come to grips with all of our past hurts and move on. Is that too much to ask?" Lamonte's eyes darted between the two. Irene balled her fists, while James just stared, his head down. "Joe is not the same man that he was when he left here, Mom. He's sought help to deal with his emotional problems."

James dipped his head into his hands. With a whimper, he uttered, "Oh God, it's all my fault. I should have handled things differently back then."

Lamonte stood and placed his hand on his father's shoulder. "No Pops, don't blame yourself. You never abandoned Joe Nathan like some men would have done. You raised him and you raised me. I think you did a damned good job," he commended.

"But I should have known my oldest son was in so much pain," James cried, looking up. "No wonder he acted out the way that he did," he added.

"Dr. Phil and his assistant," Irene sneered to her husband and son. She got up from the table and filled a glass with water, and took a big gulp. Looking at the men, she muttered, "Both of you are giving me a headache with this sympathy talk for poor old Joe Nathan." With a nod of her head, she addressed her husband. "Joe Nathan knew exactly what he was doing, James. He wanted you to leave me and go back to Roewena. A woman you fell out of love with."

Lamonte wasn't so sure he wanted to hear this conversation. It made him uncomfortable.

James said softly, "I did love her, Irene. She was the mother of my firstborn. I just wasn't in love with her anymore." He stared back at his wife.

"So your leaving Roewena caused Joe Nathan to flip out and act a fool for all these years. Please, James, give me a break." Irene sighed.

She walked back to the table and reclaimed her seat, shaking her head. "Do you know how many children grow up with divorced parents?" she asked as she glared at Lamonte and then her husband. "My own momma left my daddy and I didn't go around trying to hurt everyone in my path."

"Momma, Joe Nathan had issues that ran deeper than you both knew about. Some people handle things well and some don't. I believe him, Momma, and I am going to give him all of my support, and I suggest you do the same," Lamonte said.

His father's face filled with joy. The idea that after all these years, his boys would be together again made him very happy. On the other hand, Irene had a face straight from hell.

Noticing his mother's demeanor, Lamonte spoke gently. "Momma, you taught me the principle of forgiveness. You said if we don't learn to forgive others, how can we expect to be forgiven? Do you remember, that, Momma?" Lamonte asked solemnly.

Irene quickly looked away. He continued, "I remember you told me that when my best friend Richard and I had a falling out in high school." He watched his mother's tight expression. "I think it's time we did just that in this family, don't you?" Lamonte asked, standing up and putting his arms around his mother.

Tears welled up in her eyes. She turned to look at her son. Her face softened for a moment, then hardened. "Sometimes, son, forgiveness comes a little too late," she mumbled as she stood up and left the kitchen.

A GHOST FROM THE PAST

Joe waited in the parking lot in front of Styles by Saphire. He smiled at all of the beautiful ladies who went in looking like tired old housewives and emerged like models after the treatment they received. He lit up a cigarette and inhaled. He took a couple more puffs, then threw the butt to the ground and mashed it with his size eleven shoe. He wasn't a chain smoker, but he'd found himself smoking a lot lately. As he waited, he had a tight feeling in his chest. Making amends may cost him the very thing he hoped to salvage. A relationship with the woman he loved, and always would. Finally, he saw her. She was just as beautiful as he remembered. Saphire strolled out of the salon and headed towards her car. Joe Nathan watched the subtle sway of her hips as she walked.

Memories crept into his mind of all the times they shared. "Saphire!" he called out and she stopped abruptly.

She turned and focused. It was like she was looking at a ghost. "Joe?" she asked with uncertainty.

"Yes," Joe uttered, walking towards her.

They stared at each other for a moment without saying a word as memories took them back in time.

Saphire broke the spell. "When did you get back in town?"

"A few days ago," Joe answered, stepping even closer to her.

Saphire inhaled the masculine scent of Joe. It brought back sweet remembrances she thought she'd buried years ago. "You're looking damned good, Saphire." Joe smiled.

"Thanks, Joe, and you are just as fine as ever," Saphire said, trying to choose her words carefully. The effect Joe was having on her made her tingle.

"Can I buy you a cup of coffee? We need to talk," he asked in a serious

tone she'd never heard before.

She stared at him as if she could read into his mind. She was taken aback at his abruptness. "Is something wrong, Joe?" she asked bluntly.

"Let's just say a lot went wrong," he responded.

Seated at Georgia's cafe, a small but elegant restaurant on the west side of Crenshaw, they both sipped cappuccinos. Joe leaned in. "Saphire, I have so many things I want to tell you and I...I...just don't know where to begin." He stammered as he set his cup back onto the table.

Joe's perplexed expression made hairs stand up on Saphire's arms. What was this man going to tell her? Was he infected with some dread disease he'd passed on to her, and now he was going to ask her to get herself checked out? She'd seen a movie like that a few days ago on Lifetime. That movie had been the deciding factor in her vow to stay faithful to her husband for the rest of her life. Saphire's heart was beating so hard, she thought Joe would be able to see it through the white satin blouse she was wearing. Moving a lock of hair away from her face, she answered, "Whatever it is, Joe, just spit it out." She tightened her grip on the coffee mug as she waited.

Joe took a deep breath and leaned back in his seat. "Saphire, we have a lot more in common than you think. In all reality, I guess you could say we are actually family."

Saphire's eyes narrowed. "Now what's that supposed to mean?" she asked flatly. With a shake of her head she murmured, "I don't get this, Joe, so stop playing games and give it to me straight."

"You want it straight, well, here it is, my friend." Joe pulled himself forward. "Saphire, your sister's husband is my brother."

Saphire turned two shades of brown as she tried to process his statement. "Lamonte...is...your brother?" she stammered with a raised brow.

"Well, actually, my half-brother, we share the same father," he clarified.

With a tilt of her head, Saphire retorted, "That's a bunch of bull, Joe. You are lying through your teeth. Why are you tripping on me like this?" she bellowed.

"I'm telling you the truth," he answered firmly.

Saphire swallowed hard. She knew Lamonte had a brother named Joe Nathan. But he never came around. He was the black sheep of the family who left years ago and lived somewhere in South Carolina. That is, until he decided to come back for a hot minute to help Lamonte get his business off the ground. She'd never seen the man, and now here Joe was telling her it was him. This was sounding ludicrous.

Joe watched Saphire as she tried putting two and two together. He knew she was perplexed, and he wasn't even finished yet.

"Wait a damned minute," Saphire huffed as her mind stabilized. "Your name is Joe Burrels. Lamonte's last name is Singletary, so how on earth can you say that you are his brother?" Saphire hissed.

"I took on my mother's maiden name, which is Burrels."

Saphire fell back into her seat. "I don't believe you, Joe. You're trying to run some kind of crazy game on me," she spewed.

"This is no game, babe," Joe uttered solemnly. "There was a lot of bad blood between Lamonte's mother and myself. Family problems that ripped everyone apart for years. That's why I kept my distance," he said, picking up his cup and taking a sip.

Saphire's mind drifted back to the first day she laid eyes on Joe. It was at Clay's family picnic so many years ago. "When we met at the park and you were with Gade..." Saphire's voice stuck in her throat when she said her sister's name. "Oh my God! Does Gade know about this?"

"No, not yet, but in a few hours she will."

Saphire felt hot all of a sudden. She gulped down the ice water the waitress had placed on their table. "That day in the park, you said you were there with a friend, but you were visiting your family as well. I remember that clearly."

"I lied," Joe replied. "My family had no clue I was even here in LA. I'd been here for months without them knowing."

"You mean to tell me that you were in town and never contacted your family, not even once?" Saphire asked in disbelief. Joe nodded his head.

"This is sick, sick, sick!" Saphire exclaimed.

"Relax, Saphire, I'm not a maniac, I assure you. I was just a confused

soul at that time," Joe Nathan confessed. "Back then, I had so much going on inside my head. I didn't care what I did or who I did it to."

"Of course you didn't give a damn. How could you, Joe? You knew that you were dating your brother's girlfriend and you kept on seeing her anyway?" Saphire shrieked.

"You're wrong about that, Saphire," he said, taking her hand in his. "I didn't know at first, I swear. I found out a few months later. I didn't know about Gade and Lamonte until just before their wedding."

Pulling her hand out of his, Saphire said, "That's a stone-cold lie because Gade said she told you all about her boyfriend who was in the service and you didn't have a problem dating her. You knew, you had to know." Saphire's voice was shaky now. Her body began to tremble.

Joe fell silent. He just stared at her with a vacant look in his eyes that chilled her to the bone. She was glad that they were seated in a public place. Otherwise, she would have been long gone. Finding courage, she took in a deep breath to calm her nerves. "I believe you knew damned well you were screwing your brother's girlfriend and you kept right on doing it, just for the hell of it." She spewed this at him with disgust.

Joe Nathan glared at her. "Just like you kept right on screwing me, your sister's boyfriend," he said. Saphire could only stare at Joe with her mouth wide open. "Don't go throwing stones, baby, we both would die now, wouldn't we?" Joe held Saphire's gaze.

"Why did you do this, Joe? You knew Lamonte was your blood. Why did you do this to all of us? I don't understand. Why didn't you just come clean with us years ago. Why now, Joe?" Saphire cried as tears slipped down her cheeks.

He exhaled as if he'd been holding his breath. "I've hurt a lot of people in my past. I'm not proud of what I've done, Saphire, and that's why I am here to make amends for my mistakes and get on with my life. I'm going to tell my brother about my relationship with Gade and I'm also going to tell Gade about us," he stated firmly.

"About us?" Shaking her head, Saphire stated, "No way in hell are you going to tell my sister a damned thing about us."

"Why not, don't you think she has a right to know the truth?" Saphire again shook her head, now in disbelief. "Joe, we haven't been together in years. We can let bygones be bygones. Let sleeping dogs lie," she pleaded.

"I can't, Saphire, my brother needs to know, and so does your sister. They have the right to know, and I want to disclose everything. I need a clean slate, for once in my life!"

"No, Joe, what you really want is to destroy people's lives in your warped way of redeeming yourself. I can't believe any of this is happening to me right now," Saphire gasped as she took a gulp of water.

"It is happening, and it is as real as the seat you're sitting on," Joe Nathan replied as his eyes remained fixed on her face.

Saphire lowered her head. "Oh my God, I feel as if I'm on The Jerry Springer Show." Saphire laughed bitterly. "But there is not a damned thing that is funny, is there?" she asked under her breath.

"I'm sorry, Saphire, really I am," Joe whispered, touching her hand. "I loved you for such a long time. I wanted things to work between us but you…you were determined to marry Clay," he said with an edge to his voice.

"You were dating my sister, for crying out loud. How could we possibly have ended up together?" Saphire asked wildly. The air thickened between them as each contemplated their thoughts. Images from the past filled their minds as the reality of their future lay hanging in limbo. "Gade told me you said you loved her. So which is it, Joe? Did you love Gade as well as me?"

Joe hesitated for a moment. His lips parted, but he said nothing. Saphire pulled away. "You loved us both, didn't you?" Saphire gasped as she held her hand to her mouth.

Joe reached out and touched her hand. "Get your hands off me!" she demanded.

"You know something, I think both of you are just as sick as I was," Joe sneered as he leaned into Saphire. "There is something else I think you need to know, my righteous sister. Before my brother married your sister, she and I slept together." Saphire's eyes widened as she stared at him with a disbelieving look. "In fact, it happened just a few days before the glorious

event," he gloated.

"Liar!" Saphire spat.

"No, baby, this is no lie. I slept with your baby sister right before she walked her pretty little self down that aisle. So you see, I'm not alone in this deception, this sick game, as you called it," Joe scoffed as he leaned back in his seat.

Saphire fought for control as her thoughts raced. She and Gade sleeping with Joe simultaneously was too much for her to accept. Yes, in the beginning, it was fun for her, just a diva's game she played. But later, she realized it was absolutely wrong. She was certain Gade had long ago ended all contact with Joe. So who was fooling who? Saphire thought as her mind ran over all the possibilities.

Joe's voice brought her back to the present. "At least I can say I've been in therapy for the past two years to deal with this mess, but tell me, Saphire, how do you sleep at night?"

Saphire's eyes filled with contempt as she watched the self-righteous grin on his face. All of this was too much for her to handle, and if she could get away with it, she would kill him right then and there.

Joe's expression changed. He knew Saphire held him in contempt and he wanted to salvage some part of what they used to have. In a serious tone he said, "I know you must hate the hell out of me right now, but I came back to face my demons. I want to apologize to everyone that I've hurt in my past and the first is you, my love."

"Don't you dare mention the word love in this. You don't even know the meaning," Saphire hissed. With a low breath she asked, "As of now, Lamonte doesn't know about this?"

"No, but he will this weekend. He invited me over to his home, to meet his family. Can you imagine that?" Joe answered with a devilish grin."

Saphire couldn't believe what she was hearing. "You can't do that, Joe, you just can't," she bellowed. Holding back tears she choked, "Everything is going great in our lives. Gade and I have never been as close as we are now. My husband and I are planning on having a child, and we are very happy. I don't see how you think you can decide years later to walk back

into our lives and cause so much havoc just to make yourself feel good."

"You got it all wrong, baby, I'm doing this for all of us," he stated evenly.

Saphire's expression darkened. Her fear was now turning into anger. "Drop all of this crazy shit right now, Joe, and go back to South Carolina and leave us all the hell alone!" she said through clenched teeth.

"As good as that may sound to you, Saphire, I just can't. I've already spoken to Lamonte and I'm here to stay. We are partners again in our construction business." Joe smirked.

Saphire's head began to pound. "Okay, you are back in town now. Have a nice life, Joe, but don't ruin other people's lives in the process. Keep your mouth shut and stay the hell away from me and my sister," she commanded.

"Saphire, I have no other choice. Once Gade sees me, I will have to explain everything. I'm Lamonte's brother, for God's sake, and he doesn't even know that I'm already familiar with his wife," Joe reasoned with a nod of his head. "So you see, all of this has to be resolved here and now. There is no other way out, I'm afraid."

Shaking her head Saphire blasted, "I won't accept this. I can't accept it! We've got to come up with another plan."

"What plan?" Joe Nathan asked with tired eyes. Jet lag was creeping up on him.

A waiter passed their table and Saphire stopped him. "Two martinis, please," she ordered. This was going to be a long night.

THE CURTAINS HAVE OPENED

A couple of days later, Saphire and Joe sat in her office at Styles and More by Saphire. She had closed the salon for the day. The sign on her business door read closed due to illness, which was absolutely the truth. Since Joe's damning confession, she had been sick to her stomach. Clay thought she was having a nervous breakdown when she arrived home that night after a meeting with Joe. She wouldn't eat, talk, or look at him. All she wanted to do was go straight to bed. The next morning, she mumbled an excuse to Clay about having a virus and not wanting to be bothered. Time seemed to stand still as they waited for their important guest. She knew her sister would be dumbfounded, as she had been. She and Joe exchanged nervous glances as they heard footsteps on the other side of the door.

Gade knocked lightly on the door. Saphire crossed her office to open it. "Saphire, what's up with you, and why are you closed today? The sign says closed due to illness, who's sick?" Gade questioned, looking Saphire up and down.

"Stop with all the questions, will you, and just follow me," Saphire replied vacantly.

Joe was already seated in the brown leather chair across from her desk. He was adorned in a Kenneth Cole black satin shirt with matching trousers. His skin was smooth as butter. His light brown eyes stared in Saphire's direction, and she couldn't help but notice how sexy the man looked. She wanted to hate Joe, or Joe Nathan, as he claimed his true name was, for all the drama he was causing in their lives. But somehow, she just couldn't.

Joe Nathan's stomach was a ball of nervous energy as Gade entered the room. Just the sight of her took his breath away. She was as beautiful as the day they met in the park almost six years ago. The Michaels women

mesmerized him as he saw them both together for the very first time in years. Joe Nathan willed himself to stay focused on the matter at hand. He had to concentrate, staying within the boundaries he and Saphire had set. Damage control was what Saphire called it when they came up with their little plan last night.

Gade's heart almost failed to beat when her eyes fell upon Joe. He stood up and greeted her. "Hello Gade," he said in the same sexy voice she remembered.

"Joe, what on earth are you doing here, and why are you in my sister's salon?" Gade asked.

Saphire turned toward Gade. "Lil' Sis, as you can see, Joe is back in town…and…well, there are quite a few things he and I need to tell you," gesturing to the vacant sofa she said, "so have a seat."

Looking at her son's father made Gade tremble as if a cold draft had just blown through the room. Did Joe somehow find out about Brice, and now he was here to claim him? Fear ran through her like wildfire. Gade sat opposite Joe, her eyes never leaving his face.

"What do you want, Joe?" she asked in a cold tone. It was so cold it made Saphire blink.

Joe held her stern gaze. "Gade, I came back to make amends with everyone."

Gade clutched her Chanel purse so tightly her fingertips began to hurt. "Make amends for what?" Her eyes darted from his face to her sister's. "What in God's name are you talking about?"

Joe and Saphire exchanged glances, and then their gaze settled upon Gade's ominous stare. "You see, Lil' Sis, what Joe is going to tell you," Saphire paused as she peered into her sister's puzzled eyes. Clearing her throat, she began again, "What Joe is going to tell you now is really water under the bridge. It happened so long ago, I myself can't figure out why it should even matter." Saphire chuckled nervously. "But for some crazy reason, he wants to…confess his sins." Taking a quick glance at Joe, Saphire stuttered, "I…I…told him this was all unnecessary. What happened in the past…should stay…in the past." Swallowing the lump

in her throat, she touched the top of her sister's hand. "We've both have moved on with our lives and we are very happy now. All of this really doesn't matter anymore." She hoped Gade would agree with her.

"All of what doesn't matter?" Gade questioned. Slowly, it was dawning on Gade, this so-called lunch date was really a confession dinner that her sister and Joe wanted her to share. "You two slept together, didn't you!" Gade spat with accusing eyes. Joe remained emotionless and silent as Gade's eyes moved from his face and then back to her sister's. "Answer me, dammit!" Gade shouted.

"Yes, we have," Joe murmured. "But as Saphire said before, Gade, it all happened years ago. We were just having fun back then. We never meant to hurt anyone."

Disregarding his explanation, Gade demanded, "How many times?"

"Come on, Lil' Sis, don't go there. It doesn't matter anymore," Saphire interjected.

"Shut up, Saphire!" Gade shouted, standing up. With heavy legs she willed to move, Gade walked over to Joe. Closing the gap between them, she stared deep into his hazel eyes. The eyes of a man to whom she once gave her whole heart, mind, body and soul. "How many times have you slept with my sister?" she hissed. Joe peered over at Saphire and then his gaze focused on Gade's furious face.

"How many?" Joe chuckled as he scratched his head. Did she really expect him to tally up the times?

Gade let out a low whimper. "You know what, never mind." She dismissed it with a wave of her hand. "I don't even want to know." Tears welled in her eyes. She turned her wrath on her sister now who was perched on the edge of her office desk. "You just had to do it to me, didn't you?

Saphire stared back. "Do what?"

"Don't play stupid, Saphire." Gade grimaced. Tilting her head, she spewed out, "Every man that looked my way, you had to have him, didn't you?"

"No, Lil' Sis, that's not true," Saphire mumbled and stood.

"Liar!" Gade shouted. "I don't believe you. And while we are here

making our confessions of the soul, tell me, my dear sister, did you sleep with my husband as well? Has Lamonte been added to the long list of your bed partners?" Gade yelled out as she gave her sister a glare of contempt.

"Oh my God, no! How could you accuse me of something as crazy as that? I would never do that to you, Lil' Sis. Never." Saphire gasped.

"And why on earth not? The other men in my life weren't off limits to you, so why not him?" Gade snarled.

Saphire began to pace the floor. Maybe all of this was a mistake after all. But they all were here now, and there was no turning back. "I know you are upset but please be sensible," Saphire responded.

"Oh, I know why he was off limits to you," Gade said as if she'd had a new revelation. "You knew Lamonte wouldn't let you near him. He was a decent man with morals and you don't deal with decent men, only scum like the one who is sitting before me." Gade glanced back at Joe.

Joe felt as if Gade had stabbed him in his heart with a sharp two-edged sword. Her words were cutting, and yet so true. Saphire's eyes blazed as she looked at Gade. Trying to salvage a thread of her reputation for herself, she returned, "You can't place all the blame on me, Gade. Joe slept with the both of us with little remorse, so you have to acknowledge that fact as well. I told you from the beginning, he wasn't any good, but did you listen to me? No, you were so blind. You thought he loved you so damned much. I warned you, told you the kind of man Joe Burrels really was. If only you would have listened to me."

"But Saphire, you are my blood. Blood is thicker than water. Him," she pointed at Joe, "I can see playing me. But why did you deceive me? My one and only sister, my blood." Gade's voice dripped with pain as tears made their way down her cheeks. Wiping them away quickly, she uttered, "I knew it was you Joe was sleeping with that day I found that diamond earring of yours in his bedroom."

Gade faced Joe again. "And you denied it. You knew it was Saphire's earring all along and you lied to me, you bastard!" she shouted. "You both are conniving individuals who were hoping to keep your illicit sexing under wraps." Gade balled her fists. "You know what, I hate the sight of

both of you! Looking at you two makes me sick to my stomach!" she cried through her tears. By now, Gade was trembling with anger. Oh, how much she wanted to kill them with her bare hands. Her sister and her man carrying on behind her back. What a fool she had been.

"This is going too damned far!" Saphire exclaimed, walking over to Gade and putting her arms around her. Gade was shaking. "You don't mean that, Gade, I know you don't."

"Don't touch me!" she screamed, pushing Saphire's arms away.

"There is a lot more you don't know, Gade," Joe spoke after seeing the emotional exchange between the women.

Gade turned to him with disgust. "What else can there be, Joe? Don't tell me you slept with my mother too," she said with ice in her voice.

"Don't be ridiculous!" Joe responded, feeling anger rising up in him. Dismissing her accusation, he revealed, "My real name is Joe Nathan Singletary. I'm Lamonte's brother."

Gade felt herself sway. She could have sworn the earth moved right beneath her. She had to hold onto Saphire's office desk to steady herself. "Wh-wh-what…did…you say?" Gade stammered for clarity.

"I am Lamonte's half-brother. We share the same father. I'm the one who's been away all of this time. The one who came back to open up the business with him, the one you fell in love with," Joe Nathan managed.

Gade walked over and slapped Joe's face as hard as she could. Joe Nathan winced and then clutched his stinging jaw. "How could you deceive me like this?" Gade cried out. "My husband worships the ground you walk on, and this is how you treated him? You self-serving bastard!" Gade spat. "How could you do this and why?" Gade shouted.

"This is the reason I'm here, Gade," Joe said with his voice rising. "I want to apologize for the things I've done to all of you, and perhaps start over," he reasoned earnestly as he shook off the pain in his cheek.

"There is no amount of apologies that you can give that is going to cover what you've done, Joe, or should I say Joe Nathan." Gade smirked. "Lamonte is going to be devastated and he is not going to want anything to do with you. You are so disgusting and degrading," she sputtered with

bitterness in her voice.

It was Joe's turn to get angry. She was acting as if she had done not an ounce of wrong. He wasn't going to bear the burden of it all. Springing from his seat, he said, "I wasn't so disgusting when you slept with me days before your wedding, was I? Maybe I should tell baby brother about that while I'm confessing my soul, as you say. And I promise you, he will want nothing to do with you, either." Joe Nathan saw the hurt he'd inflicted and it stabbed him to the core. The pain he saw in her eyes pierced his heart. His voice softened. "Gade, I'm sorry, I didn't mean to…"

"Save it, Joe. You have caused us enough sorrow," Saphire lamented. Looking into Gade's eyes, Saphire said, "So it's true. Did you sleep with him before your wedding?"

Gade's shoulders slumped.

"Why didn't you tell me?" Saphire asked.

Gade's eyes fell away from Saphire's and she folded her arms. "It was a mistake, Saphire," she mumbled. "A mistake I will regret for the rest of my life." She exhaled and looked over at Joe Nathan. "Tell me something, Joe," Gade asked, staring intensely at him. "Since you bedded the both of us, which one did you like the best?" Gade said this with a cold stare.

"Lil' Sis, that's uncalled for. This is…not some sort of competition," Saphire soothed.

"Oh, is it not?" Gade spouted with a raised brow. "You could have fooled me, Saphire. One man, sleeping with two women, sisters at that. And sleeping with me," she faced Joe, "must have done so much for your ego, not to mention your libido, I may add." With pursed lips, she asked, "Tell me, did it turn you on sleeping with your brother's girl? At least I didn't know who you were, but you certainly knew who I was."

Joe remained silent. As low as he had been, he would never resort to comparing one sister against the other. And to tell who was better in bed would be doing just that.

Gade continued, "I believe all this was a sordid competition thing for you, wasn't it? Our feelings and emotions meant absolutely nothing to you," she stated, searching his face for a remnant of the man she fell so

deeply in love with. Finally, he responded.

"No, it wasn't a competition, Gade, and your feelings meant a hell of a lot to me. It's...just..." Joe Nathan paused. "If it makes you feel any better, just say it was a sick game that I should have stopped a long time ago," he stumbled over the words as he looked at them both. "You see, I fell for each of you for completely different reasons. Gade, I loved you, I know you don't believe that now, but I did. But I also knew I could never be the kind of man that you deserved. You are beautiful, loving, and so innocent."

"And what about me, Joe?" Saphire said. "You said you loved me too. Or was it all about the sex?" Tears stung Saphire's eyes realizing the web they all had spun for themselves, was entrapping them.

Joe Nathan's hazel eyes clouded as he spoke. "Saphire, you know that is not true at all. I wanted you, but you were already committed to Clay, remember? I begged you to leave the city with me, but you refused. You chose him, so I left you alone and that's when I started back with Gade."

Gade let out a soft moan. "Because you couldn't have Saphire, you came back to me!" Gade choked as pain ripped her in half. "Just like always, Saphire, men choose you first, don't they," Gade responded in defeat. "I should have known." Gade's tears trickled down her cheeks. Refusing more pain, she shook her head. "I've had enough of this charade. I'm through with both of you sorry excuses for human beings," she stated through clenched teeth. She turned on her heels. As she made her way to the door, Saphire stepped in her path. "Get the hell out of my way!" Gade ordered.

"We are not done here, Lil' Sis. Don't you walk away as if you have no sins. You haven't been the perfect little angel in this whole mess. We all have played in the dirt. Now it's time to clean up."

"This is yours and Joe's mess. Not mine. So get out of my way!"

"Surely you haven't forgotten about your husband? He can't find out about this," Saphire reminded her.

"Since when have you been concerned about my husband, Saphire? What you're really saying is that you don't want Clay to find out about your dirty little secret. For if he did, he would throw your ass out of his

house like yesterday's garbage. Poor, gullible Clay," Gade hissed, shaking her head. "I pity him for having a wife like you."

Saphire lowered her head. Gade's words hit like heavy stones. Gade continued, "If he were to find out about the sexy and dynamic Saphire screwing around with her own sister's man, he would never look at you the same again." Saphire shot daggers with her eyes at her sister's accusations. Gade was right on the money about Clay. Clay would never speak to her again, not in this life.

"Tell me something, my dear sister," Gade interrupted Saphire's reverie as she stared her squarely in the eye. "You have never been faithful to Clay, have you? I mean, in all these years you've been married to him. Was there ever a break?"

"Yes, Gade. I've been faithful to my husband for years. You've got to believe me."

"How pathetic is this? You have to beg me to take your word. What kind of trust do we have? Absolutely none," Gade concluded with disdain.

Saphire lowered her eyes from her sister's stare. If she was a magician, she surely would do a disappearing act right about now.

Looking at both of them, Gade said, "For all I know, you and Joe are still sleeping together. I feel like such a fool. A damned laughing stock. The joke is on me, isn't it?

"That's not true. I swear, Lil' Sis, I haven't seen Joe in years. Tell her, Joe."

Joe Nathan stepped in. "It's true, Gade, we have had no contact what-soever until yesterday."

Gade let out another low moan. "I can't believe this," Gade said, throwing up her hands. "You knew Joe was back in town and I'm just now finding out about it. What was it? You two had to get your little lies straight before you revealed your sinister secrets to me!" Gade cried out.

"I've had enough of this self-righteous act of yours," Saphire jumped in. "You marched in here acting like you are next to God in all your goodness. You're just as guilty as we are!" Saphire shouted. "I don't think Lamonte would be elated to learn that you slept with another man even if you didn't

know that he was his brother. The fact remains that you, my dear sister, cheated on him just days before you married him. So you see, we both have lied in so many ways, and now it all has come back in our faces. They always say, payback is a bitch, Lil' Sis." Saphire finally felt like she had the upper hand.

"And you should know a bitch when you see one. Thanks for training me," Gade returned.

"I'm not going to respond to that," Saphire said, blinking back a tear. "And as far as Joe and me conjuring up anything, you got it all wrong," she explained. "Joe wanted to tell you and Lamonte everything but I was the one who stopped him. I didn't think Lamonte or Clay need to know about any of this. It was us three who were the culprits in…this…tangled mess." With a sigh she added, "They are innocent bystanders, Gade. Why ruin their love and trust in us for something that happened so long ago? We would have nothing to gain, but a hell of a lot to lose," she reasoned.

Gade let out a painful chuckle. Shaking her head, she glared at her sister and Joe in disbelief. "I can't believe this is happening to us! Why, God, why?" she screamed.

Saphire stood in front of Gade and placed her hands on her shoulders. Peering into her eyes, she said, "Listen to me. Neither one of us is sleeping with him now. We have moved on with our lives. You and Lamonte are happy and have a wonderful son together. I'm happy with Clay, and we are planning our own little family. Let's not throw our future away by involving them in this disturbing saga of our lives, one that is over and done with."

"But how can I keep this from my husband? I'm not good at lying like you are, Saphire," Gade cried blindly. "The reason I never told anyone about that night with Joe, before my wedding, is because…" Gade stole a quick glance at Joe Nathan. Her heart was sinking like an abandoned ship in murky waters. "Is…because I buried it deep down inside." Closing her eyes she said, "I didn't want to remember it. I wanted to pretend it never even happened."

Saphire felt her own tears gather in her eyes as she mirrored her sister's

pain. "It's all in the past now. We have to concentrate on our future. You have to do this, Lil' Sis." Gade closed her eyes and sighed. "Think about your son, Brice. Do it for him."

The mention of her son's name brought Gade back to reality. Joe was his father. A secret he didn't know—and would never know, if she had anything to say about it.

"Gade, we can do this, I know we can. Joe and I have already come to an agreement. He won't say anything to our husbands." Saphire looked to Joe for assurance.

"Saphire is right, Gade. This is of our own doing, and I will keep it between the three of us, I swear," Joe reassured her.

"You see, it's all taken care of now." Saphire exhaled. Looking from Gade to Joe, she said pointedly, "We will all have dinner together Friday night at Maxie's. You will be meeting Joe for the very first time," she said evenly.

"Wait a minute. How can that be? Clay knows Joe and so does our mother," Gade interjected as her eyes narrowed.

"Let me take care of Clay and Momma," Saphire said.

Gade turned her eyes away from Joe, who was looking at her as if he wanted to take her in his arms and kiss this day away. Focusing on her sister, she retorted, "Oh, that's right, you are the Martha Stewart of lies. Clay would believe the sky was falling if you told him it was. And poor Momma, you'll probably end up blackmailing her like you did when you sent for our father."

Saphire swallowed hard. She wanted to slap the smug look right off Gade's face, but she restrained herself. Getting their stories straight was entirely too important. Ignoring Gade's insults she spoke forcefully. "Our main concern here is that our husbands will never find out about our past affairs with this man." She cut her eyes at Joe Nathan.

He cleared his throat. The women were talking about him as if he wasn't even in the room. "Ladies, I am not here to make war. I really want peace between all of us." His eyes settled on Saphire and Gade's tense faces.

"I'm just sorry you came back," Gade replied bitterly.

Joe Nathan blinked. "Before we end this thing, I'd like to ask you one important question." Gade stared at him as if he had two heads. Walking over to her, he peered into her light brown eyes once more.

She stood unmoving, planted in her spot. He whispered her name quietly, and with wet lips he asked, "What have I done for you to hate me so?"

How could she tell him the reasons behind her hatred, even after all of the years that had passed, that she'd never really stopped loving him. Deep down inside, in a hidden corner of her heart, she was ecstatic to find out that they shared a child. A child with the man she loved. In her secret world, she pretended that they were a happy family. But in reality, she knew that could never be. Yes, she loved her husband, but there was a place in her heart that craved him. Savored his love like a precious gem. Gade tried to form words, but none came from her lips as Joe Nathan's eyes sucked her in. To this day, she hated to love him. Why couldn't she stop? Saphire interrupted. The spell was broken.

"Forget him, Gade. We both are over him now, and that's what matters."

"I guess that's my cue to leave," Joe Nathan bellowed with a crooked smile. He walked over to the office door and paused. Saphire stepped aside, not wanting the remote chance of their bodies touching. Joe Nathan had an effect on her still. She too had tried to bury her feelings for him. She too had never stopped loving him.

So many nights over the years, she would dream of their love affair. His warm fingers roaming her body as if they were on a journey looking for pleasure, which he gave her so richly.

Gade stood silently as she watched Joe Nathan reach for the doorknob. His cologne, Unforgettable by Diddy tantalized the women's senses. His gaze rested on both of them, yet in different ways, sent a wave of desire racing through them. He would be unforgettable as he walked out the door, leaving his memory behind.

A BROKEN HEART

Clay stood silently, his lips trembling. The beautiful bouquet of flowers with its lovely fragrance that he once held lay at his feet. Was he hearing correctly? How could someone he loved so much orchestrate such an evil scheme? He felt pain stab at his heart like a session of little knives, slashing flesh as they went deeper within. Saphire had professed her love for him so many times. Hell, she'd married him. How could he have been so blind and so damned stupid?

He stiffened as he heard footsteps approaching. He crammed his tall frame behind the makeshift wall in the foyer of Styles and More by Saphire. He hoped like hell he wouldn't be noticed, but at his size, he wasn't so sure he could pull the trick off. Joe Nathan Burrels strolled by him, never turning his head as he exited the building. Clay wanted to snatch him right out of the high-priced Armani suit he wore and beat him down until he was just a grease spot on the thick carpet.

It took every ounce of strength within him to refrain from doing so. Now he heard voices as well as footsteps approaching. The women stood just a few feet away from him. They continued to talk and he strained his ears to hear every word. Gade was disheveled. The makeup she once wore had long ago vanished from her pretty round face. Her eyes were red and puffy as she stared into the face of his wife, who seemed as cool as a cucumber. There wasn't an inkling of any remorse, guilt or sadness. She stood calm, steady, not a hair out of place. Her smug look irked him to the point he bit down into his bottom lip and tasted blood. He fought for control, fought for his sanity.

"Don't worry, Lil' Sis, everything is going to be just fine," Saphire reassured, reaching out to give her a sisterly hug which she pulled away from.

"Don't," Gade mumbled, putting her hands up and stepping away from her. With a frown, she sputtered, "I hope you don't think all this is forgiven."

Saphire licked her lips, the strawberry lip gloss she was wearing still in place. "Of course it's going to be difficult at first, Lil' Sis, but in a few months all of this will have blown over and things will be back to normal. It will be just like the old arguments we used to have, and Lord knows we've had our share of them."

Saphire hoped to have lightened the mood a bit, but from looking at Gade's dark expression, she knew she had failed.

Gade let out a low whimper. "You just don't seem to get it, Saphire. This is not some stupid little prank you pulled in high school and got away with. You're playing with our lives and our marriages are in jeopardy here!"

Saphire exhaled. "Come on now, Gade. Don't be so dramatic. If we stick with the plan, everything will turn out just the way we want it to. Trust me," Saphire said firmly.

Gade looked at her sister in total despair. She realized that she was just wasting her strength and energy trying to get through to Saphire. And right now, she couldn't afford to waste either one. She needed her strength to get through this, and her energy to save her marriage if it all began to fall apart.

MY EYES ARE OPEN NOW

Clay sat in the dark. The street lights filtering into the building cast a soft glow on his face. He stared down at his cell, which was blowing up like crazy. His home number flashed across the screen. It was his wife calling, and he wasn't about to answer it, as he was still inside Styles and More by Saphire. The business he helped his wife attain, thanks to his grandfather's money. Before the old man passed away four years back, he'd had the chance to help them celebrate the grand opening of Styles and More by Saphire. No one could have been more proud. It meant so much to his grandfather to be able to give them something they both could cherish for years to come. He began to laugh as a single tear slid down his face. What a freakin' joke his marriage turned out to be. Saphire never loved him. How could she? Not only was she cheating on him back then, but of all people with her sister's man. What kind of woman had he married? Obviously a self-serving, lying and shallow bitch.

He replayed the scene over again in his mind. Taking in the plan they were talking about, sent chills through his body. The Plan, as they called it, was to cover up their deceitful affairs and to blind the eyes of the very ones they claimed to love. He had trouble facing what was right in front of his face. How could his own wife be this conniving? The answer to that question made him gag. He felt like a drowning man in the middle of the ocean. He could see the shore; it was so near, yet so far.

His head fell into his hands, and he wept. Slowly, as he composed himself, Lamonte's image appeared before him. His dear brother-in-law. He felt so sorry for him as well. He knew how much Lamonte had loved Gade, but he was in for a rude awakening, just as he had been. Never in his wildest dreams would he ever have thought she would cheat on Lamonte. He thought Gade was different. But how different could she be from

her very own sister. After all, they shared the same blood. Deceit flowed through their veins like rivers of water. His cell blew up again, and just like before, he didn't answer. Home was the last place he wanted to be.

ANOTHER NIGHTMARE

Gade slid quietly between the fresh, crisp cotton sheets. It was 3:00 in the morning, and she was unable to sleep so she had gone downstairs for a cup of warm milk mixed with a little brandy to calm her nerves. Back in bed, she tried closing her eyes once more and waited for the sandman to do his job and take her into a blissful and sound sleep. Instead, he led her into the clutches of a horrible nightmare. She saw her husband, Lamonte, standing before her with their son Brice in his arms. He was screaming obscenities at her as he carried him to the SUV, which was filled with luggage. She wondered why he was so upset with her, and most importantly, where were they going? She tried her best to get through to Lamonte, but he wasn't listening to her. His face was dark and stony while the face of her child was distorted like a puzzle.

She grabbed at Brice, trying to pull him out of Lamonte's arms, but he pushed her away. She stumbled back as tears raced down her cheeks. After placing Brice in the back seat, her husband then hopped in the SUV. Without giving her a second look, he sped away, leaving her standing with outstretched arms and swollen eyes.

Gade sat up and screamed. The piercing sound jolted Lamonte awake and he took his wife's trembling body into his arms. "Honey, you were having a nightmare. It's over now," he whispered as he kissed her damp face. Gade held onto Lamonte like a small, frightened child. If he only knew that her nightmare was far from over. It had only just begun.

G STREET CHRONICLES
~A NEW URBAN DYNASTY~
WWW.GSTREETCHRONICLES.COM

HOME IS WHERE THE HEART IS, OR IS IT?

Saphire had stayed up all night waiting for her husband to come home. This was so unlike Clay. Clay was dependable, truthful, and loving. He never stayed out past eleven unless they were together, and she knew that he would never put her through such anguish purposely. Her fears surfaced. Something must have happened to Clay. There was no other explanation. So at 1:00 a.m., she began calling the hospitals as well as family and friends. She even called the police, who weren't much help at all. They said he had to be missing at least 24 hours before they would even begin to look for him.

Now it was after 7:00 a.m., and still no Clay. Suddenly, Saphire heard a noise. She jumped when she saw his tall frame come into their bedroom. He found her sprawled in the middle of their bed holding the phone in one hand and her address book in the other. She was about to start calling people all over again, but instead, she flew off the bed, and into her husband's arms, kissing him fiercely.

"Oh, Clay, you had me so worried, baby! Where have you been? Why didn't you call me? I was climbing the walls!" Saphire's words tumbled out. In the midst of this, she noticed his hands hung loosely by his side. He never embraced her. He never acknowledged her tears.

Clay's eyes were dark and cold as he looked at his wife. Saphire searched his face for blood, or bruises. Surely her husband had been mugged or in an accident, but she found nothing. "Clay, what is wrong, baby? Talk to me?" she pleaded as she shook him. Still there was no reaction, no emotion. In the coldest voice she'd ever heard, her happy-go-lucky husband uttered, "I'm leaving you, Saphire. Our marriage is over." Saphire was certain her heart had stopped beating. She felt light-headed, and a gripping pain seized her.

She struggled for breath as her brain processed the information. Leaving? Marriage over. No, that couldn't be. Saphire looked into his eyes and cupped his face. "Honey…Clay…I love you. Our marriage is wonderful, baby. You're not yourself. You must not be feeling well. Come over here and sit," she cajoled as she tried to guide him towards their bed. Clay stood planted there, unmoving.

"It's over, Saphire. I'm through with you and your deceitful ways. I've had enough. I should have ended this charade a long time ago."

Saphire shook her head frantically. "Our marriage was never a charade," she spouted. "I loved you when I married you and I love you now. Please don't leave me, Clay!" she screamed as she dropped down to her knees. She wrapped her thick arms around his long legs and whimpered. She considered herself to be as classy as they come, but this man had her heart, her life, and at this moment, she wasn't too proud to beg.

"I'm sorry, baby. I'm so sorry," she moaned as tears glazed her cheeks. With his leg in a firm grip, she reasoned, "Bobby doesn't mean a damned thing to me. I swear. He never has. I don't even know why I kept seeing him. I was so stupid, Clay. You've got to forgive me. We can start all over again, baby, and have that family we both want. I love you, honey, you and only you. Please believe me," Saphire sobbed as she hung onto his pants leg.

Clay pulled his leg free, almost knocking her backward. Looking down at her with daggers in his eyes he asked, "Who the hell is Bobby?"

Saphire froze. She felt herself sinking as if she was just tossed into quicksand. Surely, he was talking about her affair with Bobby. Why else would he want to leave her? Saphire swallowed the lump that had formed in her throat. "The…the man…that I've been seeing, Clay, but it's over now," she cried, looking up at him with pleading eyes. Saphire stood up and reached out to touch him.

"Get the hell away from me!" His voice had the force of a speeding train. Saphire's arms dropped to her side. Her husband's face, etched in pain, stared back at her.

"Clay, you've got to listen to me. It's over now!" she whimpered.

"No, what's over is you and I and this farce of a marriage!" he snapped as he headed for the walk-in closet. He took out his luggage and began throwing clothes into the large suitcase.

"Stop, Clay!" Saphire cried out. "You don't mean this. I know you don't mean this. Baby, I'm sorry. I know you are upset, and I promise I will make this up to you. Clay, I will do anything you want me to. Counseling, that's it. I'll go to counseling. Anything, Clay. You just name it, baby." But all of her pleas fell on deaf ears.

Clay walked over to the walnut dresser and proceeded to take out more things, shoving them into the smaller suitcase. Saphire continued. "I can't live without you, Clay, you're my world. Please, baby, don't leave me!" she begged as she continued to sob.

Clay stopped. A shadow of irritation ran across his face. His eyes took in his wife's tear-stained face. Tilting his head, he let out a throaty and bitter laugh. "So I'm your world, huh? Was I your world when you let another man between your legs? Did my face appear in that warped mind of yours? Did the slightest feeling of guilt stab at that deceitful heart of yours?" Tears fell from his eyes, his breathing became shallow as he fought for air. "You think that I'm still your little fool, don't you? Spoon feed me more lies and I will swallow them like the good boy that I am. Well, guess what, Sugar Plum. My eyes are opened now and you leave a bad taste in my mouth."

Saphire let out a wounded moan. His words cut her so deeply. "For the record, tell me something." Clay placed his face inches away from hers. He could feel her soft breath. "How many did you have?"

Saphire's shoulders slumped and she lowered her head. She wouldn't let herself look into the wounded eyes of her husband. Lifting up her chin, he screamed, "Answer me, dammit!" The sound of his voice made her jump. Her eyes closed, but she opened them slowly. She whispered, "Two...or...three."

"Which is it, Saphire, or are you trying to decide whether or not to include your sister's ex-boyfriend Joe Nathan on the list?" Saphire could have sworn an invisible hand just wrapped itself around her throat and was squeezing the life out of her at the mention of his name.

"Uh...what? I...don't know what you are talking about," she stammered.

Clay reached over and picked up one of the empty suitcases and hurled it across the room. The suitcase hit the Victorian lamp on the nightstand and it went crashing to the floor. The lamp landed in pieces. Just like his world, he thought. "Will you please, for once in your trifling little life, stop the lyin'!" Clay screamed.

Saphire's brain was working overtime. How did he know about Joe Nathan? Did that S.O.B. double-cross her? Could he have gone to Clay first, giving him his sorry ass redemption story and now leaving her to deal with the aftermath? No, he couldn't have stooped so low. He promised her, he promised them. Saphire thought about Gade and her nephew Brice. What would happen to them if all of this was revealed?

Clay's eyes blazed with anger. He walked back to his wife and grabbed her by the shoulders. Looking her squarely in the eye, he growled, "You might as well give it up, Saphire. I know the whole sordid story. I was there in the beauty salon when you, Joe Nathan, and that sister of yours bared your dirty little souls." He gasped. His heart was racing like a man being chased by demons. "And to think I came by to take my beautiful wife out for a bite to eat. I even had a dozen roses to give to you. Oh God, I feel like a damned fool." His voice cracked. "You never loved me. I gave you everything. My love, my money, my life. And what did I get in return? A whoring woman for a wife. And to think I wanted a baby with you? There is a God and I thank him for letting me see the real you." Saphire let out a wounded cry, her eyes swollen from her tears. Clay stared into her clouded eyes. "So tell me, my beautiful and committed wife. Is it true what they say about confession being good for the soul?" he sneered. "Because if it is, I got a confession to make. The biggest mistake of my life was when I said I do to the likes of you!"

Saphire cried as Clay held her firmly by the arms. He released his grip, letting her go. He took off his gold wedding band and threw it at her. It landed in her cleavage in the silk white nightgown she was wearing. Saphire placed her hand over her chest and curled into a fetal position. Her

world was walking out on her. He proceeded to pack in silence. Once he finished, he took one last look at her.

Saphire's glazed eyes met his. "Are you going to tell Lamonte?" she managed to ask, her words barely audible. Clay stared at her and with a smug look on his face, he uttered, "I already have."

EARLY MORNING PHONE CALLS

Clay had phoned Lamonte before the crack of dawn. As Lamonte held the phone, he watched the rise and fall of Gade's chest as she slept peacefully by his side. Lamonte quickly picked up the phone the first time it rang. It was his sister-in-law Saphire looking for her husband. He assured her he hadn't seen Clay and would call if he heard from him. Now here again, the phone had rang and this time it was the person missing in action–Clay.

"Sorry to be calling you this early, man," Clay mumbled.

"Save the apologies, Clay. You're going to need every one of them for that frantic wife of yours. She called here looking for you, dude. It seems you didn't make it home last night. What's up with that?" Lamonte asked in a half-joking, half-serious tone of voice.

Clay paused a moment and then he stated, "It's a long, crazy ass story, man. But there's something you need to know."

Lamonte frowned. What did Clay have to tell him and why did he sound so grim? Lamonte clamped the phone in the crook of his neck and eased out of bed. He didn't want to risk waking Gade, so he left the bedroom and made his way down to the den.

"You're not drunk, are you?" Lamonte asked as he plopped down in the black leather La-Z-Boy chair.

"Nah, man, but I wish the hell I was, and after I finish telling you about this mess, you're going to wish you were too." Clay went through the previous day's events and the devastating news he'd heard as if he were reading a script to an upcoming movie. When he was through, Lamonte sat dazed as tears threatened to spill from his eyes.

He was so angry, yet so confused, and hurt wasn't even the word. He could comprehend the part about Saphire sleeping with his brother, even

though the situation still dazed him. But all the rest of it just didn't make sense. The idea of his wife sleeping with his brother days before their wedding ripped through him like a jagged knife. This shit was crazy. Gade knowing his brother, all of this time.

"Sleeping with him? Sleeping with him?" He kept muttering under his breath. He asked Clay a dozen times more. Was he sure about what he had heard and a dozen times his answer remained the same.

Yes, yes, and yes. So many questions. How could his brother do this to him? Hadn't he done enough already? He remembered what his mother had been telling him all these years, but he refused to listen. He didn't want to believe her words were true. Joe Nathan never gave a damn about anybody, not even him. Well, he would get his, but right now, he had to deal with his wife. Lamonte sat on the edge of the bed next to his loving wife. Waiting for her eyes to open to the break of what would have been a beautiful day. As far as he was concerned, it was the dawn of a nightmare.

Minutes ticked by, and then Gade finally stirred. Her light brown eyes flickered open and she smiled. "Good morning, honey," she murmured as she gazed into his handsome face. Gade noticed there was something different about her husband. His face was distorted. His lifeless and cold eyes stared back at her. She sat up. "Honey, what's wrong? Did something happen to Brice?"

"No, Brice is fine, but I can't say the same about us," Lamonte replied in a cool voice.

"What do you mean, honey?" Gade asked, placing her finger on his full lips.

He removed her hand. Staring blankly at her he asked, "Did you sleep with my brother? Did you know about him all of this time? What's up, Gade? I need answers and I need them now."

Gade didn't bother to ask how he knew, and when found out, because it really didn't matter. She reached behind her back and pulled out the soft satin pillow. She placed it in front of her and squeezed. She needed the support as she began to tell her husband the secrets of the past.

REVELATION FOR THE SISTERS

Saphire stood, staring blankly into space. Her life was like a beautiful home that had now been consumed by a raging fire. Nothing was left except the faded memories of the happiness she once shared with her husband, Clay. Where did she go wrong? The ultimate question was why? She had it all, money, security, and the love of a wonderful man.

Her mother's words rang true. How clearly she could see it now. She had been searching her whole life, then finally found what she had been looking for. It was right there with her since the day she met Clay Matthews. She accepted it, then she took it for granted, and now it was gone—forever.

Who could she blame for the ending of her marriage? Her mother, for constantly judging her. Making her feel as if she was nothing. Or maybe her father, for setting such a wonderful example. Then there was her perfect little sister Gade, whom her mom adored. Gade who could never do any wrong in Josey's eyes. She needed to blame someone for her pain.

Sobs escaped from her trembling lips. A revelation ran through her veins like a river of ice. There wasn't anyone she could blame for her broken life except the woman in the mirror who stared back at her now. Saphire's bloodshot eyes held her gaze in the cracked mirror on the wall.

The Victorian lamp must have grazed it when her husband hurled it across the room. With a heavy heart, Saphire dropped to her knees and she began to pray. This time it would be for real, as only God could help her. She needed His power to change her evil ways. The choices she'd made in the past were governed by her and no one else; now she had to deal with the aftermath. If only she would have turned to Him years ago. Maybe if she had, her life would have been different.

Janie DeCoster

* * * * *

Flipping through the pages of her wedding album, Gade smiled in spite of her tears. She'd married the man of her dreams, and oh, how much she loved him. How could she have ever betrayed him?

What was she thinking? Evidently she wasn't, for if she had been, that incident with Joe Nathan Burrels would never have happened.

But if it hadn't, she wouldn't have her wonderful son, Brice. A tear fell and landed on a photo of her and Lamonte. Their eyes sparkled with happiness while her heart thumped with pain. Thinking back to the confrontation between her and Lamonte earlier that morning, she closed her eyes as well as the wedding album. How could she do it? She pondered. For her lips were like bricks, as the words, 'Brice is not your son,' rolled from her tongue. Standing before her husband, failing to look into his eyes, knowing the pain she would find. Instead, she heard the moans that turned into gut-wrenching sobs from the man she loved. Accusations hurled from his lips. She watched silently as he packed his things and he walked out of her life. There were no words she could use to change anything. So why waste them?

Tears continued to fall as she wallowed in her plight. Why did things turn out this way? Brice should have been Lamonte's. Then everything would have been perfect. Just like they were until he came back. Oh how she hated Joe Nathan. But to hate him, she had to hate herself. She was a willing participant. No one forced her to be so foolish, so weak. Now she had to live with the indiscretion for the rest of her life.

If she only had herself to consider, it wouldn't have hurt so much, but she had a son. A son whose little world would be turned upside down. How could she tell him that the man he thought was his father was in all actuality his uncle? A sob formed in her throat. And that wasn't the most terrifying thing. She had to reveal to the man she'd come to hate that the son his brother was raising was his very own. How did her life go so wrong? Wasn't she a good person? She'd tried to live her life the best she could. So why couldn't her one little secret stay buried forever? She bowed her head in despair.

She knew the answer. Secrets never stay hidden forever. Like it is written in the bible, you reap what you sow. And reaping had devastated her once perfect world. Now, only God could give her the strength to face her past sins and move on. Gade was determined to pick up the pieces of her crumbling life. This time, in all honesty she would struggle to make a better life for her and her son; after all, blood is thicker than lust.

THE END

Can a man take fire in his bosom and his clothes not be burned?
Can one walk on hot coals and his feet not be seared?
Proverbs 6:27,28

QUESTIONS FOR DISCUSSION

1) What do you think of the relationship between Gade and her sister Saphire?

2) Do you think their behavior towards men stems from their father walking out on their mother when they both were young?

3) Do you think Saphire was really jealous of Gade, and not the other way around?

4) Do you think Clay saw what he wanted to see in his relationship with Saphire?

5) Do you think Saphire was really in love with Clay, or did she just marry him because she knew he was a sure thing?

6) If you were Lamonte, would you have gone out of your way to have a deeper relationship with Joe?

7) Speaking of Joe, what do you think of the role he played in the sisters' lives?

8) Do you think Joe really got help for his emotional problems?

9) What role do you think Josey played in her daughters' behavior?

10) What would you have done if you found yourself caught up in a situation similar to the Michaels sisters' plight?